ALSO BY CORINNE MICHAELS

come what may

CORINNE MICHAELS

sourcebooks
casablanca

Published by Sourcebooks Casablanca, an imprint of Sourcebooks
1935 Brookdale RD, Naperville, IL 60563-2773
(630) 961-3900
sourcebooks.com

Cataloging-in-Publication data is on file with the Library of Congress.

Printed and bound in the United States of America.
MA 10 9 8 7 6 5 4 3 2 1

To the women who are out there doing it all, feeling exhausted, but still holding it together... I see you.

CONTENT WARNING

Dear Reader,

It is always my goal to write a beautiful love story that will capture your heart and leave a lasting impression. However, I want all readers to be comfortable. Therefore, if you want to be aware of any possible CW please scan the QR code below to take you to the book page where there is a link that will drop down. If you do not need this, please go forth and I hope you love this book filled with all the pieces of my heart.

CHAPTER 1
TESSA

YOU ARE BEAUTIFUL.

You are smart.

You are loved.

You are going to do amazing things.

Doesn't matter that you're a little weird sometimes. And maybe you could use a haircut, but that's okay.

Also, you have this thing you do when you're upset—your eye kind of tics, and you should probably see a doctor, but again, totally fine.

Dating might be a good idea too. It's been like two years since you've been on one and really, it's time.

I lean toward the mirror.

"Are those wrinkles on your forehead?" I ask myself as I stare at my reflection. I sigh. "I really suck at this whole morning affirmations thing."

My roommate Brianna chuckles as she leans against the doorjamb, eating a yogurt. "What nonsense did you tell yourself this time?"

I turn, resting against the sink. "I start off well and always go off the rails. I need a haircut, by the way."

Brianna is an up-and-coming stylist who just got her first gig working for a huge brand during fashion week. She's going to do amazing things, which means at some point, I'll never get her to fix my hair.

She comes up close, lifting the brown strands and letting them fall. "Yeah, we'll do that tomorrow. Can you come into the salon after work?"

I nod quickly. "Yes, put me on the calendar!"

If she doesn't, she'll take a client and I'll never get in.

"Fine. Tomorrow at seven."

I nod once. "Thank you."

"As always, you are most welcome."

Brianna dips her spoon into her yogurt. As I open my mouth to ask her a question, I hear a deep groan coming from the room next to me.

Great. She brought another guy home.

She always gets some and I keep getting none.

"Where did we meet this man in your bed?" I ask.

She grins. "He's a model. We were doing some test work…"

"Bri, it's not a good idea to sleep with the models *before* the event," I say, immediately slipping into publicist mode. "After, fine, but not before or during. You have to be professional."

Brianna gives zero fucks and rolls her eyes. "He's from another company. Relax, Mom."

I guess that's a little different. "I'm just looking out for you. You worked so damn hard for this job."

"And I promise, I won't do anything stupid. I'll be the good little angel like you are."

I'm not an angel. I mean, I can break rules. Maybe. I haven't really yet, but I *could*. "I could be reckless and put myself out there," I tell her.

She smiles as she approaches me and pats my cheek. "Sure, you can."

I hold back a deep huff. "I need to shower and get to work."

She grins. "Have fun, honey bunch."

This time I let that huff fly, and she giggles.

I quickly shower, and since we only get maybe four minutes of hot water, I have it down to a science. You have to love tiny apartment living in New York City, right?

I leave Brianna and Antonio, who made a groggy introduction and is way too freaking pretty, and head into the Anchor Light office. Each time I walk through the doors, it's like the best moment of my life. I love being a publicist and to have been hired, right out of grad school, to work at a company like this? It's everything.

Anchor Light Corporate is a newer sub-office with a very small staff of intelligent women. The co-owners, Brynlee and Thea, are both supportive and have great visions for the company. I work most closely with the senior publicist, Aarabelle Dempsey.

The atmosphere is warm, supportive, and endlessly inspiring.

As soon as I step in, though, the energy is different.

Aarabelle spots me. "Conference room, right away," she says, her voice clipped.

"Okay," I say quickly, my heart rate jumping a bit.

We don't really have immediate meetings, or at least we haven't since I started. Something must be going on.

I walk to my desk, toss my stuff down, and rush in just as Aarabelle is sitting. The team is gathered around the table, and the phone speaker is in the middle. Brynlee is supposed to be on maternity leave, but her voice fills the room. "Everyone there?"

"Yes," Thea says as I sink into an empty chair. "Go ahead, Brynn."

"I know I'm not supposed to be working and all that, but we have an issue with one of my clients who is a real estate mogul. I don't have much information on what's going on, but it seems urgent, and our presence is needed."

"Where is the client located?" Aarabelle asks.

"Boston, but they are out of town so someone would need to meet them," Brynn explains. There is some noise on her end of the line before she returns to the call. "Sorry, the baby was fussing. The client is in Ember Falls, Virginia."

Aarabelle jumps in quickly. "I can do it. I'm from Virginia, and I have most of your clients assigned to me while you're out."

Disappointment fills me. I also have some of her clients. I push down my own feeling of failure and decide to speak up. *Closed mouths don't get fed,* as my best friend used to say. "I can also go if it's one of the clients you have me handling."

Thea smiles. "We have two eager publicists, and I think they both could do it, just depends who you think would work best with the client."

"Okay, let me think…" Brynn says as she soothes her son who is fussing behind her with *shh*-ing noises.

I wait with bated breath, hoping so much that they'll ask me to go.

"As much as I agree, both Aarabelle and Tessa can handle it, I think it would be best to send Aarabelle."

Aarabelle glances at me, and I force a smile.

Yes, I would've loved to have had the chance to do it, and I know I can do it, but I understand the decision.

I've only been here a few weeks and I don't have a ton of experience, but man, I wanted a chance to prove myself.

"Whatever Aarabelle needs, I'll be here to help," I say, tamping down my disappointment and working to sound helpful.

"Thank you, Tessa. I promise, your time is coming," Brynlee says quickly. "You both are truly talented and capable."

"There's no need to explain," I assure her.

The last thing I want to do is come off ungrateful for the opportunity to work here. Anchor Light is a well-respected company. Originally, they started off working out of California with celebrities. Catherine Cole is the owner and has allowed Brynlee and Thea to buy into the company to start a corporate subdivision, which gives us a huge advantage as Catherine's contacts are extensive and her name is respected.

We leave the meeting, and while Aarabelle is running around, getting her client folders in order so that I can help her manage while she's out of the office, I also help get travel arrangements set for her. Lodging in that town is a bit of a risk since there are literally no hotels within forty miles, but I do my best with a short-term rental I found online.

"Thank you, Tessa. You have no idea how much this helps," Aara says as I give her a folder with all the travel details she'll need.

"Of course."

"Walk with me? I need to get home to pack since it's a ten-hour drive."

I smile and fall in line with her. As we head down to the lobby, she sighs. "I tried to get permission to take you, but with Brynlee out, we really need you here."

"Oh, no, I didn't think," I say quickly, shaking my head, but I stop when she places a hand on my arm.

"I remember being a junior publicist and it sucks. Especially because you've already shown how great you'll be. Which is why, while I'm gone, I really need your help as I'm really deep in one project and, according to Brynlee, helping her client is my sole responsibility."

"Whatever you need."

"I'm in the middle of two company launch proposals. One is a relaunch of a clothing line that flopped before and no matter what anyone says, the owners are absolutely sure it will take off. Can you maybe take a look at it and give me some notes?"

I nod. "Not a problem."

"Thank you. I've tried, but I'm telling you, this is going to be a dud and I can't do a damn thing to save it. The other is the museum we just signed—they're having a big gala in about a week. All the plans are laid out, but I need you to get all dressed up and attend. It's black tie, and fancy. I assured my client I would be there, arranging the press and making sure we get them the attention they deserve. I think you'll do really well."

"I can do that," I assure her.

We exit the lobby, standing on the busy New York City sidewalk as people shove and move around each other, heading to wherever they're going.

"Oh, I know you can, and so do Thea and Brynlee. When I said I needed to offload these, they were absolutely on board with them going to you," she says with a warm smile. "You're a natural at this, you know that, right?"

I don't, but I appreciate her telling me that and mentally add it to my list of affirmations.

"Thank you," I say instead of my natural instinct to deflect any kind of praise. Lord knows I didn't grow up hearing any of it.

"All right, I'll see you in a week or two," Aarabelle says.

She turns and right as she does, I swear, her life flashes before my eyes. Her heel gets stuck in a crack and a bicyclist is coming right at her.

"Aarabelle!" I scream.

Her eyes widen for a heartbeat before she lets out a loud noise, but it does nothing to stop what comes next.

The cyclist turns his wheel to the left, but she goes that way as well, causing him to slam right into her.

Aarabelle goes down, slamming her head on the pavement—hard.

"Oh my God!" I scream and drop, trying to help her.

Her hand goes to her head and she moans.

"Aara?"

"My head," she croaks.

She tries to move, but then lets out a scream so loud I feel it in my bones.

"Don't move!" I say quickly.

Aarabelle grabs at her leg and…well…that is definitely not the way it should look.

I immediately call 911, and the ambulance arrives quickly. Aarabelle is howling in pain through the entire ride.

We spend three hours in the hospital where it's determined that Aarabelle has broken her leg, which will require surgery, and suffered a concussion. I call Thea to give her the update. She inhales deeply and then lets it out.

"Okay, you have to go."

"What?" I ask, unsure what she's referring to.

"Well, Aarabelle can't travel, and we really need someone on the ground in Ember Falls. You go down there, handle the situation, and then come back."

I blink, my heart beating so hard as reality hits me. This is it. My big break. Maybe that wasn't the best choice of words since… you know…Aarabelle *did* break her leg, but this is the moment I've been waiting for.

"Are you sure, Thea?" I ask.

"Are you saying you can't do it?"

"No!" I say a little too aggressively. "I mean…no, I can handle it."

"Good, then that's what you'll do. Go pack a bag and get to Ember Falls. We'll email you all the details before your meeting tomorrow."

———————————

Ember Falls is a tiny little town out in the western part of Virginia. It reminds me so much of my small town in Indiana. The streets are wide and homes are speckled around the countryside. More than anything, it's the smell of the air.

It's like a fresh breeze on a warm day. A mix of pollen, some animal scents, but mostly trees and sunshine.

After I left the hospital, I headed straight home, packed a bag, and got on the plane. I landed in Virginia, rented the car and made the four-hour drive to Ember Falls, yawning the entire time. I made arrangements for Aarabelle to stay in a room above a store. I call ahead to explain I'll be coming instead, but that only makes the woman who owns the place even more confused. As I hang up, I take a deep breath and assure myself I'll sort it out once I get there.

I enter Ember Falls through the Main Street area and I can't help but think how absolutely picturesque it is. There is a coffee shop, a pizza place, an ice cream shop, and a bar and grill at the end of the street. It literally looks like something off a postcard.

I find a parking spot outside of the antique store that I'm renting the room from, park, and head inside.

"Hello?" I call out, standing at the front desk of the store.

"Hello?"

I peek my head around the side of the back wall. "Yes, is Miss Thornberry here?" I ask.

"Who?" The elderly voice replies from a distance.

"Miss Thornberry?"

"Yes."

Yes, it's her? Or yes, she's here? "I'm Tessa Rivers. My coworker, Aarabelle Dempsey, reserved a room."

"I'm sorry, I don't know an Aarabelle."

Of course not. "No, I know that," I say quickly, trying to move around the store that is almost impossible to navigate. There are things everywhere. Furniture, knickknacks, stacks of old books, picture frames hanging off the furniture. It's a maze. "Aarabelle is the name that room is rented under."

"You want a room? I'm sorry, I rented it already."

I clear my throat. "Miss Thornberry? Can you come out here?"

I have finally reached the point of no return in this store.

She sighs heavily, and the most adorable woman—who reminds me of my grandma—comes out to the front. Her gray hair is cut short with big curls, exactly like Granny had hers done at the beauty parlor—as she called it—every week.

"Oh, hello, I'm Mrs. Thornberry."

I flash my winning smile. "Hello, I'm Tessa. My coworker, Aarabelle, rented your room earlier this morning. She got injured and I'm here instead. I called to explain, but I think our connection was bad."

Her eyes flash with recognition. "I see, and you're staying for a week?"

"Yes, a week at a minimum. You mentioned that you might be able to extend the stay if needed?" At least that was what she said when I booked it.

Aarabelle also asked me to meet with another client who is local to this area, Penelope Walker, who is launching a rebrand of her interior design company.

I'm not sure how long things are going to take. I don't expect these assignments to need more than a week. Therefore, I plan to blow them away and for these clients to be absolutely impressed with my professionalism and ability to get things done quickly. They'll immediately tell Brynlee and Thea that I'm a delight and they want to work with me exclusively.

I doubt that's going to happen, but hope is never a bad thing.

At least that's what I tell myself.

"Sure, Dempsey, I can do that. Strange name to give a girl," she mutters, digging in a drawer. I don't correct her because that is a conversation I don't need to have right now. She hands me a key. "Here you are, dear. Just head up the stairs on the right."

Since there's only one set of stairs here and there's no clear path to them, this should be fun. I somehow manage to navigate myself to the stairs, climbing over and under more pieces of furniture and knickknacks than I can name, and get my bag upstairs.

This place is…old.

There is a dresser that could be from the 1800s with paint peeling off the front. There is a twin bed in the middle of two windows that the center looks like it's touching the floor as it sinks—great. And the room has a strange musty smell to it.

I place my bag on the bed, which squeaks very loudly, and walk over to find the bathroom area.

Oh my God. It's pink.

Like bright pink tiles everywhere. The tub is pink. The floor is pink. The countertop is…yup, pink.

I didn't even know you could have a bubblegum pink toilet, but here it is.

And that musty smell from the bedroom? It's stronger in here.

Great.

Suddenly, I'm hoping I can get this job done even faster because staying here is going to be a freaking nightmare.

However, I can do it. I've endured some really difficult things in my life, and I'll manage this one.

Instead of standing here, surveying the uninspiring living conditions for the next week, I decide to head out and get a drink and some food.

My stomach rumbles and I sigh, thankful that there's a bar and grill just down the road.

After escaping my antique living quarters, I walk down the street, noticing more of the shops and that the coffee shop also has breakfast, where I know where I'll be each morning. Once I make it to the bar and step inside, it's exactly like I imagined. Its wood-paneled walls are decorated with various photos and neon lights, the floor is covered in black-and-white checkered tiles that are more brown now than either color, and there's a large square bar in the center.

I find an empty seat between two groups and squeeze my way in.

"Hello there," the bartender says as I settle onto my stool. "What can I get you?"

"Hi. Can I get a whiskey sour, please?" I ask.

"Sure thing. Are you new here?" he asks as he walks over to grab a glass and start pouring.

"Yes, I'm visiting for work."

He nods. "In Ember Falls? What kind of work do you do?"

"Consulting," I explain, which isn't true, but since I don't know anything about what the client needs, that seems like a perfectly good cover story.

He finishes the drink and sets it down. "Well, lots of folks around here probably need that."

I smile. "Good to know. I'm always looking to expand my reach. Are you guys still serving food?"

The bartender nods. "Kitchen is open until ten. Would you like to see a menu?"

"Yes, please, I'm starving," I explain.

"Sure thing. I'm Max and if you need anything, just holler."

I smile. "Thanks."

I take a sip of my drink, looking around at the crowd. There aren't very many people my age here, most are a lot older or look like they just turned twenty-one.

Not that I'm so much older since I'm only twenty-five, but still, twenty-one feels like a million years ago.

My phone vibrates in my pocket, and I inwardly groan, not the least bit surprised my mother texted. Lord knows she never misses a chance for her weekly hate text about me leaving Indiana—and her.

> **Mom:** Another week alone. No one has come by to even check on me. I thought you said I wouldn't be alone, Tessa. You promised your move to New York wouldn't change my life. You also said you'd visit every month. It's been four and not one visit.

Because I'm freaking living and trying to make money. I rub my forehead. Of course my asshole brother hasn't gone to check on her.

> **Me:** Sorry that Reece hasn't stopped by, Mom. I'll do my best to visit. Right now I'm on a business trip.

It's also incredibly expensive to go back home, but that really isn't her concern. I get it, she's alone, my brother is a prick, my father left when Reece was two months old, drained the bank account, and never came back. She worked hard just to put food on the table and then after her car accident six years ago, she was never the same since she couldn't work and there was no settlement.

I became the source of her frustration and have borne the brunt of it since.

And I've tried so hard to do what I can to be there for her, but I have to live my life.

At least that's what my therapist tells me.

Mom: Oh. You're traveling.
Me: For work.
Mom: Okay, Tessa. Maybe you should work on prioritizing the people in your life who have been there for you above your career. I guess I'll see you when you have the time.

I can literally feel her disdain from here and the guilt that only she manages to deliver so well.

But I'm a grown woman with a master's degree and doing it all on her own. I need to stop taking care of everyone other than myself.

I put my phone away and decide to put my past, my failures as a daughter (according to my mom), and my inability to let go behind me.

I glance over the menu again, still not sure what I want as Max is busy with the very crowded bar, and sigh. This bar reminds me of college. It was exactly like Bill's, the bar that was down the street from my apartment in Georgia. My college roommate, Meredith, and I spent so much of our time there. God, that reminds me how long it's been since I've talked to her, and I think she only lives an hour or so from here.

The door opens and for some reason, my attention drifts there and lands on the most incredibly sexy man. My jaw drops as I take in his dark brown hair that has just the slightest silver dusting on the side that's peeking out of his cowboy hat. The dusting doesn't make him look bad, no, it makes him look absolutely gorgeous. Even the scruff on his jaw adds to the allure.

He locks eyes with me and then walks straight to me.

The closer he gets the more I realize he's not just hot—he's scorching hot. Quite possibly the sexiest man I've ever seen in my life.

And then he smiles and my heart drops as he takes the seat next to me.

Have strength, Tessa.

CHAPTER 2
TESSA

I grab my phone back out of my purse, needing to distract myself. A knot forms in my stomach when I see him shift his chair, getting closer.

I quickly send a text to my friend from college, focusing my attention on anything but the hot cowboy who is sitting right freaking next to me.

It's the hat.

It's always the men in cowboy hats.

I had a thing for them in high school and apparently, it didn't go away.

> **Me:** Hey, Mer! It's been way too freaking long—I'm sorry I've been the worst. I'm actually in western Virginia for a few days and wasn't sure if you were around. I'd love to have lunch or coffee or a drink. Xoxo

Or maybe you can come right now so I don't make a total fool of myself around this guy who is flagging down the bartender.

> **Meredith:** Tessy! My love! I've missed you and I wish I could. You have no idea how much I need that drink, but I have some family drama going on and I'm out of town for a few days.

I smile. Meredith is the only person who calls me Tessy, and no one besides me calls her Mer—without a freaking earful that will ensure they never do it again. I'm sad she can't commit, but I would never make her feel bad about it.

> **Me:** Sorry about the drama. Anything I can do to help?
> **Meredith:** Oh, I wish, but no. It'll be fine. How long are you in the area?
> **Me:** Maybe a week or two. Let me know if anything changes and we can make it work.
> **Meredith:** I will. Hopefully my dad can get it figured out and we can move on.

Her dad? Wow. I didn't know she was talking to him after they had their big blow up a year ago. Sometimes, there is something to be said about blissful ignorance. Meredith did a DNA test to see if she had the breast cancer gene after her mother passed away. Only, she found out a whole lot more, like the fact that her parents had lied to her and she wasn't actually her father's daughter.

That went over like a lead balloon.

> **Me:** I'll hope for the best and it seems we have a lot to catch up on.
> **Meredith:** Thanks, Tessy! I'll call you in the next few days and let you know when I'm back in town. Jake will want to see you too.

Jake and I met my sophomore year in Psychology, and we quickly became friends. When he saw Meredith for the first time—that was it. He was in love, and she spent a year making him chase her, which he did. I was the maid of honor at their wedding, and I don't know that I've ever met two people who fit together like them.

Me: I miss you both and can't wait to see you!

Hopefully we can make that happen. It's been way too long and I'm honestly starting to wonder if my mother is right and I suck as a human for not staying in touch. Meredith was—is—my best friend. She's the only person who has always been there, no matter what I needed. She deserved better than a few months and a random text because I'm in the area.

No longer having the phone as an excuse to not look at the guy next to me, I pick up the menu, remembering that I was here for food anyway.

"I don't suggest anything with fish," a deep, raspy voice says from the other side of the menu.

Of course his voice is freaking hot too.

I clear my throat and look into a pair of eyes that could literally melt me off this bar stool. His green eyes are really light in the center and then darken as they go out to the thick black ring containing all that color.

Shit.

He talked. *I* should talk.

Yes, talking would be good.

"Thanks for the advice. Fish at a bar is never a good idea," I say, my voice sounding scratchy. I take a sip of my whiskey sour.

He smiles and my stomach does one of those flips that make my skin tingle. "That's true, well, unless you're in Boston. Then you want to get whatever seafood is on the menu."

The way he says it, with a Boston accent at the end, has me grinning. "Same in New York." I let my practiced one come through.

"You're a New Yorker?"

I shake my head. "Not really. I'm actually from Indiana, but I've been practicing to sound like a New Yorker since I live there. What about you? Are you from Boston?"

What about you? Ugh! I sound ridiculous.

"Sometimes."

"That's vague," I say back, placing the menu down and my hands on top of it.

"Is it? Sometimes I'm from there, other times I'm not."

I laugh softly. "Okay. Then how often are you here?"

"It used to be around 50 percent—now it's more like seventy."

"Interesting," I say, lifting my glass. "What keeps you here more lately?"

Please don't say a wife.

Or maybe I do want him to say that so I can go back to my menu perusing and instead of staring at the hot guy.

"My farm."

Farm doesn't mean wife. That's a start. He has no ring on, but my dad proved a ring really means jack shit.

Plus, my friend's husband never wears one because when he was working on his engine, it got caught on something and he almost had to have his finger amputated.

Farmers use their hands a lot, right? This guy could be thinking the same thing.

"I see," I say even though I don't. "So, since I shouldn't get the fish here, is there anything you'd recommend?"

He leans in a little closer, looking at the menu. "I'd also avoid their Italian food. If you live in New York, you're not going to be impressed here."

That is a very true statement. The Italian food in the city is absolutely the best I've ever had, well, other than when I was in Italy, but that's in a league of its own.

"We're really limiting my options here," I tease the sexy stranger.

Slowly he lifts his green eyes to mine and I can't breathe. I could get lost in them. I could stare into them as they looked down on me while he…

What the hell?

Where did that come from?

My God, I'm here for work, not a hookup. Not that I would even know what a hookup is at this point, since it's been about four years.

Okay, five.

In college, I was never into the dating scene. Most guys at my school just wanted to sleep with as many girls as they could find. No thank you. I did have one, but he was an asshole who dumped me after he cheated.

Then, I didn't have time between classes, tests, and working damn near full-time so I could afford college, my internship, and grad school.

I would've thought once I moved to New York City it would've been different, but again, I have goals. Big goals that don't include a guy messing up my world.

So, it just…hasn't happened.

I haven't really thought much of it—until now.

"I think having options is always important," his deep voice slides over the words, sending a shiver down my spine.

"Agreed. Options make us feel less…trapped."

He laughs once. "They do. So, let's think about your options."

The ones I'm thinking about all involve lips, tongues, hands, and…other body parts.

I close my eyes, mentally slap myself, and put my dirty mind to the back burner because this never happens. We're talking about food, not sex.

"There's a burger," I say, keeping my gaze on the menu.

"Solid choice."

"Chicken tenders."

"Ehh, can be kept on the short list."

I smile. "Salad?"

"Boring. You don't seem like a salad girl."

At that I look up. "I don't?"

For some reason, I don't think we're talking about food.

He shakes his head. "I think you're a bit more adventurous."

I lean in, unable to stop myself. "You don't know me at all."

His eyes move to my lips. "I think I do."

I raise one brow and run my eyes along that chiseled jawline. "And what do you know?"

He doesn't hesitate to answer, and I'm caught off guard by his words. "You're beautiful and smart and take what you want. You work hard, harder than you get credit for, but you don't complain. No, you're too proud for that."

My heart is pounding so hard it's almost all I can hear. He's right about so much of it and how he was able to read me so easily is… unlike anything I've ever experienced.

I hide those things. I hide a lot of myself because anytime I've exposed a part of my heart, it's been broken. By men, my family, my friends—myself.

Needing to keep this conversation back to the light and fun, I smile and return the topic to food. "And that makes me a non-salad girl?"

He moves his hand closer, the tip of his finger just grazing mine. "Do you *want* a salad?"

I shake my head. "I don't."

"Then what do you want?"

For him to take me out of this bar and make me forget about food.

But that would be reckless, and that's the one thing I never am.

CHAPTER 3
KILLIAN

THIS WOMAN.

I've never seen a woman equal to her.

Beautiful is too mundane of a word to use. She's stunning, spectacular, gorgeous, bewitching, which is really what she's done with just one smile—bewitched me.

Her long, straight brown hair rests just above the small of her back, looking like spun silk. Then there's those eyes, damn blue eyes on a brunette are my kryptonite. Her heart-shaped lips are perfectly full, not too big, not too small. Everything about her calls to me.

I've never been so viscerally attracted to anyone, and I don't even know her name.

However, this conversation, right now, has given me my first fucking break from the shitshow that my life has become in the last two days.

Her long, black lashes fan open and closed. "I'm not sure."

"You need more time?" I ask. "With the menu?"

I'm not sure what the hell I'm thinking. This is a mistake, flirting with someone while I'm in the middle of a crisis, but...God, what I wouldn't give to kiss those pouty lips.

"I think," she says, leaning forward a little, "that sometimes, you have to just take a chance...when ordering."

Yeah, except she's the only thing I see on the menu.

"Do you take chances often?"

She shakes her head. "I don't."

"That's a shame. You're too young to be so serious."

God knows at her age I was a fucking mess. I have no idea what that age is, but it's nowhere close to mine. She looks fresh out of college and at that point, I'd been playing professional football, quit, started my company, and was basically floundering.

"I have fun," she defends, looking slightly offended. "I just have dreams and goals, which require hard work."

"I respect that," I say quickly. "I wasn't judging you, just saying that sometimes, taking a chance can lead you to something amazing."

"Like our chance meeting?"

Exactly like that. "It's definitely one I'm not regretting."

She pushes her long brown hair back over her shoulder and then pulls her lower lip between her teeth. "Life is too short for regrets."

Fuck my life. I'm going to say something I pray I don't regret.

With the world's worst timing ever, Max comes back over, stopping me from speaking. "Did you want to order anything off the menu?"

Her blue eyes find mine, and she shakes her head slowly. "I don't think so."

"Do you need more time?" Max asks.

I tilt my head. "Or did you figure out you wanted something else?" I ask.

The beautiful woman smiles and tucks her hair behind her ear. "I think, I might have something, at my place to eat..."

And I'll get to fucking devour her.

Max huffs out a quick laugh. "All right, let me know if you change your mind."

He leaves us and I reach my hand out. "What do you say we go find something, somewhere else?"

Her hand touches mine, just barely, but enough I feel it everywhere. "Where are you thinking?"

I'm thinking anywhere but here.

"I live not too far from here and I can promise you a proper meal," I say.

She looks at me hesitantly. "I'm not sure that's a great idea."

Yeah, I know it's not, but she's probably more worried that I'm an axe murderer, which at least I can promise is not the case. "It might not be, but I promise you're safe with me."

Her eyes narrow. "Isn't that what anyone would say?"

"What assurances can I give you?"

"Well, your name would be a good start."

I extend my hand. "Killian."

She places her palm against mine. "Tessa."

I lift her hand up to my lips and press a kiss there. "It's a pleasure to meet you, Tessa."

"You too." The blush on her cheeks is fucking tantalizing. "So, your place?"

I nod. "Come on, you can follow me over that way so you have your car if you want to leave at any moment."

She stands and I do the same before she smiles. "Show me the way."

We get outside to where my truck is parked. "Where's your car?" I ask.

"Right down the road a little."

She's going to change her mind—I can feel it. And honestly, she should. I don't know what I'm thinking but right now, expect that my life is a series of bad decisions, so what's one more?

When we get to a small white sedan she turns to me.

Here it is.

I brace for it, knowing it's probably for the best, when she says, "I'll follow you."

I smile. "I'll go slow."

She lets out a soft sigh. "I'm pretty sure we're going anything but slow."

"True, but…we don't have to do anything you don't want to," I say, leaning into her just a little.

"I appreciate that, but…I'm ready to follow you."

Right into hell where I'm already burning for her.

"Can I kiss you, Tessa?" I ask, wanting that even if this goes pear-shaped, at least I can have a kiss to replay.

She steps into me, her hands going to my chest and she nods.

I move my arm around her, my other hand cupping her jaw and bringing her lips to mine.

It's as though a match has been lit and I'm ready to set the entire forest up in flames. I kiss her hard, wanting to be lost and out of my mind, and like magic, she silences everything that's been drowning me. Her mouth moves against mine in perfect harmony, and it's fucking torture and yet—heaven.

Too soon I pull back, needing her to want to follow me back to my place where I plan to kiss every inch of her beautiful body.

Her lips are slightly swollen and shining from the kiss. Her blue eyes slowly open. "Drive fast."

I grin. "Keep up."

I get to my truck and her headlights stay behind me as we navigate to the ranch. I swipe the key card to the gate that's midway down my driveway and she follows me through. We park in front of the main house that's way too grand for me, but since it was already here, I didn't have much choice.

It's supposed to look like a farmhouse, but the previous owners didn't do that great of a job making it blend. It's huge, white with black windows and trim, and the front has the most ridiculous landscaping. Complete with horse-shaped topiaries.

It's meant to impress, and from the wide look in her eyes, it does.

"Wow," Tessa says softly as she closes her car door. "This is your *farm*? What in the world do you farm here?"

I chuckle. "We're a horse farm."

"I love horses! I used to ride, what feels like a million years ago. When you said farm, I was picturing something completely different. It's beautiful," she says.

"You're beautiful," I retort.

That seems to bring her back to why we're here. Her cheeks redden slightly. "Thank you."

"Do you want to come in?" I ask, again needing to make sure she really does want this.

"I do."

I extend my hand, and like the sparrow trusting an eagle, she comes to me willingly.

We enter the house, and as soon as the door closes, I pull her into my arms. Tessa squeaks before her hands move to my face, pulling me to her as I do the same. Our lips crash together with another searing kiss, so much passion, so much—escape.

Her mouth moves perfectly with mine, and each swipe of her tongue feels like fucking heaven.

It's been too long.

Too many years that I've gone without, working myself until I have nothing to give to anyone else. All my time is spent between this ranch and the company in Boston. I'm always doing whatever I can to climb higher and I fall further instead.

I hate it.

I just want to be out of my goddamn head for a few hours.

And that's exactly what I plan to do.

Get lost in Tessa.

Her fingers slide through my hair, and I lift her up, her legs wrapping around me.

Thankfully, the owner suite is on the main level, and I could get there blindfolded. I walk with her in my arms, my hands on her ass, ready to have these jeans off and touch her skin. I kick the door closed with my foot and move to the bed.

Gently, I lay her down, her chestnut hair billowing out against the white comforter. She looks up at me, pulling that plump bottom lip between her teeth.

"Killian," she says my name softly as I stare at her.

She doesn't know who I am, how much money I have, or the fact that my life is falling apart. For one night, I'm just a man. Soon, she'll be out of Ember Falls and I can pretend it never happened.

Come what may, I'm going to enjoy this one night.

I climb onto the mattress and kiss her again, swallowing her moan as she grips my shirt, pulling it up. I help her, removing it, and shudder as her soft fingers glide over my muscles.

The guys may give me shit about being in my forties, but I work hard to keep up with them and most of the time, I'm stronger and faster.

Right now, I'm pretty happy I do invest so much time at the gym.

Tessa's eyes track her hands, moving up higher. "Like what you see?" I ask, hoping she does.

"Umm, yes, very much."

I grin. "Sit up."

She does and I lift the hem of her shirt over her head. Tessa is wearing a pink lacy bra that I can see her nipples through. My mouth waters and I slowly lean in. My lips press against her collarbone, then her shoulder, until I reach the strap of her bra then move to her breasts. Methodically I kiss everywhere, moving back and forth and then I lick her nipple through the lace.

"Oh, God," she gasps, her hand going to my hair. "Please."

I grin, and do it on the other side, letting the lace become wet from my mouth. I want more though. I want to draw that pink peak in my mouth, suck it and drive her wild. I bite on the edge of the lace, pulling it down and exposing the bud.

Then I do exactly what I wanted. I pull her nipple deep in my mouth, flicking it with my tongue before licking it softly. Over and over, I repeat the motions, savoring the soft noises of pleasure she makes.

I lift up, wanting to lick somewhere else even more. "Are you wet for me?" I ask.

Her face reddens slightly but she nods.

"How wet?"

Tessa leans up on her elbows looking like a goddess. "Why don't you find out," she challenges.

"Oh, sweetheart, don't you know better than to challenge a man who likes control?"

I want her to know that I'm not some little schoolboy and I like to be the one who leads the show.

"Am I to be submissive then?"

I move my hand down her front, unbuttoning her jeans. "Not submissive," I clarify. "But will you do as you're told?"

"Depends what you want me to do."

Let's test her then. "Get up."

I move off to the side, watching and waiting to see what she'll do.

She gets up, her pants undone, bra still on but the cups are now pulled below her ample breasts, letting me see them in all their glory.

"I'm up."

I smile. "Slide your pants down." She doesn't hesitate in pushing them down her legs before stepping out. "The bra." I order.

Tessa does it. "Okay."

"Take the underwear off. I want to see your pretty cunt."

Tessa's eyes flash with defiance, but she complies, pulling it off. "Now what?"

"Stand there."

I get off the bed, moving to her side, looking at her, but not touching. I'm close, the heat off her body is so appealing, but I use my restraint to keep myself from giving her what she wants.

"So beautiful," I croon. "Standing before me like a fucking queen. Do you want me on my knees for you, sweetheart? To lick your cunt until you scream my name and your legs give out?"

She sucks in a breath. "I…"

I watch her unable to think, her mind racing in a million directions, I wonder if she'll ask for what she wants. "Or do you want to go to your knees, and let me fill that pretty mouth of yours with my cock?"

I think she wants to be controlled a little. To escape the same way that I am. She needs someone to take away her worries, give her control by not having to think for one fucking minute.

Her whimper tells me exactly which option she wants, but I'll wait.

I want to hear her say it.

I stare into her blue eyes, willing her to answer. Either one of those options has us both winning.

After another second of silence, I prompt her again. "Which one will it be?"

Tessa straightens her back a little and slowly lowers to her knees. *Fuck me.*

Her hand slides up my thigh, just barely grazing my cock, and to the button of my jeans. "I think you'd like me better this way," she says, her voice is like velvet, soft and smooth.

"Know that after you suck my dick, I'm going to lay you down and lick every drop between your legs until you scream my name." I move her fingers away and work at my button and zipper. I lower my jeans and boxers, letting my cock free.

"Promise?"

"Cross my heart."

Her eyes drink me in, and she runs her tongue along her lips. I'm not sure how I don't lose myself right then, but I take her face in my hand, pushing her lips apart.

"Open for me," I tell her. When her lips part, I push the head of my cock into her hot mouth. "Now suck."

She takes me deep, running her tongue along the vein of my cock. There are no words to describe the pleasure she gives me. Not just from the blow job, but from looking at her like this. Her tits on display, hand around my cock as it disappears in her mouth.

So fucking hot.

So good.

So perfect.

I moan, my head falling back when I feel the back of her throat. Then my need becomes frantic. "Stay still," I say to her as I take her face in my hands. "Just like that, let me move."

I move my hips back and forth in a slow motion. My thumb grazes the corner of her lip, wiping spit leaking out. "You have no idea how beautiful you are. I could come just like this, seeing you on your knees for me, my cock deep in your mouth. Touch yourself. Go ahead, feel how wet you are." Tessa moves her hand down between her legs and moans. I have to bite my tongue to keep from coming again. "Don't touch your clit, sweetheart. That's mine tonight."

When her eyes close and she again makes a low sound, I know I can't keep up. I need to make her come.

I pull out and she gasps. Then I'm on the floor, moving her to her back, pulling her legs apart and then putting her feet on my shoulders.

"Oh, my God," she pants.

"Keep your feet there. If you move them, I stop. Understand?"

"Yes."

I don't hesitate or go slow—I'm fucking ravenous for her. I want to taste her, bring her to climax over and over again.

I don't care that we're on the floor. That I have a very large, very comfortable bed. Right now, I need her.

She's spread open and I move to her clit, flicking it slowly and then adding pressure. She's dripping for me, and I lap it up. I can feel the tremble in her legs as she fights the urge to close her legs.

That's it, stay just like that.

I reward her for fighting it, inserting two fingers deep inside her as I keep up the pressure against her clit.

Tessa is so responsive and her muscles contract around my fingers.

"Killian. Oh, I can't. I'm going to come. Oh, God."

Her head thrashes back and forth, fingers sliding through my hair and tightening around the strands. I groan, sucking her clit into my mouth and pumping my fingers deeper. She groans loudly as she releases. She gasps and then her hands are fisting my hair. I coax her through it, wanting every second of her climax to be powerful.

When she finally stops, I pull my fingers out, licking each one, savoring the taste of her as her eyes flash with surprise.

I don't say anything. Instead, I come to the side of her, scooping her up as her arms go around my neck. I walk us to the bed, laying her down in the center. I reach into the bedside table and grab a condom.

"If you want me to fuck you, put it on me," I say, handing it to her.

She huffs out a short laugh and tears it open with her teeth. Her small hand wraps around my cock and she rolls it down my shaft. "I want this," she says with steel in her voice. "I want you."

Then have me she shall.

I climb up, pushing her thighs apart, and line up at her entrance. "Look at me, Tessa." Her eyes come to mine in a heartbeat and I push inside of her, feeling the greatest pleasure I've ever known.

Fuck, this girl is going to wreck my world.

CHAPTER 4
TESSA

BEST. SEX. EVER.

Like in the whole wide world. No one has ever had sex like I just did.

I didn't even know that it was possible to come so many times. However, here I am, in the afterglow of a night I will never forget with a man whose last name I don't even know.

Since I'm relatively unfamiliar with this, I'm not sure what the next move is. I have my car so at least I don't need to ask for a ride, but like, do I stay? Get dressed? Thank him?

I really wish I could call Meredith. She did this our freshman year of college when I didn't.

However, that's not possible so I need to be a grown-up and make a decision.

Leaving it is.

I sit up as Killian lies beside me, still working to even out his breath. I climb out of the bed, moving to where my discarded clothes are, and the sheets ruffle behind me.

"Where are you going?"

I can do this. I can be all cool and flirty about it. There's no way this man wants to cuddle or anything. This is a one-night stand, so now I need to do the stand and leave part.

"It's getting late and I'm starving," I say as I grab my shirt and slip it over my head. "You know, you sort of disrupted my food ordering."

Killian chuckles. "I did, but I also promised we'd get food."

Okay, maybe he doesn't want to toss me out immediately. Feeding me would be the nice thing to do at least. I have no food in the room I'm renting and no idea where the closest option for a meal is since the kitchen at the bar is now closed.

"You don't have to," I say, not wanting him to feel forced.

Killian climbs out of the bed, naked, and dear Lord I feel a tingle between my legs at the sight of him.

His body is pure perfection. Zero percent body fat and one hundred percent hot.

He stands before me, grabs my pants and tosses them behind him. "I know I don't have to, but I want to. Come on."

I take his offered hand as we walk out of the bedroom. I didn't get a chance to really admire the house since he devoured me as soon as we got inside, but this place is magnificent. The large, planked wood floors go perfectly with the cream-colored walls. There's a huge natural rock fireplace in the living room with a sectional creating a separate space for the kitchen.

Now *that* is a work of art.

Natural wood cabinets with a hunter-green island. The nine-burner stove that has a plaster hood above it. Every detail is meticulously planned and meant to impress, which I am.

And even as gorgeous as the house is, I can't help but continue to sneak a peek at Killian—who is still naked.

He walks me to the monstrous refrigerator, opening it wide. "You're welcome to anything I have."

This is totally awkward, but my stomach rumbles as though punctuating its need for food.

This place is stocked. It has every fruit or vegetable imaginable. There is a whole section, yes, section because it's that big, of yogurts and dairy products. To the left is an array of already cooked meats. Who lives like this?

"Do you have a chef?" I ask.

Killian shakes his head. "I like to cook. I eat as healthy as I can, so I always keep things ready to grab."

"I see. Can I have a yogurt?" I ask.

"Yogurt?"

I nod. It seems like the easiest and quickest thing.

Killian laughs once. "Go sit on stool at the counter," he instructs.

I have never been a girl who likes to take orders, but with him, it feels different. Like he wants to care for me, not boss me around just because.

So, I go over to the stool and jump up. "Now what?"

He smiles. "Now I'm going to make you a proper meal."

"Fish?" I tease.

"No fish, sweetheart, but how do tacos sound?"

I purse my lips, pondering it in a playful way. "Hmm, tacos on a Tuesday? I guess that sounds...perfect."

Still naked, Killian grabs supplies from the fridge and lines them all up. "Spicy or not?"

"Medium spice? I'm like a three-pepper girl."

"Since I'm going to be touching jalapeños, I need clothes. I'll be right back." He walks over, kisses me on the nose and heads back in the bedroom as I stare at his tight ass.

He returns after putting on a pair of gym shorts and gets to work.

I sit here, munching on some chips and salsa since he didn't want me to wait the fifteen minutes it might take to assemble some tacos, and I appreciate that.

Our conversation is surface level at best. We talk about the house, the farm, the options for food in town and that's it. Killian makes me a plate with three soft shell tacos, and he sits next to me with his.

"So, what brought you to Ember Falls?" Killian asks as I grab the taco and take a bite.

I chew, not wanting to be rude, and then answer, keeping up

with the story I told Max seems to be the smartest idea. "Work. I'm a consultant and there's a client in the area that needs some help."

"That's great. How long are you here for?"

I shift in my chair. "A week or two? I'm not sure yet."

"Well, I'm sure we'll see each other—the town is small."

My cheeks heat and I look over with a smile. "I hope so."

"I do too," he admits before taking a bite.

I do the same, hoping that maybe I can avoid saying something stupid. When we're both done, he grabs the plates and puts them in the sink. His phone buzzes, and he makes a face that clearly says he's not happy and looks up.

"I need to make a work call. Are you okay to stay here?"

"Sure, is everything okay?"

He sighs heavily. "No, but…it will be. I pay people to handle these things."

I understand that since I get paid to fix things. "Okay."

"I'll be five minutes."

A part of me wonders if maybe he's calling a wife or something, but I do my best not to think about that. The last thing in the world I ever want to do is sleep with a married man. I've seen the realities of what infidelity can do to a person.

My mother was an absolute wreck when she learned the truth about my father and even though I didn't love my ex, his betrayal hurt.

I…can't be like him.

I refuse.

Even though I have no idea what Killian is doing, my mind starts to race, and I feel sick. What if he is married? I didn't even ask.

I just went back to his house and fucked his brains out.

To be fair, if he was going to cheat, I'd think going to my place would've been the more logical thing, but sometimes, I've learned, men are not logical.

They often think with one body part.

He returns and I'm now mid–panic attack. He stops as soon as he meets my eyes. "What's wrong?"

I could lie. I mean, he wouldn't know, but then this part of me, this ugly, dark part of my soul revolts and demands answers. "Are you married?"

He jerks back slightly. "No. I've never been married. Why do you think that?"

He said no and…at this point, the onus is on him, right?

"I just hate cheating, and I don't know, I wasn't thinking when we…hooked up. So, I thought I should probably ask, even though I should've done that before the hookup. Anyway, you said you had to make a work call and I didn't know if that was code for wife."

Killian is in front of me a moment later, taking my hands in his. "I've never been married. I was engaged once, to a woman I thought I *should* marry, and then she cheated on me. I don't lie. I don't cheat. I would never do that." Then he gives me his phone. "Look at the call list—call the last number or ten if you need to. There's no one. I'm single and it's been a really fucking long time since I've been attached to anyone."

I stare into his green eyes, looking for the tell of a lie. The shift of his gaze, the twitch in his jaw, anything, but there's nothing. Either this guy is the best liar or he's telling the truth. I place his phone back in his hands, not looking.

"I believe you."

He kisses me. "Good."

The kiss was unexpected but cute. Honestly, this entire day hasn't gone like I expected, so why I'd think me not being awkward after casual sex would be normal, I have no idea.

I get off the chair, my hand on his chest. "I'll wash since you cooked."

"What? No."

"It's the least I can do." I push past him and go over to the sink. My mother always had the rule that whoever cooked never had to clean. Once I learned how to make dinner, I really loved that rule since Reece always had to wash dishes.

I turn the faucet on and grab the sponge that rests on the counter. Before I can even get soap on the sponge, Killian is behind me, wrapping his arms around my middle.

I squeak and then he turns me.

We're face-to-face, and I get lost in his eyes again as the colors deepen and almost shift. He moves his hand to my face, his thumb grazing my cheek. "I don't want you to do the dishes."

"You don't?"

He shakes his head, bringing his mouth to mine for a soft kiss. My hands move to his bare chest, resting on his hard muscles. He pulls back. "I'd rather do something else."

"What's that?"

He grins, lifting me up onto the edge of the counter. "You."

Then we do it again because the night isn't over.

Sunlight streams through the window, and I go to move, but Killian's arm is wrapped around my middle.

I smile, remembering all the freaking amazing sex we had. Then, he tucks me in next to him and pulls me to his chest.

It seems Killian is a cuddler.

My phone vibrates on the bedside table, and I groan, knowing I need to answer. I was supposed to get an email with the details of the client and what they need, but I didn't. I'm hoping the call is Thea or Aarabelle so I know what the hell I'm doing here in Ember Falls.

Killian moves, releasing me, and I reach for it.

Only it's neither of them.

It's Brynlee—the owner.

Shit.

"Hey," I say quickly, pulling the sheet up with me to shield myself.

Not that she can see me, but it's sort of weird talking to your boss when you're naked.

"Hi, Tessa, sorry to call so early, but the baby had a horrible night and I couldn't email, then I figured I'd just call. I know you're totally capable of handling this and just wanted to make sure you have everything you need."

I actually don't have anything I need, but I don't say that. She's a new mom, dealing with having the baby early, and, well, my boss.

"I'm here now, so whenever you have the info, just send it over."

"I'm so sorry. I…yeah, I didn't send you anything so you have nothing. Great. I would be there, but Crew has put his foot down that I am not going to put myself or the baby at risk by freaking out, and…you know, being me."

"Of course, and I have to agree with your husband here."

She sighs. "Yeah, yeah. I just have worked with Mr. Thorn for a long time. He hasn't disclosed any of the info about what's going on. So, when you get to the client, I need you to assess his issue, and then you'll need to form a plan. According to him, the sky is falling, his business is falling apart, and we have to mitigate it, if at all possible."

"Of course, I can do all that—" I check the clock "—what if I call you before lunch and fill you in, make sure you approve of the plan?"

"Yes. Yes, thank you," Brynn says, letting out a huff. "I know you were working on a new client proposal, and I can take over whatever you have on your plate to get that accomplished." Someone, I'm assuming Crew, in the background starts to argue. "I am perfectly capable of sitting my ass on the couch and doing a damn proposal, dear. Relax. I'm not getting on a plane," Brynn grumbles. "Sorry, I'll help if you need it."

No way in hell am I accepting that. I'm going to manage this crisis and also get my very first client signed. Brynlee and Thea have built this company on their backs and part of why they hired me is because I promised I would work hard and bring in new clients.

Proving myself, my value, my worth to her and everyone I know is what matters.

"If I need it, I'll definitely ask. Send me the address and I'll reach out to meet with them."

"Perfect, I'll text the address for the client."

"Thank you."

"No, thank you, Tessa. You're a lifesaver. Talk soon."

We hang up and I need to get my butt moving so I can prepare, but before I can get out of the bed, his strong arms wrap around me, pulling me against his chest. I squeak and giggle. "Killian! I have to get up."

He kisses the space between my neck and shoulder. "Stay. Just a little longer."

Oh, how I wish I could. I look at him from over my shoulder. "I can't. I need to shower, get changed, and deal with work stuff."

"Mmm," he grumbles against my skin. "I think the shower is a great idea. I can make sure every inch of you is clean."

Don't say yes. Don't say yes.

But I really want to. This could be my opening to finding out if maybe this doesn't have to be one night—maybe this whole week could be spent having fantastic sex.

My insecurities are screaming at me not to be needy and ask, so I keep myself in check and let it be his choice. "I can't."

His lips move up my neck to rest on my ear. "You're sure?"

No.

"Yes."

"How about breakfast at least?"

I sigh. God, this guy is so sweet. "Fine. Breakfast and then I need to leave and get ready before my meeting."

He runs his tongue along the shell of my ear. "Too bad I can't eat you."

This is becoming impossible to extricate myself from and the way his voice rumbles against me sends sparks shooting everywhere. I melt into his embrace. "Killian...I...want you again, so much."

He lets me go and then rolls himself on top of me, caging me in. "We both have shit we need to deal with today. Let's at least have this."

I purse my lips and stare into those stunning fucking eyes. "Ten minutes."

He grins. "Then I better get to work."

And work he does. Oh, God how he works.

We finish and I get dressed. I had to force him to leave the room so I could actually get my clothes on this time.

Thankfully, he listens and promises to feed me so I can tackle the day. I'm going to need sustenance since I am lacking sleep and have expended a hell of a lot of energy.

I walk out of his bedroom, and he has a plate with eggs and bacon, a yogurt cup with fresh fruit, and another plate with pancakes sitting on the kitchen island.

"What's all this?" I ask with a smile.

"Breakfast."

My eyes widen as I look at the spread. "This is...well, a lot."

He shrugs. "Pick one then. Whatever we don't eat I'm sure one of the ranch hands will want."

Okay. I go for the yogurt and Killian takes the eggs.

"So, you mentioned this is a horse ranch?"

"It is."

"What kind of horses?" I ask before taking a bite.

"We board, train, and breed racehorses, but we also have horses who are old and just want a pasture to roam. Our bread and butter is breeding, though."

I nod as if I have a clue what that means. "That's fun. I went to a horse camp for a summer and learned to ride and care for horses. I can't imagine how amazing it is to be around them all the time. It sounds like a dream."

"I love it here. It's...well, it's a lot of work and stress, but it's important to me."

"My boss always reminds me that if we love what we do, we do it well. From what it sounds like, you love it even with the stress, so it's worth it and I bet you're great."

He clears his throat. "I try to be."

"Then, I'm sure you are."

Killian reaches his hand up to my face, brushing the corner of my mouth. "You had some yogurt." I run my tongue along my lips, and he nearly growls. "I think you might be trying to kill me."

I smile. "I promise, I'm not." My phone buzzes, and Brynlee's text comes through with the address and a phone number for Mr. Thorn. "But I do have to go."

"Now?"

"Like an hour ago." I laugh softly. "Thank you for breakfast and dinner last night and...you know, the sex."

He smiles. "You're welcome and thank you." Killian pauses and then brushes his thumb across my lips. "Can I see you again?"

My heart races because it's what I hoped for and also didn't. I'm pretty sure this is not a good idea, but at the same time, I'm not staying here. My job, my life, and everything I'm working for are all in New York so...what's the harm?

"Yeah, I'd like that." I get to my feet, pushing my hair behind my shoulder. My phone buzzes again.

Brynlee: Thanks for handling this, Tessa. I got an email from Mr. Thorn that said he'll be ready in fifteen.

Shit. Now I can't go home and change.

"Dinner?"

"Dinner sounds great."

He stands and kisses me softly. "I'll see you tonight. Let's meet at the bar at seven?"

I have no idea where I'm going and how long I'll be out, but I nod. "That sounds like a plan. I really have to go—my client is waiting."

"Of course. I have someone on their way here to work on the ranch so I should get dressed."

"Okay, but tonight at seven?"

He grins widely. "Yes, and this time, pack a bag."

I smile and put the address of the location I need to head to and press "find route."

The voice on the GPS cuts through the room. "You have arrived at your location."

I look up and he looks down at the phone.

No, this can't be.

I…he…us…no.

Killian takes the phone, looking at the address, and then his eyes come back to mine. There is a look of horror that must mirror my own because I realize that I slept with our client.

CHAPTER 5
KILLIAN

I keep looking at the phone, waiting for this to be a joke.

Brynlee said a girl named Aarabelle was coming. That she'd be here this morning and she is her top publicist.

Tessa looks up. Her chest rises and falls and the sexual bliss that filled her eyes just moments ago has morphed to a mix of horror and regret. "Is your last name Thorn?" she asks hesitantly.

"Yes. I'm Killian Thorn."

Her hand covers her mouth. "Oh, God. Oh. Right. Okay. Yes. You are. I'm." She swallows and puts her purse down. "Mr. Thorn. Killian, I'm Tessa Rivers. I work for Anchor Light as…a publicist… maybe *former* now but, umm, yeah, this is awkward."

That's a fucking understatement.

I can't believe this.

I fucked my publicist.

How much more can I screw up this entire situation?

I wasn't sure it could get worse.

In walks my next mistake.

She's uncomfortable, and I need to make this right. "We're both professionals."

"We are."

Although not even twenty minutes ago I was between her legs.

Real fucking professional.

I can't make this worse than it is, although I'm sure if you give me five minutes, I'll manage it. I push aside my feelings and do what I can to mitigate her look of distress. "Yes, and I'm not your boss. This is just...two strangers who spent a night together."

Tessa straightens her back. "Yes. One night and that's it."

Message received. Any plans we had for another go are off the table now. I should be pleased with that, but fuck, I'm not. I wanted more with her. One night is not going to be enough, but it has to be.

How the hell did this happen? This doesn't even make sense. When I spoke to Brynlee, she never mentioned... "Wait," I say quickly, putting the pieces together. "Brynlee said a woman named Aarabelle was coming?"

Not a girl named Tessa.

Maybe this isn't the same girl who is supposed to be here.

Her eyes drop her to shoes. "Yes, and she was going to be the one who came here, but as she was leaving the office in New York, she was run over."

"Run over?"

"By a cyclist! Sorry, she's fine, but she broke her leg and got a concussion. So, they asked me to step in. I'm sure this sounds like it's completely nuts, but I promise it's true. Brynlee trusts that I can help and I swear, I would've never, we would've never...if I knew who you were. God, please just kill me now. You should fire me—call Brynn and tell her you want another publicist to work on this."

I fight the urge to move toward her, to touch her, to comfort her, but I don't think I'm the person who can do that right now.

"I'm not going to do that, but I'm just...stunned."

"But you should!" Tessa bursts out.

I run my fingers through my hair and sigh. "Do you want that? Truly?"

Tessa moves toward me quickly, almost as if she realizes she spoke those words aloud. "No! Please. Forget I said that. I can do this. We are both adults and we didn't know who the other was, right? There's no reason why we can't put that behind us and focus on what you need for your ranch. I'm able to do my job, no matter what happened here last night."

"And this morning."

Her cheeks redden. "Yes, and this morning. We don't need to talk about it." Tessa lets out a deep sigh, straightens her back, and nods once. "I'm here to help you so that's all that really matters, right?"

The only issue I have is that I can still taste her on my tongue. I can hear her sighs, moans, and the way she screams when she comes. That I can feel her body under mine, my dick in her mouth, and the sting of her nails as they scored my back.

But, sure, we'll just not talk about it.

"If you think you can do it," I say, trying to pretend I wasn't thinking how hard it would be to not be with her. No pun intended.

"I can." She lets out a deep breath through her nose. "Umm, do you think you should…" Her eyes move down my bare chest and to the shorts that are hanging low on my hips.

"What?" I push.

Tessa tucks her hair behind her ear. "Maybe it would be better for our meeting if, you know, you had some pants on."

I lean against the counter. "I wasn't expecting my publicist so early."

"Yes, and I wasn't expecting to be in yesterday's clothes, but these are the cards we've been dealt."

I'm being an asshole. I'm just so mad at myself. At her. At the fucking universe for dropping her in my lap and yanking her away.

There's no way we can sleep together again. Not if she's working for me. I'm a lot of things, but someone who sleeps with a coworker or those here to fix my entire crumbling business is not one.

So, that's that.

I push off, ready to eat crow and also put her at ease. She didn't know who I was and the last thing I want is to have to find a new

PR team. "You're right. My office is down the hall, the third door on the left. If you want to wait for me there, we can go over everything. Or you can go back to your place, shower, do whatever you need to do, and meet me here in two hours?"

"Can it wait? Brynn said it was urgent."

I give her a reassuring smile. "It can wait a little. Go home and do what you have to do."

She pushes her purse up on her shoulder. "Thank you, Killian. For everything."

I watch her walk out the door, and I head into the shower, washing away the remnants of the night.

———————

Tessa comes back an hour and a half later.

In that time, what went from pretty shitty has escalated to out of control.

"Okay, so as of right now, the concern is that your trainer has sort of gone missing and you're losing sales in rapid succession?" Tessa asks as she follows me into my office.

"Basically, but none of it makes sense."

"Why don't we start at the beginning?"

I grip the back of my neck and motion for her to sit on the cognac-colored leather couch that is against the floor-to-ceiling windows, overlooking the ranch.

This room is my favorite in the house. It's masculine and the only one I actually gave a shit about and decorated myself.

I had all the wall space created into a library. It's warm wood tones with a rolling ladder flanking my massive desk that was my grandfather's. My kid said it was too manly the one time she came here, and she added a plush rug to "soften" it. Whatever that means.

"The beginning?"

She nods. "I want to help, but Brynlee didn't have any

information, just that it was urgent and I needed to drop everything and come here."

Right. The beginning. "Six years ago, I hired one of the most renowned horse trainers in the industry. It was a big win for me since I was able to persuade him to leave a training facility that was producing some of the top racehorses in the country. It brought me some enemies, mainly one."

Tessa writes a few things down before looking up. "I'm guessing the owner of the farm or ranch you were able to persuade him to leave?"

"Yes, and some owners of the horses he was working with."

She shifts. "Why would the owners care?"

I chuckle. "Well, either they kept their horses at that farm without the trainer or they had to come to mine and pay my fees."

"That would do it," Tessa notes. "Okay, so you get the trainer to come here, igniting anger with owners of the horses and the facility, then what?"

"We forged a pretty straightforward and lucrative team. I allowed him a lot of free rein—he had contacts in this industry that I didn't."

She nods. "Makes sense."

"This place was never really meant for any of this. I bought the ranch for a family member, and it grew into something more. I became even more passionate about horse racing and thought this would be a great side gig. I figured I'd have some fun, be around the animals I love again. It was truly never meant to grow into something."

"So how did it?" she asks.

I laugh, remembering how we went from being a sort of unknown to much bigger. "I got lucky."

Tessa leans back on the couch, draping her right leg over her left. Her long lashes sweep across her cheek and then lift again. For a moment, my breath catches, and her beauty absolutely floors me.

As though she can sense my desire starting to mount, she

clears her throat and tucks her hair behind her ear. "By getting your trainer?"

I shake my head. "No, by my horse winning a major race. I have six personal horses and my one thoroughbred just…dominated. He won and won and won and then won a major derby. He's been incredible and he's built all wrong according to everyone. My jockey said he couldn't explain it, but that horse just *wanted* to win. You can't train that, you know?"

"If you say so," she says with a smile.

"I do. It's inside of them, a desire to succeed. It made me a fuckload of money, and I knew I couldn't reproduce a season like that, but I knew I could breed him. People would pay a lot of money to have a foal from him and the right mare. Which is where I feel like things changed for me.

"I brought Travis, my trainer, in to help me create a breeding program where we figured out some markers that, when crossed, started to produce winning racers. We had, in two years, produced multiple winners and it put us on the map. Our mares and studs, when paired correctly, started to prove we were a great breeding facility. Then, we knew we could make even more money because he would train them, study their habits and tendencies, correct what he could, and sell them. Most of the buyers wanted Travis to train them, so then they boarded them here. We became a one-stop shop for quality prospective racehorses that you could buy, keep here, have trained, and cared for."

Tessa sighs. "I'm not seeing anything illegal or that would cause a PR crisis yet."

No, she wouldn't.

"Well, that's because there isn't anything in that sense. We aren't doing anything illegal. However, Travis is gone. He took off a few days ago, and I didn't think anything of it. Maybe he wanted to see another horse to buy. Maybe he had an emergency. Who knows, but it's been a week. Nothing. His phone is now off. He lives in the guesthouse back there. It's empty. Completely empty. As though he never lived here."

"I see. Okay, so he's gone, and you said something about the buyers?"

I nod. "So we have buyers lined up for the next year, but at least half are now pulling out of their contracts. Horses that we had in the program that were ready to sell in the next few weeks, they canceled the sales and the promise to board and train. No warning, no explanation—nothing. I spend about half my time between here and my home in Boston. Travis runs everything, and when I'm here, I check in and help out. Most of the day-to-day running is by him and the staff, but he's gone. I wasn't overly concerned until two days ago—I found this."

I push off the desk and walk around to the safe that looks like it's a part of the bookcase. I open it and pull the note out, coming over to where she's sitting. Our fingers brush as I hand it to her and pull back, opening and closing my fist as I try to ignore the tingle.

However, I notice the tremble that runs through her.

Good. At least I'm not the only one who felt that.

Tessa focuses her attention to the note and lifts her eyes to meet mine. "What the hell does that mean?"

"I don't know."

The note reads:

Get your house in order before the story breaks and you lose
it all.

"Okay, so there's a story coming and we need to find out what it is. How much does each of your horses go for?"

"It depends. A horse from a proven winner or combination foal can go for anywhere from $100,000 to $400,000. The other stud we have, who has never won, his foals go for less since he doesn't have the same winning record. Most of the time Travis can make a good arrangement with the buyers he knows."

"And how many sales backed out?" Tessa asks, writing more notes down.

"Six."

"That's a lot of money."

Yeah, I know. "And we lost eight of the horses we were boarding."

She stands, biting her thumb and pacing. "Okay, then let's dig in and see if we can uncover whatever story is brewing before the press or whatever the hell this note is warning you of. I can't lay out a PR plan when we're already on our back foot."

"I don't even know what foot we're on," I admit.

All of this is odd, and I don't have a great feeling about it. I don't know if Travis was stealing money, harming the horses, doing something illegal, or just finally had enough and quit. Maybe another farm grabbed him, and he didn't want to tell me. Although, he has stock in this ranch. He's not just a trainer—I gave him partial ownership of the breeding program.

Not a single fucking thing adds up, and I'm hemorrhaging money. I need to figure this out and find new buyers or I'm going to end up losing the ranch.

"We'll figure it out and then we'll create a plan, okay?" she says with determination.

"All right."

"Great. In the meantime, I want to go through any paperwork you might have on the horse sales and Travis. Also, I'd like to see the ranch. Is that possible?"

A whole day with her where I'm unable to touch her? Sure, sounds like a great day.

"Yes, that's possible."

CHAPTER 6
TESSA

"You should stay here," Killian says as we approach the front door of his home so I can head back to my room, which was even worse in the daylight when I went to change. I need to do some more work and it's late, I'm exhausted, and tomorrow I'm spending the morning with another of Aarabelle's clients since I'm in town.

I stare at him, sure that I misheard. "I...what?"

"I have plenty of room. This house has six bedrooms."

"Killian," I say quickly. "That's probably a bad idea."

No, not probably. It definitely is.

Today feels like one of the most intense and horrible workouts I've ever had. My muscles are tight, my body is aching, and my mind is unable to fully make decisions.

No matter what, though, I know that staying on the ranch is not a good choice.

"You are going to have to be coming and going all day as we keep digging. Do you really want to stay in the antique store where it smells like mold?"

We spent pretty much five hours going through the notes, dates, paperwork, and anything he had regarding the horses.

After that, he once again made sure I had a meal while I did some preliminary research on Ivy Thorn Farms and Killian, hoping to find some good press here.

I didn't.

Nothing bad, but nothing like he saved orphans from a fire that I could use in some way.

Killian is just a normal businessman. He has the ranch and his real estate company in Boston that he started with his friend, Nathaniel. Nothing that stood out as a red flag.

As much as I hoped for some good news, I'm glad it's not bad.

"It doesn't smell like mold," I argue. Just dust and feet.

He sighs. "Tessa."

I should not like the way he says my name, but oh, I do. Because for one night, I was able to not be Tessa Elizabeth Rivers. The girl who never feels whole. The one who fights so hard just to be the total opposite of her parents—a man ruins everything he touches, and woman who takes what she wants without caring about others.

But last night, I was just a girl who met a man at a bar and escaped the never-ending worries I face.

Only that girl is fiction, and I have to live in the reality. "You can't honestly think that after everything, we should be staying together in your house."

"Why? We're both adults."

I laugh once. "Yes, and professionals, but even I have a freaking limit. Plus, no, I can't."

He sighs heavily, and I can tell he's frustrated. "You won't even know I'm here."

Yeah right. I've only been able to notice him. Think about him. Imagine his lips on mine or the way his cologne smells. Absolutely ridiculous and out of the question.

"I appreciate the offer..."

"You'd rather stay in that building that doesn't have a working kitchen and God only knows what else. It should be condemned!"

Sure, it's not a five-star resort, but I'm here for a week, two tops. I can suck it up. "I'm sure it'll be fine."

It's bad enough all day I've smelled his cologne, watched his muscles beneath his shirt as he moves. I've seen his naked body in my mind more times than I care to admit. So, nope.

Not happening.

No. Freaking. Way.

"The bedroom is the first door on the right. I'll bring some clean towels," Killian says after bringing my bags upstairs.

I'm out of my damn mind for coming back here, but I was not staying in that room any longer.

After the second cockroach crawled onto my cup, I was done.

I would've slept in my car, but I didn't think that was all that smart. So, I'm here.

Like a dumbass.

But I'm a smart dumbass.

I can do this. I'm professional. I know how to hold myself together because I'm going places in life. This is a hiccup in my plan to make this trip into my big break.

My job is literally to handle things.

So, I'll handle it.

I mean, what could possibly go wrong?

"Thank you," I say as he flips the light on.

Dear God, this is a guest room? It looks like a five-star hotel room. There is a large four-poster bed that faces huge windows that has the view of the back property. I walk over to look out and my breath catches.

It's gorgeous. The outlines of the mountains are still visible as the sun is making its final descent, casting the sky in oranges and pinks. There's a faint shimmer off the river that runs along the back of the property and a few horses are wandering in the open corral.

"This is really stunning," I say softly.

"It is."

I turn to find him right there, eyes locked on mine, and the warmth of his body is so close. I remember how it felt to be in his arms and wish I could just lean in and feel it again.

But I can't.

I need to stay right here.

He clears his throat and steps back. The loss of his warmth sends a cool shiver down my spine. "Thank you for letting me stay here."

"Of course. It works out for both of us."

I'm not so sure of that, but…I don't say it.

I think this is going to end with me either on my back, under him, or in my car, running the hell away and quitting my job.

"Hopefully we have everything wrapped up quickly," I say, walking over to where my bag is. I bite my lower lip, feeling really uncomfortable with all this. "Do you want me to pay per night or can I invoice it as my hours?"

Killian's jaw tightens. Oh, boy. "I'm not charging you. Putting aside the fact that we spent hours having sex less than twenty-four hours ago, you work for me. You're here, on my request, to help me save this damn ranch. I'm not asking for compensation—this is what I should be billed regardless."

I didn't expect him to react that angrily, but I'm sorry, there are a million reasons why I would think the way I do. "Take aside the sex comment, I have no idea what your contract with Anchor Light is. I'm helping out Brynlee, who is your publicist. So, if I were going on basic business principles, I would not assume you would be responsible for my lodging expenses." I huff. "And not to mention, Mr. Thorn, it is because of the sex we had that I think we'd want a strictly contractual arrangement regarding money."

He takes two steps closer. "I don't have a contract with you."

"My *company* then."

Hopefully it'll remain my company because if they ever find out about what we did, I'll be fired.

There are strict company policies that we have to adhere to.

No drugs, absolutely no discussing anything about our clients with anyone outside the company, we have morality clauses, and no sleeping with clients or anyone in the office.

Killian pinches the bridge of his nose. "I just wanted you to be comfortable and close in case this whole damn situation goes to shit."

That part I understand. Today there was a reporter who called asking where Travis was because he wanted to get a quote.

I wouldn't have been concerned since Travis is a very well-known trainer, but when I suggested he speak with me or Killian, he said he would as soon as he had the rest of his story straight.

Which means something is up.

It's why we started to go through all the sales contracts, but there are just so many and so far, nothing has jumped out at either of us. My hope is to find a pattern, something that shows the house isn't in order. If not, at least I can build a list of people who recently bought horses and then canceled, if I reach out to one of them, there could be an answer there.

"I appreciate it," I say. "I need to do a little more work and it definitely will be easier here."

Killian smiles and nods once. "I'll let you get to it."

"Thank you."

"I'll be downstairs if you need anything."

He leaves and I have to grip the pole on the bed to stop myself from collapsing. I'm exhausted and my mind is a clusterfuck.

Still, I grab my laptop and start to work. I sit on the bed, legs crossed, and go through my notes. After speaking with Thea, we agreed that putting any kind of statement out at this point is a mistake.

We don't know anything.

Saying something could be seen as admitting to guilt.

What we need to do is find Travis, and I need to know why all these people are pulling out of the sales they'd agreed to.

I put together a list of possibilities. Sometimes it just helps to think through the scenarios.

> • *Travis was recruited by another farm and left.*
> • *Travis stole something we haven't uncovered and ran off.*
> • *Travis is in trouble.*
> • *The buyers were only dealing with Travis, and he was doing something nefarious, which spooked them enough to cancel.*
> • *The ranch didn't actually produce any winners and they're pulling out because of it.*
> • *God only knows the other reasons.*

As I tick them off, I start to make arguments and counter-arguments to each one. Hours later, I'm unable to turn my mind off.

I hate this about myself, but I'm a perfectionist to a fault.

The clock shows it's eleven. I'm never getting to sleep at this rate. Unable to lie here anymore, I get out of bed and grab my laptop. The house is dark and quiet, so I head out to the back deck to sit on the porch swing.

It's one of those perfect nights, thick with the summer air wanting to come in.

I love the end of spring.

I lift the top and the screen comes to life. I pull up my search results about Killian, reading through some of the notes I highlighted.

He was a professional football player who left when the company he invested in started to take off. The article talks about the injury he sustained his rookie year and how he didn't see a lot of playing time after it.

After leaving football behind, he invested in his best friend from college's company and together, they grew their real estate firm into a huge success. I look through photos of him and Nathaniel that have been shown over the years. Nathaniel is a good-looking guy—not anything like the specimen that Killian is, but not ugly.

Yet in every other photo there's a woman who could be a supermodel on Nathaniel's arm, where there's not one of Killian with someone.

It's funny to me because he's ten times better looking, so why is he single?

Lord knows he's a freaking god in bed. He's smart, financially secure, in perfect shape, and has a fantastic dick. Which again begs the question, why isn't there someone standing next to him?

Why do I care?

Why am I now remembering his dick?

Oh, I know, because I want him to come out here, strip me naked, and make me forget my name again.

"You're going to get eaten alive," a deep voice says from the darkness.

I scream causing my laptop to fly in the air, which clatters on the ground, and I nearly leap out of my skin. My heart pounds so loud it drowns out all sense of reason.

"Easy, it's just me." Killian steps into the light, his hands raised. "Sorry, I saw a light and the motion detectors went off, so I came to check if everything was okay."

"Right. No. Sure, I'm just…having a heart attack." My hand is gripping my chest as I try to get control, but I'm shaking.

"Please don't do that. I can't handle the press claiming I did something to my publicist." He leans down and grabs my laptop off the ground.

"Did I kill it?" I ask.

He checks it over. "No, it looks fine. I had no idea you'd throw the laptop."

"Well, it's late, dark, and all of a sudden someone was here."

He grins, handing my computer back to me. "I didn't want to scare you by just walking onto the porch in the middle of the night either."

I'm not sure which would've been better since I'm…in my freaking pajamas. Great.

I hold my laptop against my chest, hoping to hide the lack of bra under my tank top. I remind myself that he's already seen me naked, but still, we're not doing that again. "I was just going over my notes."

He shakes his head. "Did something change?"

"No, no. I just wanted to make sure I didn't miss something. Sometimes, after a little time has passed, we're able to see things better, you know?"

Not that I didn't already spend three hours doing exactly that.

"Did you have an epiphany?"

I smile and laugh. "I felt one coming on, but then this creeper came on the porch when I was thinking about things and scared the shit out of me."

"I'm sorry about that, Tessa." He grins.

Again, my body reacts to the way he says my name and a shiver runs through me. No, that's the wind. At least, I'm going to tell myself that.

I clear my throat and step to the swing, grabbing the blanket to cover myself. "Don't be. It's your house after all. But I do think we'll figure out what's going on. I'm sending an email to a friend who knows some guys who can do some digging to find Travis. Thankfully, my laptop didn't break in my mini panic attack, or we'd have another issue to deal with."

"Yes, but that would be the least of our worries since I have a laptop you could use," Killian jokes and then walks closer. "Can I sit?"

"Sure," I say, hating that I ever got out of bed. At least then I would be able to pretend I'm not at all attracted to him. That last night was just a dream and I didn't love every second of just being with him—in and out of bed.

I liked our talk, the way he took care of me with food—and the other way.

Killian sits on the swing, and I shift, keeping to the corner with the blanket securely around me.

The two of us stay in the silence for a minute, staring up at the sky. It's so beautiful and I feel so nostalgic sitting here. "This is the part I miss the most being in New York City. There are no stars."

His eyes meet mine. "Boston isn't much better." I'm sure it's not. All the cities have this as their one great flaw. "It's why I come here so much. Life is simpler here. People are kind, we care about our neighbors, no matter where they came from. If someone needs something, we're there to lend a hand."

"My childhood was like that," I say with a smile. "I grew up in a small town, and I remember a time when we didn't have—well, anything. We were struggling, and all of a sudden, a neighbor came with a casserole, then the next day, another one came. For a week, there was a stream of food delivered and then someone would offer us a ride when Momma's car broke down. Since we didn't have the help we should've had, we had our community."

He shifts in the chair, his leg just brushing against mine. "I'm sensing there's a story there."

I laugh once. "You have no idea, but…things work out the way they're supposed to. Anyway, my favorite thing to do with my mom was sit out at night and talk to the stars."

"Did they talk back?"

I smile. "I think they did. I would ask for things, wishes and dreams and hopes. I think they came through for me."

At least parts of them did. I wanted out of the town, away from my past. I needed a fresh start and college allowed me that.

"Maybe that's what I need to do then, wish for this nightmare to be over," Killian says with a laugh.

"If only it were that simple."

Killian chuckles. "If only. This farm, it means the world to me. I love the horses, the land—this is where my heart is."

I glance at him from the side, our knees now completely against each other's. "Did you suspect anything was going on with Travis?"

He sighs heavily. "I keep asking myself that same thing. I keep trying to find a moment in time where there was a shift, but I can't. Travis was tough, he trained those horses hard, and that was often an issue between us. He produced a lot of winners, though. That allowed us to get much better prices on each horse we sold. Other than that, I thought we were great partners. He was running things here, selling horses, which made me happy. I didn't push back on much, so he seemed pretty content. The only thing I ever questioned was why so many of the horses that were sold stayed here to be trained. Travis was great, don't get me wrong, but his costs were astronomical, and he'd always been a one-horse trainer."

"What does that mean?" I ask. "A one-horse trainer."

"He only worked with one winner at a time. It was his entire motto. Then suddenly he started training anyone who bought from us. It was weird, and when I asked, he said money was money and we needed the brand awareness. I should've known something was weird."

I reach out, resting my hand on his. "Killian, it's not your fault."

"It's my ranch. Of course it's my fault. I should've been more involved, but I was so damn busy in Massachusetts. I had to work, sell more properties and I just let Travis do his thing because it was working."

"Well, tomorrow we're going to buckle down again and keep looking. Hopefully I'll get an email back and maybe my contact can uncover something."

"You really think we're going to figure this whole thing out?"

I nod. "People don't usually disappear without a trace. They always leave some kind of clue—we just have to find it."

"I don't know that I agree with that," Killian says, looking up at the sky. The way he says it leads me to think we're not talking about the ranch. There's a softness, almost an ache to his voice. One that says we can't erase last night either. "When I was a teenager, I had someone disappear and it took me over two decades to find her again."

"It's always a girl," I say with a smile.

"You are beguiling creatures. Men can't seem to resist the pull."

I wish that were true because I've been alone a very long time. "The downfall of humanity."

Killian chuckles. "That and money."

"Very true, but you kind of made my point."

"How?"

I grin. "You found her again."

His smile is bright, and he leans close to me. So close I can smell the mint on his breath. My throat grows tight, and the warm air now feels stifling. I need to walk away before I do something stupid like kiss him.

"It's late. I should...sleep."

"What time do you need to be at Penelope's tomorrow for your meeting?"

"Early. I set up a meeting at eight so I could be back here by ten and we can work again."

Penelope wanted to do earlier, but I really don't want to show up at the meeting looking ill-prepared.

His emerald eyes find mine. "I hope your meeting goes well. Goodnight, Tessa."

"Goodnight, Killian."

"Sleep well."

Fat chance of that happening.

CHAPTER 7
KILLIAN

"So, it's pretty bad, huh?" Everett asks as we're walking to the field for our Ultimate Frisbee practice.

I pull my bag up on my shoulder. "It will be if we don't find Travis. Another boarding client left. It's as though they know something and no one will tell me."

He clasps his hand around the back of my neck. "It'll work out. I know you and how you feel about the ranch—the truth will come out."

I sure hope so.

"I'm going to hire a company to do some digging."

"Oh?"

"I mean, I'm going to have to. Or I'll lose everything."

Tessa has someone doing it, but Miles mentioned his brother-in-law to be and they are one of the best in the country. They don't just dig, they unearth the truth.

"What are you two bitches talking about?" Miles, one of the other Frisbee team members, calls out, running up behind us.

"Your mom," Everett tosses back.

"Really? That would be hard since she died when I was four days old."

I wince. "Low blow, Ev."

He shakes his head, not phased. "I take it back. We were talking about your woman."

Now he's done it.

Miles may be the nicest guy out of all of us, but there is nothing he loves more in this world than Penelope and her son Kai.

I nudge Everett. "Maybe go back to insulting his mother."

He laughs. "Relax, we're just kidding."

I raise one hand. "I didn't say anything."

"You live another day," Miles tells me.

I'm not quite sure if that's a good thing since each day just shows me another layer of hell I'm being buried under.

I toss my bag down and the three of us start to get our cleats on and stretch. Lachlan comes up behind us, the last member of our team. "I swear, you fucks are always late."

We look at each other. "Umm," I say first. "You're behind us."

He lifts his foot, showing his cleats are on. "I've already done two laps. We were supposed to start at noon."

"Well, some of us have real jobs," Miles says. "You know, with students and teachers and a schedule."

Lachlan rolls his eyes. "Yeah, being the fire chief is a fucking dance. I mean, my free time is just abundant."

I raise one brow. "Do you have office hours?"

"Says the one who doesn't have an office in this state," Lachlan tosses back.

Miles steps forward. "Don't be mean to the old guy. He's preparing for retired life."

These assholes really need some new material. "For fuck's sake, I'm only ten years older than you. It's not that much."

Everett jumps in. Of course he does, the sarcastic asshole can't resist. "Isn't it though? I mean, you're what? Forty-two?"

He knows exactly how old I am. They love to remind me.

"He's forty-three," Miles says.

Lachlan is the next one. "No, no, he's forty-four."

I grin. "And yet, I don't look it. Unlike you assholes."

"Those gray hairs say otherwise, brother." Everett snorts and claps me on the back. "They're saying, 'look at me, I'm old as fuck.'"

I flip him off and start to stretch my legs.

Yes, I'm forty-four, but no one ever thinks that. Most of the time, they think I'm in my mid-thirties and my body is that of a twenty-year-old, so I don't give a shit what my birth certificate says.

"Hey, guys," Miles says as he pushes his arms out, like he's going to hold the other guys back. "It's not nice to be mean to our elders. Especially since he could be our dad."

This again.

"I always forget about his daughter." Lachlan grins. "She's our age, huh?"

"No, she's younger than you assholes, so unless I had you at like thirteen, no, I could not be your father. And God help me if I had you jackasses in my family tree. I'd be cutting off those limbs," I say, pushing up off the grass, thinking that might end this.

I should've known better.

"I mean, that still makes her closer to our age than…yours."

"Shut up."

Miles chuckles. "All right, all right, let's lay off Killian—he's going through enough."

Damn right I am.

He continues, "Although, I heard, he brought a girl home and… she hasn't been back to the room she rented. Did you kidnap her?"

I used to feel bad for these three. When they were each trying to find the people they love, the rest of us picked on them.

Now, I don't regret any of it.

They deserved it and worse.

"Sometimes, I really hate Ember Falls," I say and run out onto the field to warm up.

I start my jog, thinking about Tessa. Her smile, the way we fit together as though we were made for one another. I remember the way she looked at me in the bar, how my desire for her was like a living thing. How her heart-shaped lips were swollen after my kiss and those blue eyes became soft when I entered her.

Hopefully no one pieces together that she's the girl from the bar.

Max would know, but one of the things Max prides himself on is that a bartender is equivalent to a therapist in some cases, and he would never share his patient's information. It's a stretch, but he's discreet.

It's the rest of the town that is relentless with their gossip.

A few seconds later, all three of my friends are running with me. "Don't be mad, Pops," Lachlan says.

"I swear, I could kill you."

"Yeah, but you won't. We are the four best friends that anyone could have," he quotes the line from our favorite movie we've seen one too many times.

I scoff. "When did you become my best friends?"

"When you decided to join our team," Miles explains. "It's an *implied* best friendship."

"Like fight club," Everett tacks on.

"Only we disc it to them," Lachlan supplies this time.

Everett laughs. "Dude, that was terrible."

"Seriously," I say, speeding up, hoping to lose these fools.

It doesn't work, they keep pace.

"Listen, we just want to know about the girl you brought home. I've never heard about you hooking up with anyone." Everett appears beside me, irritating me once again.

I roll my eyes. "Because I don't kiss and tell."

Also, because I don't usually do it. Tessa was an anomaly. A woman who I just couldn't look away from. Now, I have to physically force myself to do exactly that. Not that I succeeded last night. No, I went out there and spent time with her when I should've been in my room, pretending she wasn't staying only a few rooms away.

Right now, the last damn thing I need is a story saying I'm

sleeping with her. I'm sure the town gossips, also known as the Disc Jocks, would find a way to spin it into something ridiculous like I'm in love with her and we're having a baby.

"What's her name?" Lachlan asks.

My God. "Are you all so bored you have nothing else to do than worry about me?"

"Someone needs to."

The last thing I want is this damn conversation. I stop running, turning to face the three idiots. "Her name was none-of-your-business. It was one night. Thank you all for the concern but it's not needed. If you want to help, please find out why the hell I'm losing sales on the ranch."

Miles's eyes narrow. "I'm sorry. Wait, it's true? You really did bring a girl home from the bar?"

Lachlan laughs. "Well, I didn't see that coming."

Ironically, it's Everett who puts a stop to it. "Let's leave him be. He's got a lot of shit going on and we can always make fun of Lachlan—it's easier."

"Seriously, he's stupid," Miles agrees.

"Fuck right off, assholes."

I snort. "Go get the disc. I have an hour before I need to pick the pieces of my life back up."

Then we play Ultimate Frisbee and I forget for just a bit about all my troubles.

After an hour of running myself ragged, I'm back at my car and Miles calls my name.

Great, this again.

I really don't want to have another round from earlier. I'm physically exhausted and just want to enjoy the feeling for a minute.

"Killian, wait."

I stop walking, releasing a heavy breath, and wait. "What's up?" I ask, a little too tersely.

They don't know that their teasing about my age brought up

another layer of self-loathing I've been struggling with. I don't know how old Tessa is, but it's clear she's not in her forties.

She's at least twelve years younger, but if I were guessing, it's more than that. She's just starting out in her life and here I am, fucking things up for her. I really need to keep away from her and my mind off anything more than a professional relationship.

Miles chuckles. "I promise, I'm not going to give you shit."

That's a relief. "I appreciate that."

"I just want to know if you're all right. I know all the shit with the ranch is weighing you down, but…it seems like there's more."

I lean against the quarter panel of my car and shrug. "I'm fine."

I'm not. I'm worried about everything and nothing feels as though it's going right.

The ranch is going to fall apart, and I can't find a way to stop it. Not to mention, I don't even know what the hell is going on. I can't fix something if I don't know how it's broken.

Miles raises one brow. "You aren't fine, dude. I wouldn't be if I were you."

"I guess I'm not, but I need to face all of my mistakes."

Lord knows I've made a few and one of them happened two nights ago.

So much for not thinking about Tessa.

"We all do at some point, but it's also why friendships are important. All of us will do everything we can, even if you just need to vent," Miles assures me. "I won't judge."

I huff a laugh. "I think people always judge."

He shrugs. "Maybe, but I'll at least pretend I'm not."

We both laugh. "How kind of you."

"Hey, I'm just a nice guy. So, seriously, I'm worried. I've known you for years and I've never heard a damn rumor about you, but now the whole town is talking about you and some young girl leaving the bar."

Of course that one word is now the only thing I can hear. "Young, huh?"

"Is she not?"

"I appreciate the concern, Miles, I really do—"

"But you don't want to talk about it," Miles finishes for me. "And I get that. However, I don't see how hooking up with someone can be bad. Is she underage?"

I jerk back. "What?"

"I'm just asking. Otherwise, what could have you so tight-lipped?"

I really don't want to explain this, but at the same time, I don't know who the fuck to talk to. Nathaniel will lose his shit since we also employ Anchor Light, and I don't want Tessa to lose her job. I'm not talking to my daughter about it, and I'm not even sure that any of this even is a damn thing.

"She is my publicist."

His eyes widen. "The one at my house right now?"

I nod. "The same one."

"Did you know she was when you slept with her?"

"No!" I say with a huff. "I didn't know her damn name. We met at the bar, flirted, and…we spent the night together. Then, in the morning, I found out who she was."

"Okay, so what's the issue?"

"She works for me. I don't sleep with employees," I explain.

"Yes, but she's not your employee. She's a contractor who works for you."

I roll my eyes. "Semantics."

"They matter," Miles says with a shrug. "I'm just saying. You didn't know who she was when you slept with her. She's a grown woman and you had consensual sex. I don't think you need to be so worried about it."

"She's also staying at the ranch in my damn house."

He barks out a laugh. "I'm starting to think you're just trying to make your life harder. Penelope said Tessa was staying at Mrs. Thornberry's, which is almost as bad as the Brickman shit shack."

I nod. "No shit. So, I told her to stay with me."

"Again, you're not doing anything wrong. Ease up, Killian. You've got enough real issues going on in your life, don't make this into one." He clasps my shoulder. "You're both adults and it's not like she's staying in Ember Falls forever. So, get through this week and it'll all be behind you."

He's right.

Tessa isn't staying in Ember Falls and we're not going to make the same mistake again.

Unfortunately.

"Thanks, Miles." I approach the subject I wanted to talk with him about earlier, but didn't want to say it in front of the other guys. "Penelope's brother, he works in top secret security, right?"

"Clearly it's not all that the top secret, but I know people. Why?"

When his fiancée was in trouble, he went to Virginia Beach to find her brother and then, though I don't know how, they were able to locate her. He made a few mentions when we've hung out about her brother being a SEAL and doing security for an elite company. That's who I want working for me.

"I might need his help. Will you do me a solid and reach out to him?"

Miles nods. "Yeah, no problem. Is it Travis?"

"Yes, we need to find him."

"I'll call today and let you know what he says," he promises.

"I appreciate it."

"Of course, and I should warn you, Penelope was asking Ainsley and Violet over when Tessa was there. So, I would prepare for a lot of questions from her."

Great.

CHAPTER 8
TESSA

KILLIAN LETS OUT A LONG GROAN AS HE STRETCHES HIS ARMS OVER his head. "God, I can't look at any more of this. The words are just starting to blur together."

My neck is stiff, and I feel the same way. After I got back from meeting with Penny, where we discussed the launch of the new interior design service, Killian and I dove headfirst into the purchase orders.

Travis handled most of the sales and since that's the first thing that was being affected in the business, it made sense to begin there. Whatever the issue is, I need to know so I can do some damage control and hopefully fix the image issue.

"I'm going to keep looking. We're close, I can feel it."

"Tessa, you need to rest. We're not going to solve the puzzle today, unfortunately."

Each day seems to be costing him money and my job is to help him strategize and help him mitigate the damage.

I stretch my neck side to side and sigh. "Maybe not, but I have to try." My phone rings and it's Meredith's name on my screen. "Do you mind if I take this?"

"No, I'm done for the night. I'm going to grab us something to eat. Take the call in here."

Killian leaves, closing the office door behind him, and I let out a sigh and then answer the phone.

"Hey, Mer," I say as I answer.

"Tessy! I've missed you. How are you? Are you still in the area?"

I smile, remembering her rapid fire question mode. "I'm good. I miss you too. Yes, I'm here, I think I'll be here at least another week."

"Oh, problems at work?"

I look over at the papers on the floor. "You can say that."

"Well, whatever the issue is, that company should be eternally grateful they have you there to fix the mess."

I don't think that's the case, but her support is appreciated. "Thank you. Are you back? Can I come by? Dinner maybe?"

"Yes, I got home earlier today and would love nothing more than to catch up. Do you want me to meet you, or do you have a car?"

"I do, I rented one," I tell her. "How about we plan for dinner on Saturday? It gives me the rest of the week to work through this without worrying."

She squeals. "Absolutely. We'll make Jake grill since I bought him one of those fancy ones that looks like an egg. I'll also order takeout because"—she drops her voice to a whisper—"while he thinks he knows what he's doing, he either undercooks the meat or overcooks it. So, you know, I'll make sure we have a contingency."

I laugh. "I can't wait."

"Me neither. I'll text you the address just so you have it—and see you Saturday, whatever time you want to come."

"It's going to be so great seeing you again."

"It's been too long."

Well, now I'm excited. I haven't seen my best friend in what feels like forever, and it gets me to spend some time away from Killian and the ever-mounting temptation that is him.

When I lift my head, I look at the paperwork and something catches my eye.

On one of the bills of sale, the signature is off.

I reach down and lift it up. Killian's signature has been on a bunch of sales, and even though he can't recall each one, he said that when it came to bills for any foals that came from his stud, he often signed those.

But this one…doesn't look like the others. There's something in the slant of the "T" and the price looks like it was changed.

I start to examine the other ones a little closer and there are slight differences. I start to sort them into piles.

"Killian!" I call for him.

He enters a few seconds later. "What's wrong?" he asks as he looks down at me, sitting on the floor surrounded by piles and papers.

"Look at this," I say, giving him the bill of sale to a guy named Andrew Bennett. This horse should've been double that cost. It was from his stud, and bred with a mare that produced a very successful racehorse. It should've been one of the highest sales, not the lowest.

He reads it over. "What am I missing?"

"First, look at the horses and the price."

Killian half snorts and half scoffs. "What the fuck? I didn't sell this one."

"You signed it."

He flips the paper over and shakes his head. "That's not my signature."

"I didn't think so. Look at this one." I hand him another.

This price is a lot higher than the others, which I didn't think anything of when I started digging. I wasn't aware of what drives some of the prices up, but this foal comes from Killian's second horse, a great stud, but nowhere near what his derby winner is, and the mare is also untested.

"This doesn't make sense." Killian starts to pace. "I didn't sign this one. I would've asked why the hell this one went for so much."

"Are any of these your signature?"

He takes the pile, sits on the couch behind me, and starts going over them. "This is me." He pulls one out.

I take it and put it in another pile. We go through each one, trying to organize it the best way possible.

At the end there are about ten bills of sale that were signed by someone other than Killian but bear his name.

"Could it be Travis's signature?"

He shakes his head slowly. "I mean, it could be. But I don't know why he wouldn't just sign his name. He did on half of these. This is a fucking mess."

I rest my hand on his forearm. "Let's look into these first, then we can sort everything out."

His eyes move to where my hand is, and when his eyes meet mine, I feel it everywhere. I pull my hand away and he runs his fingers through his hair. "This is a start."

I tamp down my feeling and nod. "It is."

"Let's stop now, and we'll look at it tomorrow with fresh eyes."

Normally, I would be all for that. We've been at it for hours, and honestly, my mind isn't firing on all cylinders. However, this means we're not working and we're staying in the same house.

What the hell are we supposed to do?

It's late. I could just go to my room, which is probably the safest option.

But then Killian stands and extends his hand. "Come on, we need to eat and then I want to show you something."

I look up, unsure of what to do, but there's something in his eyes, an excitement that calls to me. So I take his hand and allow him to lead me into the living room.

"We're going to order in and then go out to the barn."

"The barn?" I ask, not really sure that's a good idea.

"I want to show you a few of the foals."

When we did a tour of the place yesterday, it was more about where things were and overall layout. I saw a few horses because it's pretty much impossible not to, but I didn't get to see any babies.

"I would really love that."

He smiles. "Pizza or Chinese food?"

Oh, that's a hard one. Still, I don't know that I trust small-town pizza. "Weren't you the one who warned me about Italian food here?"

Killian laughs. "I did. So, Chinese food it is. Why don't you go change and I'll call it in."

I write down my order for him and then come up to my room.

This has truly been such a strange few days, but I actually have a little hope that we're on to something. With us finding something abnormal, it almost feels like maybe we'll get some answers.

I grab my jeans and change into a T-shirt—I didn't really pack a lot of options, so I have to make do—and head downstairs. Killian is sitting on the couch, reading something on his phone and wearing a pair of wire-rimmed glasses.

Okay, why do the glasses just make him look hotter than usual?

I inwardly groan and put aside my thoughts of his sexiness as I enter the room.

"Hey," he says when he looks up to see me.

"Hi."

"Food should be here in about five to ten minutes. Do you want to watch something?" Killian asks as he lifts the remote.

I shake my head. "No, I'm good. Thank you though."

He smiles and puts it down. "Not big into TV?"

"Oh, I love watching ridiculous reality shows, but it's what I do on the weekends when I have hours to just put it on."

He chuckles. "I can't sit still that long. I tried to watch a series once and after two episodes I had to go outside and work."

"I can lie on the couch on a Saturday for twelve hours and not even notice." It's not my finest quality, but it's really sometimes what I need. To zone out, forget the world, and watch mindless television. "All week long I focus so much, I have to be one hundred percent tuned into work, so when I get the chance to just…veg…I do it big."

"Do you like being a publicist?"

"I do. I mean, I love parts of it. I think my work is meaningful, especially when I can help others. I don't hate it," I answer in the most vague answer I can give.

While I do love the company I work for, it's not my end game. My dream is to help people in a different way, more giving them the tools to avoid needing help fixing issues. It's not something I'll be able to afford to do, but...being a publicist isn't something I went into life dreaming of.

Killian pulls his glasses off, tossing them on the coffee table. He shifts, facing me more directly. "I don't hate a lot of things, but that doesn't mean I like them. What did you dream of doing?"

I smile softly, trying to think how to answer this where I don't sound like an idiot since this is my job. "When I was little, I was never a girl who knew what she wanted, you know? I didn't have this dream of growing up and being something. I just wanted to make a difference, and then I thought I was going to be a therapist. I wanted to help people, really help people at their core."

"So what stopped you?" Killian asks as he drapes his arm across the back of the couch.

I pull my lip between my teeth as I let the weight of the question settle. There are so many things that contributed to it, but really, there's just one big one. "My father."

"Your father?"

"Yeah. It's complicated and honestly, it's not a fun story."

"Do you want to tell me about it?"

God, not really. "Maybe another time."

Killian's smile is soft and his fingers graze my arm. "Whenever you want to talk about it, I'd like to hear it. To go from wanting to fix people's lives to saving a horse ranch from whatever bullshit is going on seems a little similar. You're helping people's lives by being a publicist and stepping in."

I laugh. "It does when you put it that way."

There is a buzzing sound on the security panel. "That's probably the food," Killian says as he gets up. He says something back and forth through the speaker and then buzzes the driver through.

He opens the door, waiting for the car to approach and then exchanges the money for food. I get up to help and also offer to pay, but he, of course, won't hear it.

Killian lays out the food and hands me chopsticks. I grab a container, sit back on the couch, and dig in.

"All right, so I know I said I'd wait, but you gotta give me something. How did you end up as a publicist?"

I pull my right leg up and cross my left under my butt. "I got really lucky. Out of undergrad, I was kind of floundering, and I took a job as a nanny. It was for a pretty famous baseball player in Indiana. He's represented by Anchor Light, but the entertainment division out of California. I met Catherine, the owner, and she said I was a natural at seeing a problem and creating a solid path. Offered me an internship while I was in grad school and then I got hired full-time by Brynlee into the new corporate side."

They both assured me that my instincts were spot on.

Although, my current situation would say otherwise.

I'm living with the man who was supposed to be a one-night stand. Who also is my client. And is probably a bit older than I'm allowing myself to admit.

"Egg roll?" Killian offers.

I shake my head. "No thanks, I'm not a fan of egg rolls. All right, I answered your question—tell me about your other business in Boston."

Killian puts his container down. "Not much to tell. We're a real estate investment company. My partner handles most of the business, while I just look at what he's interested in and decide if it's a good financial move. I'm pragmatic, where Nathaniel is more emotionally driven. I do think that's why he's successful, though. Where I follow the numbers, he goes with his instincts. We started it after I decided professional football wasn't for me and he offered me an opportunity because he saw I was lost after I gave up the sport I loved."

"He seems important to you," Tessa notes.

"He's saved my life more times than I can count. Nathaniel is like a brother. When my sister was sick, he didn't say a single word when I said I needed to come down here and split time in Boston. He picked up the slack, never complained, and he still doesn't. He's truly my best friend."

I smile at that. "I think we all need people like that."

I know how much my friends mean to me. If it weren't for them, I would've fallen apart multiple times.

Killian nods. "I agree. Nathaniel has great instincts for what will make money and what won't. When we started, he was flipping houses for the most part. It did well, and we reinvested that into buying up commercial and residential real estate. I don't know, it pays the bills and I really focus on the financial side of things where Nathaniel is the salesman."

"Sounds pretty...boring."

He chuckles. "It is. It's why I love this ranch so much, and over the past six years, I've spent more and more time here. With the sales of the horses and the board and train option, this ranch has become more lucrative than the real estate company and that's saying something."

And now he's losing money like crazy. Sales are dropping, people are pulling their horses, there is no trainer, and if we make any big moves, the story could sprout wings and take flight.

It's why I need to find Travis.

He's the lynchpin in this grenade.

In the meantime, I need to bring customers here and save his business. I have ideas on ways we can do community outreach and start to get the word out. Of course, he's going to hate all of them, which is why I'm trying to pin down which one I want to approach first.

"Are you finished?" Killian asks, looking down at the food.

"Yes, I'm stuffed. Thank you. Let me know how much dinner was."

He rolls his eyes and gets up. "Sure, I'll put it on your tab."

I'm pretty sure that means he will not do that.

I help him clean up and then I follow him out to the barn.

He pulls the big door to the right, and we walk through. This barn is huge, with a half-open loft at the one end and at least fifteen stalls. Killian walks over to an area and grabs a bag.

"Here." He hands it to me. "Apples are a horse's best friend."

I smile. "Thanks."

We walk through, stopping at a few stalls, giving apples to the horses and petting their necks. Each one is beautiful, but I'm completely enamored with the last one we come to. She's taller than the others, but lean and the most stunning shade of black. Her mane is as dark as her coat.

She's stunning.

"This was my first horse," Killian says as he rubs her nose. "This is Midnight. She's been with me a long time, right girl?"

"How did you get into horses?" I ask.

"My sister, Alicia. We grew up in Colorado in this small town called Infinity Ridge. Anyway, they have a horse ranch there and she would go over after school, muck out the stalls, and talk to Mr. Stone about one day being able to buy one of his horses."

I smile. "Did she?"

Killian sighs and shakes his head. "No, she never could. My family was poor. We could never afford to take care of a horse, let alone cover the price of it. However, Mr. Stone was one of those men who believed in hard work and he allowed her to pick one horse she loved and he promised to let her ride anytime she wanted, if she promised to take care of him."

I lean against the stall door, reaching my hand out to pet Midnight. "He sounds like an amazing man."

"He is. My sister was there every single day, taking care of her horse. Of course, as her younger brother, I wanted to be there too."

Sounds like my brother. "Ahh, little brothers and their need to be annoying."

He grins. "I asked Mr. Stone if the same applied to me—it didn't."

I burst out laughing. "I didn't see that twist."

"I wasn't half as dedicated as Alicia. However, about eight years ago, when my sister was diagnosed with cancer, I went to the Hart-Stone Ranch and bought her Midnight."

My chest tightens and I keep my gaze on his. "You bought her this horse?"

"Yes. And I bought this ranch when she got sick so I could keep them both here."

I gasp. "Wow, that's...beautiful. You bought a farm for your sister?"

"A few other reasons too, but yes."

This ranch clearly means more to him than I imagined. Of course all people love their businesses and no one wants to see their work fall apart, but there's a deeper meaning too.

"Did your sister live here?"

Killian looks at Midnight and rubs her nose. "She did. It was her dream to live on ranch like this."

"How so?"

"We left Colorado as soon as we both could. I went to college in Boston at eighteen and never came back. Alicia met a guy and moved a town over from here. He left her when she was diagnosed, said he didn't sign up for years of agony, whatever the fuck that meant. Not that life with him was all that great. They barely got by and then she was sick and without anything. By then, my company in Boston was doing extremely well, so I came here, bought the ranch so she could be around her horse and not have to worry about finances."

I reach my hand out, resting it on his arm. "Killian, that's so... amazing. I hope you know that. For her to have that peace probably meant the world to her."

"I hope so."

"I can assure you, it did."

He smiles. "Thank you."

I nod once.

"It's why I can't lose it, Tessa. I need to save it. Whatever we have to do, I'll do it. I love this land, the barns, the horses."

The way his voice quivers sends an ache through my heart. "I know, we'll figure it out."

His big green eyes lock on mine, and I pray I can deliver on my promise.

And now, my professional feelings just got personal.

CHAPTER 9
KILLIAN

I ROLL OVER, HEARING A BUZZING ON THE NIGHTSTAND, SEE WHAT time it is, and force myself to grab it.

Who the fuck is calling at four-thirty in the morning?

Nathaniel. That's who.

"Do you ever sleep?" I ask, rubbing my eyes.

"I get a solid four hours a night."

"You know they say sleep is necessary to be a functioning human."

Nathaniel laughs. "We sold six more houses this week, and by we, I mean me. Plus I'm on mile six of my morning run. I'm pretty sure I'm functioning just fine."

"I'm glad one of us is," I grumble and sit up, leaning against the headboard. "What can I do for you this fine—ridiculously early—morning?"

He answers without any huffing and puffing. "I wanted to see how things are going down there."

"I'm not really sure. For now we have no answers."

"How is that possible? You're the smartest man I know. You can always see the puzzle pieces."

Not this time apparently. "Normally, yeah, but right now, nothing adds up."

"Is there anything I can do to help?"

If I thought he could, he would've been one of my first calls. Nathaniel and I have been friends since college. Just two football players who got bunked up from completely opposite sides of the world. He grew up in New York City, came from money, went to a private school with tutors and all that shit. I came from small-town Colorado with not a pot to piss in. What we did share was a love for football—and girls.

"Just don't let our business go under or I'll really be fucked."

"Do you need a loan?"

The fact he even offered it shows how he's more of a family member than a friend. "No, I appreciate it, though."

I've always been a planner. My entire life I've always seen my future goals and done the work to get to them. When I bought this farm, I took a huge gamble because it was the first time I didn't have a real vision.

All the money I'd saved, the years of busting my ass and putting everything away, I used to buy this place.

The goal was to use my investments to invest in this place and then sell it when my sister was gone. Only nothing went to plan. I fell in love with the land and no longer wanted to get rid of it. It's special to me, it holds memories of Alicia, and it became lucrative. I was rebuilding the nest egg I cracked wide the hell open to give me back some savings.

That has now been flattened as I've had to cover the costs out of that to keep this place afloat.

"I'm serious, Killian, I can give you whatever you need. If you're uncomfortable with it being a loan, we'll work out something business-wise. Sell me some shares or whatever the fuck you need to feel better about it," Nathaniel offers.

I sigh, hating that this is even a possibility. "If it comes to that, I'll let you know."

"All right."

"How are things going in Boston?" I ask, hoping at least that company is doing well.

"Things are good. We just got another warehouse space listed. Hopefully that sells quicker than the last."

I always worked the more residential side, but Nathaniel really thought we should go into commercial sales. We decided to sort of split the business and each focus on what we were most passionate about. I also do the financials, because the one thing this man is not good at is budgeting and accounting.

"I'm sure you'll get it done."

He lets out a long puff of air, and I know he's done with his run now as the sound of the machine ends, not that the man is out of breath or anything. "I'm going to check on your properties this week, and since this thing in Ember Falls seems to be a bigger issue than you anticipated, I'm going to bring in Craig, the guy I mentioned that I met at the last auction to help a little. He'll be able to do more than I can on my own. Are you cool with that?"

"Do whatever you have to. I don't want clients upset, so if Craig can help, that's great."

"All right. Go take care of your things. I need to swim a mile or two and then get to work."

"Thanks for the wake-up call."

"Anytime."

We hang up, and as much as I'd love to just go to sleep, that's not going to happen. I have a lot of things I need to do on the ranch.

I hear a noise coming from the kitchen and head to my door, opening it.

There is Tessa in the kitchen in a pair of shorts and a T-shirt that's been cut in half, allowing me to see her flat stomach perfectly.

I lean against the doorjamb and smile.

She looks so beautiful, her earbuds are in, and she's dancing around silently. She moves to the stove, stirring something, and then shakes her ass.

God, I want to walk up behind her, grab her hips, and kiss her neck.

Instead, I have to stand here like a creep.

I clear my throat, hoping she'll hear me, but she doesn't—if her ass shaking is any indication.

I walk closer and rest my backside on the counter.

Tessa moves her body side to side, and I can see she's making eggs.

Her arms go up in a V, head falling back, and then she goes to grab the pan off the stove and turns.

When she does, those eggs go flying as she screams, holding the pan like a bat.

"Oh my God!" she yells.

I lift both hands. "It's just me."

Her chest heaves and she slowly lowers the pan. "Don't ever sneak up on a girl."

I grin. "I tried to get your attention."

She looks down at the eggs, that are now on the floor, and sighs. "Damn it."

I walk over, grabbing some paper towels, and laugh softly. "What were you listening to?"

Her eyes go wide and now I'm really intrigued. "Nothing really."

"No? You seemed pretty into it."

"I wasn't."

"Really?"

Tessa shrugs. "I mean, sure, I was into it, but it's music. You're supposed to be into it."

"I agree. I love music." My tastes are pretty eclectic. I love everything from country to rap to certain pop songs. "So, what were you listening to?"

"My brother said that it was his job to ensure that I was well rounded so my playlist is mostly Dr. Dre, Eminem, Biggie, and DMX."

I grin. "Some of the best."

"You like rap?"

"I do. I usually go for country, just because it's what I prefer, but my workout mix is pretty much all rap."

She smiles. "I love that. I would've pegged you for a metal guy for the gym."

I step toward her. "Nope."

"I'm sorry if I woke you up. I was trying to be quiet."

"You didn't wake me." Another step. "It's early—why are you awake?"

Tessa sighs. "My mind never shuts off." I understand that issue. "I was lying in bed, thinking about everything. I feel like while we're waiting for some information on Travis, we should reach out to previous buyers in the last year. Maybe we can find a connection."

She inched forward as she spoke, and her body is now so close. I know she's telling me what we need to do to work on the ranch's issues, but all I can do is focus on her lips. How they move as she speaks. The way her eyes widen slightly at the end, when the idea seemed to excite her.

I don't think she knows how absolutely beautiful she is.

I clench my fists at my side to keep from reaching toward her, touching her when I know I shouldn't.

Then she tilts her head to the side, letting out a heavy breath. "Killian?"

Right. She was talking.

I lift my gaze to meet hers. "If you think that's a good idea."

Tessa crosses her one leg in front of the other and then bites her lip. "I do. I think if we can talk to a few people, find out how their experience was, their process, almost as though we're doing an internal audit, we might unmask some information to help us. Also, I want us to do some community outreach stuff. The goal is to get some horses sold, right?"

"Right."

She runs her hands through her hair. "Cool. I'm going to come up with a few more ideas and we'll try to get something going right away."

I'm not sure how she thinks that's going to happen, but I'm not going to argue. I'm much too busy focusing on her.

"You have something..." I say lifting my hand and pulling it back.

"What?"

"Egg. It's in your hair."

Tessa runs her hands through her hair and the piece of egg is still there.

Without thinking, without remembering that I'm not supposed to want her, to touch her, to be this damn close to her, I step closer. Her big blue eyes lift to mine as I stare back at her. She's so fucking beautiful, and I want nothing more than to pull her against me and crush my lips to hers.

But I can't.

So, I raise my fingers, touching the silky brown strands and pulling it out, but my hand rests on her neck.

Her breathing hitches and those blue eyes widen. The desire is like a physical pulse between us—I can feel it pounding in my chest.

Tessa's lips part and her gaze goes to my mouth.

She wants the same thing.

"Killian," she breathes my name as I move my hand up higher.

I rub my thumb against her cheek. "There's egg..."

"Where?"

"Your lips," I lie.

Her chest rises and falls quickly.

I should be stronger than this. I should step back, go in my room, lock the door, jack off, and then go about my day.

What I definitely shouldn't do is lean in, but that's exactly my next move.

Tessa's gaze doesn't waver and her voice is barely above a whisper. "You should get it off then."

I don't wait for any further confirmation, I move my lips to hers and kiss away all my fucking self-control.

Her body moves into mine, hands resting on my chest as our lips move against each other's. She is so damn perfect. I've never wanted anyone the way I want her.

Our tongues move together, and I hold her face with both hands, needing her to stay with me. In a moment, one or the both of us will remember why this is a bad idea. She's too young, she's not from here, I'm in the middle of my entire business crumbling around me, and…she's my publicist.

Pretty sure this is not exactly part of the package.

However, right now, none of those reasons exist for me.

All that matters is her.

She lets out a soft moan as her hands move up to my neck. I don't know how long we kiss for, but it's not enough.

Too soon, she pulls back, her eyes wide, heart-shaped lips swollen, and then she covers them with her hand.

"Oh my…I shouldn't. We shouldn't," Tessa says, stepping back.

"Maybe not, but I don't regret it."

And I walk out before I do something I really will regret.

But I hear her as I go. "Neither do I."

"Mr. Thorn?" Gary, my ranch hand, calls my name as I'm walking through the barn.

"Yes?"

"Do you still want to ride out today?"

I nod. "Yes, can you saddle up two horses for me and tie them out back?"

"Two?"

Before I can say anything, Tessa's voice calls from behind me, "You have like three barns and an arena—you didn't tell me which one."

I grin. "Yet you found me."

She huffs. "I did."

After our kiss this morning, I took a cold shower and sent her a message to meet me in the barn. Today, I want to take her out of the office and show her the land in full. If she's going to help me save this place, I want her to see it in its entirety.

"Do you remember how to ride?"

Tessa looks at the horse and back to me. "I do."

"How about we skip going through papers that don't make sense and go see the land?"

Her long lashes flutter a few times and she smiles. "All right."

I glance down at the sundress she has on. "You may want to change."

"Right! Shit. Okay, I'll be back."

I help Gary saddle the horses and head inside to grab a few things to eat. We're going to be gone most of the day. I put the stuff in the bag, and Tessa comes down the stairs. She's wearing a pair of skintight jeans and a white shirt, pulling her hair up as she's descending.

I swear, the air feels thin as I look at her.

She stops when she gets to the bottom. "Hey, sorry I took a bit. I got a call."

I shake my head and put on my cowboy hat. "No problem. It allowed me to pack lunch."

"Oh! We'll be gone all day?"

"Yes."

"All right then. The call was from Brynlee—she wanted to see how things were. I gave her an update, and we brainstormed the ideas I had about ways to bring in some profit at the same time as getting people in to see the available horses. I'm assuming you'll do some auctions?"

"Yes, I have one set for next week."

I have no fucking choice. I have to sell at least four horses this month to not be completely screwed. One of the biggest issues I have is that Travis was supposed to take a deposit for each sale, he assured me he was doing that, but it turns out he wasn't doing that or if he did, it was never deposited into the bank.

I never noticed it because we had such an influx of sales.

Now all the pending sales for the next six months are gone with no recourse.

"Hopefully the auction proves fruitful. You do have a very high success rate. I did a lot of reading yesterday and I think it'll be good. In the meantime, we'll talk about some options we can do here."

I have no idea what options she thinks I have. This is a breeding, training, and boarding ranch with no trainer and all but three promised sales are canceled.

There's really nothing I can do to bring income into the barn unless I can get some locals to board with me.

I extend my arm back to head to the barn. Tessa smiles and we make our way to where the horses are tied up after Gary saddled them.

She immediately walks to the chestnut mare, extending her hand. "Hi, girl. What's your name?"

"That's Billie-Jean."

"You're just a girl, huh?"

I laugh. "She's not my lover, that's for sure, but it seems she's taken with you."

Seems to be a trend on this farm.

"Well, it's nice to meet you, Billie-Jean."

She looks over to me. "You're not going to ride Midnight?"

"No, this is Bentley. He's a bit of a nightmare but needs some exercise. Do you need help up?" I ask, hoping she'll say yes so I can accidentally touch her ass.

Tessa grabs the horn, puts her foot in the stirrup, hoists herself up, and smiles. "I got it. Can you hand me the reins though?"

"You know, you should've done that first."

She shrugs. "I know, but I have a capable friend on the ground."

I chuckle. "Yes, you do."

I untie Billie-Jean and hand Tessa the reins.

After, I get the food put in the saddle pouch on my horse and tie the blanket on the back, then I give Bentley a look that tells him I will not appreciate him making me look like an idiot.

Thankfully, he seems to get the point and allows me to untie him and get up without rearing or bucking.

I turn him in a few circles and glance over at Tessa who is just sitting on the very sweet and docile Billie-Jean. I give her a nod. "Ready?"

"I'll follow you."

CHAPTER 10
TESSA

THIS FARM IS BEYOND WHAT I EVER IMAGINED. I'VE NEVER BEEN happier to go on a horse ride than I am right now.

Killian owns over forty acres, and I am blown away as we climb a little part of the mountain range and trot down into a small, wooded valley.

There is a large clearing, which is one of the pastures, but there are huge evergreens around and I swear it's as though we're the only people in the world.

"This is so peaceful," I say softly.

"It is."

For the first time in so many damn years, I feel at ease. It's as though all the struggles just melted away as we rode farther and farther away from the chaos.

"You know, I can't thank you enough for this."

"It's me who should be thanking you. I haven't had a lot of time as of late to just come out here and ride. You gave me the perfect excuse."

I grin, liking his words way more than I should. "I forgot how much I loved to ride."

Killian comes up beside me on Bentley, eyes slightly hidden under that sexy hat that I want to rip off him and ride him instead.

Bad idea, Tessa. Get your head out of the gutter.

"How did you learn how to ride like this?"

Oh, the whole story is definitely not one I'll share, but there are bits and pieces I can give.

"When I was in high school, I really hated everyone. My dad, he's the worst and caused so much turmoil in our lives. He left when my brother was little, but really used the two of us to manipulate my mother. He'd show up before disappearing, leaving Reece and me trying to understand what we did wrong. My junior year of high school, I was a mess. I went from being a really great student to skipping class all the time and…I needed help."

I needed so much help.

"Is this where the horses come in?" Killian asks.

"My teacher, who is an absolute saint of a human being, stepped in. She spent her summers working with an equine therapy program for kids from broken homes. It was a lot of money, and we didn't have any. However, she got me a grant or—" I snort out a laugh "—knowing Mrs. Knoll, I would bet she paid for it herself. Anyway, I went for the summer, and it was the single best thing I ever did in my life. It completely changed me. I ended up volunteering during the summers when I was home from college."

Which was a whole other thing because when you are working just to live, taking two months off really messes with your cash flow.

Still, I didn't care. It paid for itself in other ways.

"You made it sound like this was just a camp, not that it was so life-changing. Why didn't you tell me how much the horses meant to you?"

I shrug. "I don't know."

I do know—it's because my life was a mess. I've worked so hard not to be that girl. The one who was angry at everyone, wanted to burn the world down because nothing was fair. Life isn't fair, I know this, but I had a victim mentality until I went to that camp. I saw people who had it way worse than me. All of that changed me, but it was my therapist there who gave me the permission to make my own decisions.

To go to college because I deserved it.

Feeling unworthy my whole life was hard, but being told by my parents I didn't deserve better broke me.

I saved me by believing in myself.

Who the hell wants to say all that to a guy she banged and is trying to be professional with?

Not me.

"I'm glad you told me now," Killian says with a grin. "We have two more things I want to show you."

"Oh?"

We ride a little deeper into the forest and we emerge into a meadow. It's not like the other pastures, this one is…untouched.

"Come on." He smiles and then dismounts.

We've been riding for over three hours, and I don't know that my legs will work. Instead of having to worry about my body betraying me, Killian is there, his hands outstretched, and I hook my leg over Billie-Jean, allowing him to help me down.

"Thank you."

I clear my throat and drop my hands that were resting on his chest.

"I'd like to show you something that means a lot to me." Killian extends his hand, palm up.

This is a bad idea, holding hands and walking through this beautiful vista, but, well, I'm an idiot, what can I say?

I put my palm in his, and we walk through the meadow. This is one of those movie scene meadows too. It's lush, green with sprinkles of different colored flowers. The wind blows softly, causing it to sway back and forth. We get to a three-rail fence and I look around, waiting for whatever it was that he wanted to show me.

"It's just on the other side," he says.

Of course it is. Thankfully, I'm in jeans and since I'm staying with Killian, I can wash my clothes. I climb over and he follows, then takes my hand again. We walk through and there's the sound of rushing water.

We get through a clearing and I gasp as I see the most beautiful waterfall. It's at least a twenty-foot drop, and while the water rushes, it then hits the pool and is calm and beautiful. "Wow, this is spectacular."

He chuckles. "It is. The funny thing is, this isn't even *the* Ember Falls."

My eyes narrow and I tilt my head. "What? There's more than one?"

"This town is full of old folklore, all of it is stupid, at least the bits and pieces I know. Apparently you have to have grown up here or be married or dating someone who did to get the full story."

I cross my arms over my chest. "That is ridiculous."

"Yup, so this is Falls Ember, as I call it."

"Ember Falls in reverse? Cute."

"The legend has it that the falls by Lachlan's house have a magical pool that can make you invisible or some shit if you go in. So, this pool doesn't do that, but it will make you an exceptional lover."

I burst out laughing, not expecting that. "Really?"

"I'm pretty sure you can attest to that being true."

My cheeks heat and I look away because I sure can. "Anyway…"

"I own it, so really, I'm the only one who reaps the benefits of this waterfall, which is why when we were together, it was as good as it was."

"I see, you were storing up your powers and I was the lucky woman who got to release them?"

"Lucky, huh?"

I roll my eyes. "Poor choice in words. I guess I should say, one of the many women."

I don't want to even think about how many women he's used this asinine story on.

He takes a step closer. "I haven't been with a woman in a while,

Tessa. There's never been anyone to tempt me to want more, not until you. So, lucky is the right word."

A flutter in my stomach feels as though it could take flight. I gaze up into his green eyes. "You were lucky then too."

"I know full well I was."

"Right, and…you know…so the falls," I stumble through my words as I shift.

The sex. The kiss. The almost moments. The stupid butterflies and nights I dream of him are a mistake. I have to resist him because come what may, in a week or two, I'm going back to New York and he's staying here.

We are client and publicist. This is literally the definition of bad publicity.

If Aarabelle—or, even worse, Brynlee—found out that this is what I was doing, I'd be fired. Hell, I should fire myself at this rate. I've broken several rules in my contract and I can't even claim I didn't know anymore because I let him kiss me in the kitchen.

So, no, I won't do anything else to jeopardize my career.

Killian returns his gaze to the water. "The falls are part of what I love about this land. Everything around it is exactly like it's meant to be, and when I use this part of the farm, I want it to be for something truly special. Something that has meaning, you know? I don't want to just have this be another pasture."

I smile. "I do. You'll find that something."

"I think I will." My chest grows tight as he stares at me before smiling and stepping back. "Come on, let's head back. We should probably dig into the piles."

I place my hand in his and let him lead me away, praying we find something so I can leave before I become enchanted with this place.

———

Our ride yesterday was amazing, but we lost a day of work, which means today, I'm paying for it. I woke up early, got dressed, and thought I'd get a jump on things. After I spent three hours going through the documents, I decided I needed a break from it all. I need to stop having breakfast with Killian where he cooks and I tell myself that I feel nothing for him. It's a lie. There's nothing professional about any of this.

If this were any other client, I wouldn't be staying with them, eating meals, dreaming of them, and also having slept with him, wishing for it again.

So, I came into town for breakfast. There were a bunch of adorable shops and I want to explore.

Or—escape.

Either term is applicable.

I pass the antique store and shudder—no need to go in there— and keep walking down Main Street. There's an ice cream store, a pizzeria, the bar is over on the other side—none of those are good breakfast options.

Finally, I stop outside a cute little store called Prose & Perk that has a coffee cup on the logo. That's promising. Maybe they have breakfast items.

"One second!" I hear someone yell from the back as I enter.

It's really cute. There are three big bookcases that have a bunch of books, the tables and chairs are all mismatched in an old-world type of style. My favorite part is that the walls are papered in the old pages of books, overlapping.

I instantly love it here.

"Can I help you?" A sweet voice calls to me.

"Hi, sorry." I make my way to the back of the store where a woman who is probably early thirties with long blond, curly hair is behind the counter. "I was just admiring the store."

She grins. "Thank you. I'm Hazel, I own the place."

"I'm Tessa. It's nice to meet you."

"You too. Did you want to order anything?"

I look at the menu and purse my lips. "Hmm, what's your favorite coffee here?"

"It's not on the menu."

"Really?" I ask.

Hazel nods. "Do you like strong coffee?"

"Absolutely." It's the only way I made it through finals in college.

"Then I'll make it." Hazel turns and starts to get to work, moving levers and grinding coffee beans. "So what brings you to Ember Falls?"

"I'm actually here for work. I'm a publicist for a company in New York City."

"That's great. How long are you here for?"

I was hoping I would already be in my car heading home, but that's not happening.

"I'm not sure—depends how long my client needs me. Probably another week though."

She glances at me from over her shoulder. "Oh, then you must be here to help Killian."

"Who?" I pretend I'm misunderstanding. Part of my job is discretion, and I have no idea who this woman is.

Hazel laughs softly and then turns with the coffee, placing it on the counter with a muffin. "Killian is a good friend of mine. I really hope he has you on his team. Especially since you so expertly dodged my question. Lord knows small towns aren't known for keeping secrets."

I smile softly. "Yes, I grew up in one and I learned that lesson well. Thank you—for the coffee."

"You're very welcome, Tessa."

"For the love of God, Hazel!" A deep voice yells as the door opens. "You're going to be the death of me!"

The man with dark brown hair in a pair of scrubs walks in with Dr. Everett Finnegan embroidered on the left of his shirt.

He's tall, stocky, and super cute. Not as cute as Killian, but I'm starting to think that's not even possible because no one measures up to him.

I need therapy.

Hazel rolls her eyes and sighs at the outburst. "Everett, meet Tessa. Tessa, this is my idiot best friend who clearly has no damn manners as he's yelling at me for no damn reason."

Oh boy.

He huffs. "Right, no damn reason." Everett looks to me. "Do you know what she did?"

"I don't even have a clue."

"She told Violet, my fiancée, that I agreed to renovate her house starting this weekend. Her entire freaking house she wants to do. Now, as someone who has a full-time job saving *lives*, do you think I can do that?" he asks.

I purse my lips, not really wanting to enter the fray. "I'm going to guess no."

"You would be right." He turns to Hazel. "Care to explain?"

Hazel sighs heavily, looking completely unrepentant. "You owe me."

"I owe you?"

"Yes, for about four years of free coffee, for fixing your ever messed-up love life—well, before Violet came back—having to go to your dumb games, and I could probably name a million other things. So, you owe me, and your saint of a fiancée agrees." Her smile says she thinks she just played her winning hand.

"What's my total that you feel you're owed? I'll write you a check."

Hazel grins. "Not a chance. Now, we're being rude arguing in front of a customer."

I lift my hands and chuckle. "Oh no, this is great. Reminds me of me and my brother."

Hazel slaps Everett's chest. "He's an idiot, and it's my job to fix him and all the other dumbasses who live in this town."

"There's a lot of them?" I ask.

"All of them, and coincidentally the four biggest ones who reside in Ember Falls happen to be on the same Ultimate Frisbee team."

I pull my head back. "What is an...Ultimate Frisbee team?"

Everett huffs. "Seriously, the women in this town need to learn more about sports. For fuck's sake, it's a very serious league. It takes an extreme amount of athleticism as well as mental concentration. We are elite athletes."

At that Hazel bursts out laughing. "Oh my God! You said that with a straight face? Oh, I can't wait to tell Ainsley, Penny, and Violet what you said."

"I hate you," Everett retorts.

"You don't, but you're ridiculous." She turns to me. "It's Frisbee with goal lines. You should come by and see their intense athleticism and absolute dialed-in concentration."

"I'm a little afraid now," I confess.

I'm not really afraid, but they seem pretty intense about this. I need to occupy myself a little, and if this is a league and there are games or something, that could be fun.

Maybe.

I love sports, don't get me wrong. I used to sit on my grandpa's lap and watch football every Saturday and Sunday before he passed away. He didn't discriminate between college and professional. Saturday we listened to him scream about his alma mater continuing to suck each year and Sundays it was the same thing.

But no matter what, I would go in my room, get my jersey and sit with him, yelling and repeating whatever he grumbled about. It carried on through college by going to home games, even though we lost all the time, I just love sports.

This doesn't really sound much like a sport.

"Oh, they're harmless, don't even worry, but it's fun and the girls bring wine and charcuterie, make fun of everyone. I know you're only here for work, but a week is a long time to be holed up somewhere in this town. Isn't there a practice tonight?"

Everett crosses his arms over his chest. "Yes, at six."

She grins. "What do you say, Tessa? Want to come watch middle-aged men pretend they're still in their twenties?"

I laugh. "I wouldn't miss it."

CHAPTER 11
KILLIAN

"Absolutely not," I huff. It's just past lunch and Tessa and I are in the middle of a heated debate on how to save the farm.

Tessa rubs her temples with her two fingers. "You need this."

"Not that much. I'd rather eat nails."

She glares at me. "That's going to be all you can afford if you don't do something to start bringing income in. I have four options. Pick one."

I'm not doing children's horse-riding parties. Absolutely not. We're a freaking award-winning horse breeding operation. We don't do parties.

The second option is out of the question. "A rodeo?"

"You have a huge arena, it wouldn't be that hard to add some bleachers," Tessa says with a grin.

I'm glad someone is enjoying this conversation because it sure as fuck isn't me. "No."

"Killian, that's probably the most lucrative of the options. We can charge for admission, the participants can pay a fee, all you have to do is provide some food, which I bet we could talk to the bar and grill to see if they'd donate, and it would help the town by bringing people in."

I clench my jaw. None of this would even be a conversation if it weren't for Travis. Which reminds me.

"We'll come back to this list in a second," I say lifting it. "Where were you this morning?"

She bristles. "Working on that list and acquainting myself with the town. I went to the coffee shop, checked out a few other little stores, which is why I think the rodeo is the absolute best option."

"I didn't realize you weren't going to be here when I got back from checking on the horses."

Tessa lets out a long sigh. "I didn't know I needed to tell you when I was going to be out?"

"You don't." I pull back my feelings about it. I don't know why I'm fighting her on it. She doesn't have to inform me, but for a minute, I was worried and I've started looking forward to seeing her in my kitchen.

Which is really stupid.

"Okay."

I need to shift gears away from this list for a minute. I can't even wrap my mind around doing any of this. "I spoke with a company in Virginia Beach today about looking into Travis's whereabouts."

Her eyes widen. "You did? I hired someone as well."

"Yes, I know you said your friend couldn't find anything so far, but the company that I was put in contact with is known for this. It's going to cost me a bit, but we're on a time crunch and bleeding money. Time is of the essence."

"I agree. I pushed my friend again, but he said he can't find anything after the day we last had him here. So, either he was planning whatever the hell this is or he's missing and needs help."

Both explanations suck. All I can hope is that he has a damn good reason for screwing me if it's the first and we find him quickly if it's the second. Well, honestly both require me to find him.

At this point, I'm pissed and don't understand how he could do this to me. I trusted him, gave him the reins to do as he thought and he fucked me. Took off with a vague note and a mountain of problems.

Now I need Cole Securities to do their magic that Miles assured me they can, since it's going to cost me a small fortune.

That's with a friends and family discount.

"Hopefully this yields some results."

"Okay, so back to what we can do at this point, look at the list," Tessa urges.

I exhale and go back again.

"You're kidding me, right?" I ask as I look at the third option.

"It'll be fun! Bachelorette parties, girl's nights, women love a cowboy, and I'm sorry but you've got Stetsons and boots running rampant on this ranch. Think of all the money you could make while we work on the bigger picture."

"No."

I'm not hosting these parties.

"I heard while I was in town that there are at least two women getting married—just think about that. You can charge one big fee, and we could set up a program that requires little financial up-front cost."

I know she's trying, and all of these ideas are exactly the point of her being here. To help unfuck the issue and also create a way to bring some income to the ranch. But I meant selling horses.

I didn't mean this way.

"Tessa, I know that this is your job, but I don't want to be a sideshow. I want to sell these horses. I want to make large amounts of money. We have the auction Sunday. I'll have six horses that I'm going to put up. Three of them are my top dollar options and the other three are mid. My hope is that I can get a really good influx of money quickly."

"And if that doesn't happen?"

Then I'm fucked. "I'll figure it out."

She stands from the chair and walks to me. "That is why I'm here. I'm trying to figure it out for you, Killian, but you're fighting me on everything. Is there not one thing on that list you'll put as our backup?"

"The rodeo, I guess."

Tessa's lips lift into a soft smile. "Okay, we'll see how the auction goes and then we can go from there, does that work?"

No, but...I'm going to come off like a prick, so. "Sure."

"Okay." She glances down at her watch. "I actually have to be somewhere in about twenty minutes. Do you mind if we get back to this tomorrow?"

"No, I actually have plans tonight as well."

My phone buzzes in my pocket—probably yet another response to the damn text thread that I have been ignoring all day.

"Perfect. Also, I'll be gone all day Saturday, but on Monday we can go through more of the paperwork."

"No problem."

She smiles. "Perfect."

Tessa starts to gather her things, and I grab my phone, ready to walk out and read some of the texts.

Miles: You're coming tonight, Killian.

Everett: I know I am.

Miles: Me too.

Lachlan: I did twice already today.

Everett: Yes, I'm sure you rubbed one out during lunch because from what I hear, Ainsley is pissed at you.

Lachlan: She's not pissed at all. I made it up to her.

Miles: What did he do this time?

Everett: He told Caspian that he could come stay with them for a few weeks without talking to her.

Lachlan: That's a secret, by the way. That Caspian will be in Ember Falls.

Miles: Yeah, this town is going to be really great about keeping the location of one of the newest music stars quiet. Maybe you should've told him to hide out somewhere his sister and best friend aren't living.

Everett: That would've made too much sense. We know Lachlan is a little low on that.

Miles: True. Speaking of low on smarts, where's Killian? He's not replying.

Everett: He's probably with Tessa.

Great. Fuck my life.

Lachlan: Who is Tessa?

Everett: I'll let him tell us. I met her today, and since I'm a genius and can put two and two together, it's clear why he went home with her after not even knowing her last name.

Miles: I'm sure Violet will love hearing that you checked her out.

Everett: Violet knows there's no other woman in the world who could tempt me from her. However, I have eyes.

Lachlan: Killian? Where are you, lover boy?

Miles: Maybe he's coming too.

As I start to reply, I bump into Tessa, the two of us almost wedging into the door frame.

"Shit!" she says as she drops the papers.

"I'm sorry."

I immediately lean down to help her pick them up and she does the same, causing her to bump into me and start to lose her balance, I grab for her quickly, pulling her against my chest and I break her fall, slamming my back on the ground.

But she's in my arms.

Her warmth, the scent of her perfume fills my senses, causing everything inside of me to awaken.

God, I want her so bad.

She squeaks and tries to roll to the side, pushing her hair out of her face. "Sorry! Damn it. I…" Tessa lifts her hand, wincing just a little.

"It was my fault. I wasn't watching." I let her go fully, the loss of her is a physical ache, but she's still close. I lift my fingers, brushing an errant strand of her back.

She sucks in a breath, and I can see the war raging inside of her beautiful blue eyes. "No, it was me. Shit, my hand hurts. I got it caught when I fell and tweaked it a little."

Her lashes flutter, and I move my hand down her delicate neckline, over her smooth shoulder, down to her wrist and lift her hand. "Right here?" I ask as I rub the area softly.

Tessa nods.

"Does this feel better?"

"A little," her voice cracks at the end.

"What about now?" I move my hand up to her palm, massaging it gently.

"Yes."

I lean in, inspecting her soft, delicate skin. There's no marks, no swelling yet, and while I may not be a doctor or know shit about this, I was an athlete. I had my fair share of sprains and tears. Nothing feels out of the ordinary, other than this tightening in my own body. Slowly, I lift her arm up and press my lips to her skin.

Tessa gasps softly, and I look into her blue eyes that are filled with desire.

I could kiss her.

She'd let me.

But she'd regret it.

So, I release her arm. "I think it'll be fine."

She nods. "Okay."

I get to my feet and extend my arm. "Here, let me help you up."

With her other arm, she grips my wrist and I get her to her feet. She doesn't release me immediately. "Thank you."

I nod and then she lets go. "I'll see you later."

"Later."

———————

"Tournament is coming up in two weeks. We have the first seed," Miles says as he's looking at the website.

"Well, we're undefeated so I would hope we'd be at the top," Everett notes as he tosses his bag on the grass.

We've had a great run this season. Our first year in this league was absolutely terrible. I honestly didn't have a lot of hope, but we turned it around. Going from a larger team to a smaller one was an adjustment after we were kicked out of the college league thanks to an anonymous complaint.

Next year we're considering bringing someone else onto the team and playing in a new league.

"Does it show the other teams registered?" I ask.

"Nope, just where we're seeded."

That's dumb.

Miles puts his phone down. "Doesn't matter. We'll practice and be ready for whoever it is."

Everett snorts as finally Lachlan gets here. "Oh, look who's late this time!"

"I know, I know." He has his hands raised.

Before we can say anything else another group walks over. Great. The girls are here.

I chuckle because they always make these practices more fun. I don't have to bust anyone's balls because they handle that for me.

Since I don't have anyone to impress, I don't have to worry about how I play, but these idiots go full-cocked and someone always ends up on their ass.

Miles groans and drops his head back.

"Yeah, that's why I was late," Lachlan says, turning to look at his wife. "Ainsley informed me she and the girls were coming and apparently, it's someone's fault."

I look over at Everett since he's the most likely culprit.

"Look, I went to see Hazel because she roped me into helping with her house renovation, and then she started saying the girls were coming, but I didn't encourage this. God knows I prefer them not to see us," he says and then waves.

I glance back and Violet lifts her hand.

Then...

Wait.

I count. Ainsley, one. Penelope, two. Violet, three. Hazel, four.

Fuck. There's a fifth.

Tessa.

Lachlan bumps my shoulder as I stare at her, coming toward us. "I'm going to guess based on the look on your face that Tessa is the girl you banged from the bar."

"Yup."

"The same one who is a publicist here to help save your company?"

"Yup."

He chuckles. "Oh, dude."

I turn to look at him. "Don't make me look bad."

Lachlan grins. "Fat chance, old man."

I should've stayed home.

CHAPTER 12
TESSA

"I had no idea this was so intense," I say to Hazel, who is trying to hold back a laugh.

"Oh, girl, this isn't normal. This is the guys trying to make Killian look like a dumbass in front of you."

"Are you serious?" I ask.

Penelope answers, "Yup. This is a little much, even for them."

"They're equal opportunity idiots," Violet adds. "Bullying is their love language. It's almost a rite of passage to look stupid in front of the girl you're dating."

I shift quickly. "Oh, we're not dating."

Hazel sighs. "Doesn't matter. You're here and they are going to take advantage of that."

I laugh softly. "Okay then."

We sit and watch, and I'm completely lost. You throw the Frisbee to someone, but once you catch it, you can't move your one foot, and then if you drop it, then it's over. I don't know, I guess when they play another team, it's different.

"Trust me, it doesn't get better," Ainsley says. "I've been to enough tournaments, and I promise, you just drink wine and hope no one gets hurt."

I go to grab a glass and hear a chorus of winces. "Oh, that's going to hurt," Ainsley says before yelling to Lachlan, "Are you okay, honey?"

He stands, wiping off the grass from his shirt. "Never better, babe."

"He says that now, until he can't move later and he's icing his knee," she grumbles and the other girls laugh.

As much as I know they said this is all for me, or to make Killian look stupid, so far, I'm not seeing that. He's caught pretty much everything, scored twice, or at least I'm assuming he did because the girls were cheering, and looks like he's completely fine, while Miles is starting to pant a little.

"So, Tessa, how is it staying on the ranch?" Hazel asks.

"It's been fine. So much better than the antique store."

Hazel shudders. "I can't believe you were going to stay there. I swear, Mrs. Thornberry is so sweet, but no one should pay for that place."

"Or the shitshack I stayed in and almost caught on fire," Ainsley adds in. "You know, maybe that's what you should open, Penelope."

"What?" she asks.

"Some kind of lodging for Ember Falls. There are no hotels, no apartments or houses that are in decent shape. You could make a killing," Ainsley says before turning to me. "When I came down to write my article on Lachlan, I ended up in what they called a cabin. The pictures were great, looked fine. It was not. After I caught the generator on fire, kind of, Lachlan moved me out and into his house."

"After the roach crawled into my cup of water, that was it for me," I say, with the ick running through my body. "I was so grossed out."

I still am. I swear, I can see it and I just...can't.

"I would be too," Hazel agrees. "Oof, Penny, it's your man this time."

Penelope shifts up onto her knees. "Miles, can you get up?"

He lifts one hand, still on the ground. "Just need a minute, love."

"All right." She sits back down and pops a grape in her mouth. "Men."

COME WHAT MAY 109

I chuckle.

Their practice continues and so does the girl talk. I didn't realize how much I've missed this. I had my friends in college, but after we graduated, we all went our own way. In grad school, I really didn't have anyone, and then I went to New York where I just have my roommate. She and I don't get to hang out like this since she's so busy with work and when she's home, I'm usually at work. Our schedules allow us to get along so well, but I do miss hanging out and shooting the shit with a friend.

"Oh, thank God," Ainsley says with a deep sigh. "They're done and we didn't need to call for medical help."

Everyone gets up and starts to pack up. "Tessa, if you're still here next week, I hope you'll come hang out with us," Penelope says.

"I'd like that, thank you."

I don't say that I really hope I won't be here, that by then, I'll have figured out what's going on with Killian's company and a way to save it. If not, I'm pretty sure Brynlee is going to either fire me or keep me as a junior publicist forever.

The guys approach, and I really take a look at Killian. His dark brown hair is pushed back and he reaches for the hem of his shirt, pulling it up and wiping his brow.

God, I forgot how perfect his body is.

That small glimpse, the little peek at his body has mine overheating, and it's really not that hot out.

He laughs at something Miles says and then looks to me.

The connection is so intense, so powerful, I forget where I am.

It's like tunnel vision where the only thing in the world that exists is him.

Someone bumps my arm. "Tessa?"

"Huh?" I say, taking my gaze away from Killian.

Everett chuckles. "I asked if you were impressed?"

I'm pretty sure he's asking about the practice and not the insanely sexy man I'm mentally undressing.

I smile. "Absolutely. Your skills were not exaggerated at all. This game is absolutely a testament to all of your athletic abilities."

He grins. "I like this one." Then he looks to Hazel. "She's nice and appeals to our masculine ego."

"Right, she's not sarcastic *at all*. Besides, your ego is big enough. All right, I need to get home, start knocking down some walls." Her smile widens as she turns to Everett. "I'll see you tomorrow—bring your tools."

Killian walks over, pulling his bag over his shoulder. "What's tomorrow?"

"You and I have to help Hazel," Everett says.

"What?"

"Yes, tomorrow, on my one damn day off, we have to go over to Hazel's. She needs help on a project and I told her you'd be able to help."

I want to laugh so much, but I manage to hold it in. Not only was Everett coerced into doing this thanks to Violet, but now he's doing the same thing to Killian.

"I can't," he says quickly.

"Why not?"

"I have a ranch."

Everett doesn't seem to care about that. "So? I have a veterinarian clinic. Good for you. Our friend is expecting us."

Violet huffs. "Oh, for the love of God, Everett."

"I know, Killian is being selfish when there's a friend in need." Everett's voice is filled with disappointment.

Killian turns to me. "Don't we have some work to do? With the ideas?"

I'm sure, as his publicist, it's my job to get him out of sticky situations and I should throw him a line, but this has been one of the best days I've had in a while, and I love these people. "No, I'm heading out of town for the day tomorrow."

Everett claps him on the shoulder. "I'll pick you up at eight in the morning."

"Goodnight, Killian. Goodnight, Tessa," Violet says, pulling her fiancé with her. "Come on, you freaking troublemaker."

And with that, it's just Killian and I.

"So," I say, kicking the ground. "That was something."

"Did you find a new love for Ultimate Frisbee?" he asks.

I laugh softly. "I did. I didn't realize this was even a thing."

His green eyes shimmer with amusement. "Oh, it's really remarkable. It's growing a real fan base too."

"I bet. The women must come in droves to see your insurmountable skills."

"It's not as easy as it looks."

I'm sure that's true, but then again, it's Frisbee. I mean, sure, the guys were doing all kinds of weird moves, if you can call them that, but it's not all that difficult.

"If you say so," I tease back.

He puts his bag down and digs in for the disc. "Come on. We'll do a quick tutorial."

"I'm good. I'm not dressed to play."

Killian's eyes roam my body from top to bottom. "I promise, you won't ruin anything."

Just my resolve.

I let out a long sigh. "Promise?"

He crosses his heart and lifts two fingers. "Scout's honor."

"I'm pretty sure that's not the sign."

"Probably not. Trust me?" he asks with his hand outstretched.

It's not him I don't trust, it's me. I'm weak around him.

However, I'm unable to stop myself from reaching out and taking his hand. He leads me onto the field, handing me the disc.

"Okay, you got me here, now what?" I ask.

"Take the disc in your dominant hand, and I want you to flick it to me."

Sounds easy enough. I step forward the way he did, as I was pretending I wasn't watching, and flick my wrist. It flies right to him.

"Like that?" I ask as he catches it effortlessly.

"Exactly like that. Ready to catch?"

I nod. He tosses it right to me, and I should've caught it, but as it hits my hand it bounces before I can grab it and it flops to the ground.

"Well shit."

Killian chuckles. "Try to catch it with two hands to start."

Right, not that I saw him do that once, but then again I've only ever done this on a beach with my brother on the one family vacation we went on.

I throw it back to him and again, the ass catches it with one hand and he had to jump because it was definitely not a good throw.

"Sorry!" I say quickly.

"You're fine. You've done this one time, you're already better than Lachlan."

I laugh. "He didn't look that bad, I mean, I don't know what good looks like, but…"

"Trust me, he's our weakest link."

"I'll take your word for it."

"Ready?"

Right. I have to catch it. "Hit me."

He tosses it right to me again and I do my best to use both hands and clamp it, but I miss.

"Okay, maybe this isn't so easy," I note.

I grab it off the ground and focus, thinking maybe it's like softball and I just need to keep my eye on the target, and what a target it is…

I shake my head, dislodging those stupid thoughts, and throw the disc again.

Only this time, it makes a hard right and rolls for a good twenty feet.

Killian jogs after it, and I take a moment to admire his ass.

He heads back but doesn't stop where he was, coming right to me instead. "It's in the wrist." He moves behind me, his front to my back. "May I?"

Not trusting my voice and what might come out of it, I just nod.

His hand runs down my arm before his fingers lightly grip my wrist. I watch as he lifts my arm up and his other arm wraps around my front, handing me the Frisbee.

I somehow force my limbs to work and hold it.

"Now, when you pull it toward your chest," he murmurs, his voice rumbling against my ear, "I want you to think of your wrist like a bow. You have to hold it, let the tension build."

The tension is definitely building. However, I'm not feeling it in my wrist.

"Okay," I manage to get the one word out.

"Do you feel like it might snap?"

"Yes."

"Good." The heat of his breath slides down my neck, and I shiver. "Focus on the release. If you want it to go to the right, you release it when your wrist is almost slack. Left, you release before the middle. Where do you want it to go?"

Who the hell knew that learning Frisbee would be my breaking point. I definitely didn't see this coming.

"Straight," I tell him.

"Then when your wrist hits this point, I want you to let it go," he instructs and moves my wrist to where he wants it. "Turn your hips." I move to be further against him. "Good. Plant your left foot and take the step with your right. Use that power and let it go."

I close my eyes and absorb the feel of him against me, remembering the night we spent together, the kiss, the way he made me come alive under his body. I would very much like to do that right here, in the middle of this field, and I wouldn't care if anyone saw us.

"Tessa," his soft, seductive voice is low in my ear. "Are you paying attention?"

My eyes fly open. "I am."

He chuckles, probably knowing I am not, in fact, paying attention to this, but to him. "All right, let's let it go."

His hand stays on my wrist as I mimic the action he showed me, focusing on tightness in my wrist and remembering where he told me to release.

I step forward and Killian comes with me, then I flick my wrist and watch as the Frisbee goes right where I wanted.

"I did it!" I yell and then turn around, jumping into his arms. "I did it."

"You did," he chuckles, holding me against him.

I grin and then, no longer caring about my rules, the reality of our situation, or the fact that I'm going to lose my job when his ranch goes under because I failed, I plant my lips on his and kiss him.

CHAPTER 13
TESSA

"AREN'T YOU A SIGHT FOR SORE EYES," MEREDITH SAYS AS SHE opens her front door.

"I have missed you, bestie."

She opens her arms, and I wrap mine around her. We do that rocking hug that girls do, holding on tight, our weight shifting side to side.

After a minute of this, she steps back with a huge smile. "You look amazing."

"As do you."

"Come in, come in."

I haven't been here since they moved in three years ago. "Wow," I say when I enter the living room. I came shortly after they bought it and it was painted very dark, making the rooms feel small, but now it looks as though it doubled in size.

The walls are white and beautiful wood beams stretch across the vaulted ceiling. It's stunning.

"We've worked hard and done a lot of DIY-ing, but I'm happy with everything so far."

"It's beautiful, Mer. Truly."

"Thank you. I found that I stress paint."

I've never heard of that before, but it's better than me with stress eating. At least it's more productive. "That must be fun for Jake."

She laughs and then sighs as she flops onto the couch. "He gets over it. Although, two weeks ago I woke him up as I was painting the guest bedroom. Please, sit."

I sink into the plush sofa beside her. "I can imagine he loved that."

"He did not, but he puts up with me. Now, tell me all about you and New York and your mother...?"

Oh, my mother. "She's the same. New York is amazing, it's unlike anywhere I've ever been. I really love it, and I have the most amazing and unhinged roommate there ever was, but she keeps it interesting."

"Do you remember the girl we lived with sophomore year? Arianna."

I groan inwardly. "Yes, I remember the girl who tried to beat you with her curling iron."

That was the worst year we had. After that experience, we decided no new roommates and it was just the two of us. It worked much better for everyone.

"All because I ate her sandwich," Meredith muses. "If only I could go back in time and have those issues be what I worried about now."

There's something in her words that pulls at me. I may not see her often, but Meredith is my best friend and that's the second comment that has me wondering why she's so stressed. "Are you okay?"

Meredith's eyes meet mine. "Me? Yeah!" She shifts forward. "I'm fine. I was just being dramatic."

"As much as that's a very Meredith thing to do, I call bullshit."

She reaches out, taking my hand. "I promise, I'm fine. It's been a lot of...change in the last year. Jake and I have been trying for a baby, and it's been hard because it's not working. You know me, I am...a 'work hard and get it done' girl. I don't like failing at anything."

I shake my head. "You're not failing."

"I know. Jake tells me the same thing, but I had a plan, and I like things to go the way I want. It's...just everything. Jake's parents

COME WHAT MAY 117

are getting divorced, which has been stressful for him because his mother wants him there all the time to help—he's there now. Then you know my drama last year in taking that DNA test to see if I had the BRCA gene only to find out so much more, like my dad wasn't my dad. So, I stress paint and remind myself it'll be fine. Now, I need to focus on someone else's drama—spill it."

I jerk back a little. "I don't have drama."

She laughs, head falling back, and it's very clear she doesn't buy it. I guess that whole intuition thing I have about her, it goes both ways.

Well, shit.

I can't talk about this. It's…wrong, and I kissed him again yesterday. Like a freaking idiot who just can't seem to stop doing it.

His lips are just so damn kissable.

Thankfully we were outside, on the field, in the dark, so it couldn't go anywhere.

But it's more than that. It's how sweet he is, how he looks at me, how he makes me smile. It's the way that he does little things, like always making sure I have food. I like him.

He makes me feel good about who I am, what I can do, and he believes in me. To him, I'm smart, capable, worthy in ways that I never felt before.

All of it keeps me going in these damn circles.

What if…what if I could tell someone? Or maybe tell her but also not tell her…?

I clear my throat. "I don't have drama, per se, but I have a hypothetical thing that I think you'd actually be really good at helping with."

Meredith straightens. "Oh? Who is the hypothetical about?"

"A girl at work," I lie.

She grins. "Okay, tell me about this girl and her issue."

This is going to be the advice I need. She's going to tell me exactly how to handle it, and Meredith is brilliant, so we will for sure feel the same.

Bad idea. Stop it.

"There are strict company policies that she had to sign. She mentioned a morality clause that specifies and no sleeping with clients or coworkers."

She nods. "I have the same at my job."

"Right, pretty standard stuff, but she fucked up. She slept with one of her clients, without knowing he was a client at first."

"How did she fuck the guy and not know?"

"They met at a bar, not knowing who the other was," I explain.

"Then she didn't do anything wrong," Meredith says, surprising me a little.

Yes, at the time they—I mean, I—didn't do anything wrong, but now it's wrong. Now I'm knowingly kissing my damn client and living in his house while I dream of him entering my room and taking me.

"She slept with the client," I say again. "You know, bad idea and all. Against company policy."

Meredith taps her finger on her lips. "The client or *her* client?"

"Does it matter?"

"I think so," Meredith says. "If she met a guy in a bar and didn't know he was a client, then that's that, right? There's no way the company can hold her responsible for sleeping with a guy she met at a bar. Now, I would argue, if he's not *her* client, specifically, she's not breaking the company guidelines anyway. However, let's say he is. Why would anyone ever have to know?"

I really thought that I was going to get good advice here—seems that's not the case.

"Meredith, she shouldn't keep sleeping with him."

"Why not?"

"Because she..."

Meredith laughs through her nose and comes to sit beside me. "Your friend, she's probably not the type of girl to sleep around, right?"

"No."

In my college time, I was only with two men. I didn't date. I didn't sleep around. I didn't do anything that was considered risky or fun.

That's just never been me.

Even in New York while I don't have the heavy burdens of school or working to pay for school, I still don't go out.

Aarabelle, Brianna, Thea, everyone I know in New York all go to the bars, dinners. They're on the dating apps and at least doing something.

Not me. I have no desire to put myself out there only to be left or told how worthless I am. I've had enough of that my entire fucking life.

"Okay, does your friend like him?"

"She doesn't know what she feels."

"No?" Meredith asks with a knowing smile.

"Well, maybe she likes him more than she should. As you know, she doesn't just hook up with guys randomly, she has to at least feel something. However, it's stupid to do something she knows will only end in heartbreak."

"Does this client live close to her?"

I shake my head. "She probably won't see him often, if ever again. Since he's not really even her client."

"I see. So, then, I think you should tell her that she's a grown ass woman and no one has to know about it. Tell her to have some fun, not get too attached, but enjoy feeling something good for a change. Not to mention, she already did it, so you can't undo that. Might as well keep doing it."

"Keep doing what?" a deep voice calls out as the front door closes.

"Tessa is banging her client, and I'm telling her that it's not only a good thing, but a necessity for her to continue to do so."

I groan. "Hi, Jake."

He walks over and kisses my cheek. "Hello, trouble." Then he kisses his wife and sits on the opposite couch. "So, Tessa, seems you're enjoying your time in Virginia, huh?"

We all laugh and I toss a pillow at him. "I hate you guys."

"You don't."

No, I don't. Not even a little.

I feel different.

I can't explain it. I can't even really understand it, but something after tonight feels different. It was the simple act of seeing my friends, telling someone about what happened with Killian, and them not making me feel worse. If anything, Meredith was pretty adamant that I wasn't doing anything wrong.

She asked if I can be objective and do my job, regardless of whatever is going on with us personally.

The answer is yes.

I can.

Whatever happens between us doesn't change how or what I will do to save the ranch.

Also, she pretty much agreed we're going full steam ahead toward it anyway.

So, why stop it?

I don't think we will stop it, and we can have it on our terms this way.

Plus, it's going to end soon.

All of these things are what I've told myself over and over as I made my way back to the farm.

Now I just need to get out of the car…

I pull the visor down and stare at myself in the mirror.

You are beautiful.

You are smart.

You are loved.

You are going to do amazing things.

Or at least have amazing sex, which is equally as important. I mean, mediocre sex is awful. Truly.

You deserve to have some fun, although fun can often lead to trouble, but we're not going to talk about that.

Now, get out of the car and go talk to him.

That is so much easier said than done.

I have no idea how he's going to feel, but there's only one way to find out.

I exit the car, making my way inside and…it's dark and he's not here.

Well, that's…anticlimactic.

I send a text to Meredith.

Me: So, I planned to come home and, you know, do it. Or him. Or whatever we're saying, but he's not here and now I feel stupid.

Meredith: Get naked and go wait in his bed.

Me: Okay, now that is really dumb and no thanks.

Meredith: Jake agrees.

Me: Well, I'm definitely not going to take his advice since he also said we should get naked and swim in the campus fountain, which…we learned was also dumb.

The things we do when we're drunk.

Meredith: This is true. Okay, then maybe this is a sign. You should go to bed—alone and not do it.

Me: That's probably the most likely scenario. Okay. Love you! I'll do my best to see you again before I leave.

Meredith: Love you most.

I sigh and walk to turn the light so I can go to bed. But as I do, there are headlights in the window, pulling up beside my car.

I should go. I should run up the damn stairs, get in my room and fake sleep.

I don't.

I stand here, like a statue as I hear the car door close, then the front door open.

Killian flips the lights on as I'm just finding my ability to move and am three steps up, not even close to the top.

I turn, and his eyes meet mine. In that split second, I know that the resistance I was very thinly holding on to, the lies I told myself about it being a sign, disappear.

The energy in the room is so tense, and I can feel my heart racing. Killian stares at me, and I do the same.

At the same moment, we both snap.

I move toward him and he's coming to me. As though thunder and lightning strike at the same time, I'm against his chest, his hands are in my hair, and our mouths fuse.

The storm that was rolling in has arrived and we're unable to seek shelter.

His tongue pushes into my mouth, and I welcome it. I hold on to him, gripping his shoulders, pulling him closer.

My back is pressed against the wall, and he anchors himself around me. Hands on each side of my head, caging me in.

We kiss, fiercely, as though there's nothing else in the world than the need we have for each other.

"Tessa," he groans against my neck as he moves his lips against my skin, lightly kissing and then sucking. "Tell me you want this."

"I need this," I admit.

"I can't...fuck...I want you more than anything."

I feel the same. A part of me, a very small one, resists the temptation of telling him to have me. I know that the thinly veiled excuses I have about this not being wrong are stupid. I can spin my tale any way I want, but the reality is that there won't be any plausible deniability if this ever gets out.

"No one can know," I say as his hand moves down my side.

"Not a soul."

"Just us."

"Only us."

I take his face in my hands, our eyes meeting. "Take me to bed, Killian."

He lifts me up in a heartbeat, carrying me, just like he did our first time, back into his room.

With each step, I feel more and more eager. These last few days have felt like torture trying to resist him.

However, I want this one night with him, more than anything I've ever wanted.

He stands before me, hands on my hips. "You're sure?"

I nod. "I am."

"I never want you to regret this, Tessa." He brushes my hair back behind my ear. "I don't want to be something you look back on and wish you had chosen differently."

I run my fingertip against his collar. "I think I'll look back on this and regret it if I walk away."

"Swear it."

I stare into his stunning green eyes. "I swear."

He kisses me again, this time slowly, tenderly, and I get lost in it. I allow my hands to move up his chest and hook behind his neck. I hold on to him, losing all sense of thought as he moans into my mouth.

I drink it in, loving that I give him pleasure.

Killian moves us backward until my knees hit the edge of the bed. "Lie back for me, angel."

I do ask as he asks, his eyes never leaving mine. "Killian," I sigh his name.

"Take your shirt off." I slowly lift the hem up over my head. "Now your pants, remove them—slowly."

I try to slow my movements down, but I am so ready for him. I've been ready since I arrived, which only grew stronger when I saw him.

"I don't want to go slow," I tell him.

"What do you want?"

"You. Now."

He grins. "Then remove all your clothes and let me see how much you want it."

I pull my underwear down with my pants, tossing them off the bed, then my bra. However, seeing how turned on he is, based on the very large erection pushing against his pants, I do move my knees apart extremely slowly.

Inch by painful inch, I stare at him as he waits for what he wants. "Like this?" I ask.

"Wider."

I lean back on my elbows, keeping my knees just a little bit apart. "More?" I ask when I just barely budge them.

"Lay your knees flat on the bed," Killian commands.

I toss my head back, arching my breasts up, and he groans. I bite my lower lip and look up at him. "And then what?"

"Then, I'm going to lick every drop of you until you come. After that, I'm going to fuck you so hard that you won't be able to move without thinking about what my cock feels like inside of you. After that, I'm going to do it again, making you come until it hurts because your body is so wrung out. Is that what you want, Tessa?"

Oh my God. I want it, and I want it more than I want to breathe. "Yes."

"Then spread your knees all the way out so I can have what I want."

I part my knees, no longer wanting to play a game, just wanting him—and also knowing he likes to have control. I've been toying with that, and he's going to make me pay for it—hopefully in orgasms.

When I go to move my legs, he rests his hands on each one, keeping them apart.

His eyes find mine. "Get ready to beg."

Before I can ask what he means, his mouth is on me and he's licking and sucking on my clit. He moves his tongue in circles and I'm already so damn close. I feel myself starting to build. His assault on my clit is relentless and I'm panting so hard. I can't move my legs, he has me completely pinned.

My head thrashes back and forth as I struggle for breath.

Then his tongue moves to my entrance as he fucks me with it. "Killian, please."

He chuckles against me and keeps going. As he holds me apart, he moves lower, his tongue swiping at my ass, and I gasp before he moves back to my clit.

"Oh, please, yes," I moan, and then he stops.

"Are you close?"

I whimper. "Yes."

"Good. Tell me, angel, has anyone ever had your ass?"

I shake my head.

"I'm going to take this part of you that no other many has had. Will you let me make you feel good?"

"You already are."

"Better than good?"

"I'm…not sure…I'm afraid it'll hurt."

Killian leans down, running his tongue against my clit again, back and forth, over and over and then slides a finger inside me. Slowly he pumps, driving me higher and higher. Then, he removes his hand and I feel it against my ass.

He runs his finger along the rim, just barely pushing inside.

"Relax," he says softly. "Stay loose, baby."

I try to let my head go, not paying attention to anything but the way he makes me feel as his tongue flicks at the bundle of nerves.

Killian sucks hard and my hips lift, at the same time, he pushes a finger inside my ass. I cry out, the feeling is so much.

It feels so good, so different and intense.

"Does that hurt?" he asks.

"No, God, it feels so good." Better than good. I'm close again. "Please don't stop."

He goes back to it, his tongue moving in glorious patterns, bringing my orgasm back to the forefront. He removes his finger from my ass and he fucks me with his tongue, pushing deep inside of me and then back to my clit where he sucks. "That's it, keep your knees there. I'm going to make you come, but only if you obey. If you take your knees off the mattress then I stop."

I won't move any part of me if it means he's going to keep going.

"Tessa, do you understand?"

I glance at him. "Yes."

"Good girl. I'm going to take your ass again, baby. I'm going to make you come so hard."

He moves his hands off me and starts again. I'm so fucking close. I want to come so bad. He flicks his tongue again and then I feel him push his fingers deep inside me. I groan, feeling so full and yet wanting more. As he pumps his hand in and out, adjusting the angles, my sanity starts to float away, but I focus on keeping my knees like this.

I don't want him to stop. I need more.

He rubs my clit with his thumb as I feel his mouth again at my ass. He licks there and it feels so good. A little different, but still incredibly good. I'm not sure if I should like it this much, but I do.

Then his mouth is back on my clit and his hand is moving there, he rims my ass with a finger again, all while his mouth is doing amazing things to me. A long moan falls from my lips as he toys with me, bringing me to the brink of an orgasm. "So close," I pant.

Then he pushes inside my ass as his mouth latches onto my clit. He sucks so hard, flicking at the same time as he pumps his hand.

I detonate.

There is no other way to describe it. I no longer have thought, breath, or feeling other than the most intense pleasure I've ever had.

My mind is gone as my body goes in a million directions. I scream or I think I do, I'm not even sure, but he doesn't relent.

He keeps pushing in and out of my ass while he takes my clit between his teeth. "Killian!"

I'm not sure if it's another orgasm on its heels or just one incredibly long one.

After time ceases to exist, he finally slows, letting me come down. I'm panting, my hair is now in my face, and I think my heart may have come out of my chest when he stops.

I feel him shift on the bed, and I open my eyes to see him removing his clothes. He grins down at me. "Good?"

"Umm, that's a word for it."

"Let's see if we can find a better one. Get on your hands and knees, angel."

While my muscles may feel like jelly, I do as he says. His hands grip my ass and he squeezes. "One day, if you trust me, I want to fuck you like this." He pushes a finger in my ass again and my head flies back as I rock into it. "I think you want it too, but right now, I want inside your cunt. Are you ready to come again?"

I groan. "Yes."

And then he's inside of me, and he makes me come—two more times.

CHAPTER 14
KILLIAN

TESSA IS ASLEEP AFTER OUR LAST ROUND OF SEX. THE SUN IS JUST starting to come up, and I haven't been able to close my eyes. Part of it was that I didn't want her to slink out of my bed, ready to pretend last night didn't happen. The other part is that I'm pretty sure when the light of day breaks, and she realizes what we did again, she's going to regret it and I want to assuage her fears.

I roll over, pulling her against my chest, and she nuzzles closer. My fingers move up and down her back, and her eyelids lift gently.

She grins. "Hi."

"Hi."

She ducks her head, hiding from me, and then looks back up. "What time is it?"

"About seven. I have to go out to the barn, but didn't want to just leave you."

"Okay."

I smile. "Are you okay?"

Tessa blinks. "Tired, but yes, why?"

Because I don't want you to say what I think you're going to say.

"I just want to make sure."

She sighs heavily and pushes back, keeping her hand over my heart. "I'm completely okay. I think we were both heading right back here and at least this time we're aware of the situation. You're okay with it, right?"

I laugh a little. "More than okay. I think us fighting this every day was making it harder to work together."

"I agree." She smiles up at me and it's like the sun cresting the horizon.

"Good."

"But I have questions…" Tessa pulls back, but I hold her close, not wanting her to move away. "I've never done this."

"Done what?" I ask. "This" could mean a multitude of things.

She sighs, her fingertips brushing over my collarbone. "Casual… sex or whatever we're calling this. I've never slept with a client or coworker, and I just…I want to prepare myself, you know? I want to have the expectations in place so that when it comes down to it, there are no surprises."

I wait for a heartbeat, not really sure what to say to that. "Okay… well, I don't really do this either. I've never slept with a work acquaintance either. I find mixing the two never bodes well for anyone. This is a new one for me."

As for the casual relationships, that's all I've had in the past. After my fiancée cheated, I really wanted no part in anything serious. It's easier to just keep things surface level. Not to mention, the woman who lied about having a child and kept her from me. I've never been able to trust much, but that put me over the edge.

"Same."

Something she said has me smiling. "So you've never done casual sex?"

Tessa groans and drops her head on my chest. "No, not really. I've been in two relationships, and that's it. I kind of have trust issues. When I meet a guy, it takes me a long time to open up."

I rub my fingers up and down her spine. "Really? You had no issues with me."

"I know."

"So you're saying I'm special?"

She laughs. "Something like that."

I'm going to pretend that's a yes. "Why does it take you a long time?"

"You don't really need to be bothered by my baggage."

She doesn't get it. "Tessa," I say her name softly. "You're not bothering me. You're not boring me. You're not irritating me by telling me about who you are. I want to know everything that makes you who you are."

Her eyes swim with emotion and she sighs. "Killian."

"I'm serious. Why does it take you a long time to open up?"

I sit and wait while she worries her lower lip before finally explaining. "My dad…he walked out, which you know, every girl seems to have daddy issues, but he would come back when it was convenient for him. Never when I needed him. My brother, he cut him off long before I did, but I held out hope." She laughs softly, but it lacks all humor. "There was a daddy-daughter dance that he promised he'd come to and then just never showed up. I was in my dress, sitting on the steps outside, telling my mother she was wrong and he'd come. I was so sure that there was a reason. He told me later that week he got busy and forgot."

"Tessa," I say her name, wanting to ease her hurt. "He should've been there."

She shrugs. "It doesn't matter. It was like that until I was about eighteen and I decided that I didn't want to be an afterthought after my father told me that's all I was ever going to be. He didn't say it in those words, but he may as well have. I haven't heard from him since I told him how I felt. He didn't care and still doesn't."

My stomach churns as I think about what she must've felt. To be ready, eager to have something special and then be told she wasn't worth it.

I'd like to punch her father in the fucking face for it.

"You're not an afterthought, Tessa. Not ever," I say, holding her chin so she can see the sincerity on my face.

Her blue eyes shimmer with unshed tears. "Don't make me cry."

I grin and kiss her gently. "All right, well, to answer what I think was your point, we're not defined. You live in New York and I'm in Boston or here. Whenever we're together whether it's with work or in bed, just know that I will never lie to you. I'll be honest if I can or can't give you something. I won't lead you on or make you think there's more if there can't be. Does that work for you?"

Honesty is the one thing I will always offer her. She won't have to wonder where we stand or what we are, I'll be transparent with her always.

"I'll give you the same," she says with a smile.

"Good. For now, this is amazing sex and fun when we're not working. We can hang out, go out, whatever we want. At least now we can stop resisting." I kiss her nose.

"Oh, you think we're going to do this again?"

Her saucy tone already has me hard. "I do."

"And why is that?" She asks.

"I'll show you why."

I roll us until I'm on top of her, my cock already hard and wanting to push inside of her. To feel the warmth of her around me, her heat, her scent, her taste, I crave it all.

Her legs automatically fall open, and I adjust so I can rub my dick against her. I rock slowly. "Tell me why I wouldn't think that," I demand.

Her perfect lips part and she gasps. "I don't know."

"No?" I rock again, making sure I rub her clit a little harder. "You're already wet, aren't you?"

"Yes," she confesses.

Not that I needed her to confirm what I already feel. "And could I push inside of you if I wanted?"

I don't have a condom on, so I only do the tip, just enough to let her feel me, to know I'm right there.

"Oh, please, fill me," Tessa begs. "Please fuck me."

"No, angel, I think you only get this right now." Keeping myself from plunging into her is the most difficult thing I've ever done. "Just this, until tonight, when I know all day you've wished for my cock. You'll have to look at me, think of me, imagine this." I push just a little deeper, despite myself. "How much do you think you're going to want me tonight, Tessa?"

Tessa scores her nails down my back, moving for my ass and pushing, trying to get me to give in, but I don't.

I want her desperate. I want her to have phantom feelings of this.

"Please, baby. Please...I need you."

I pull out completely, and she practically cries out, but I bring my lips to hers, kissing her softly and then, wanting her to have a little more satisfied, I reach between us and rub her clit. "You'll have me later, but I want you to wait." She moans as I increase the pressure. I stare down at her with her brown hair fanned out against my pillow, her heart-shaped lips forming a perfect O as she struggles for breath. When I started this, I planned to stop right before her orgasm hit, but seeing her like this, I want to watch her in full glory.

I finger her, my thumb moving to her clit, pushing in and out, no longer thinking my plan was all that smart.

Instead of being inside of her, I'm punishing myself by not giving in.

"Killian," she moans my name. "Please."

"That's it, angel. Let me give it to you," I coax.

Her fingers dig into my arms, her body lifting off the bed. "I'm so close."

I can feel her cunt pulsing around my finger. I give her more, sliding in a slow rhythm, wanting to make this last as long as I can.

"You're so beautiful," I tell her. "Watching you like this...God, I wish I could sear this into my brain. Every inch of you is perfect." She pants and her body starts to tighten. "Just like that, Tessa. Let me see you come. Let me feel you fall apart around my fingers."

Her head tilts back, eyes closed, as I rub faster, pump harder, and then she releases. Her rough cry fills the room and all the empty parts of my soul.

Before I can move, her hand wraps around my cock and she starts to pump. Fuck. I can't hold back.

I was already teetering on the edge after watching her, feeling her, touching her, but this...

I move her hand away, but she protests.

"No," she says firmly. "I want this."

"I know you do."

Keeping my eyes on hers, I pull my fingers up between us and slowly lick the taste of her off. Her pupils dilate as I moan, wishing I had my face there so I could have more.

"Well, that's not fair," she murmurs.

I glance down at her with a grin. "What's not?"

"You got to taste me, I think I should as well." She pushes against my chest until I roll to my back.

I want to deny her, but I don't.

I grip her arm gently as she starts to kiss down my chest. "Only your mouth," I command.

"For now."

And then Tessa gives me a blow job I'll never forget.

"Killian, it's good to see you," Desmond Sanchez says as he extends his hand.

I return the handshake. "Desmond, how are you?"

"Good. Can't complain."

Desmond and I have had several business dealings over the past three years. I've sold him three horses, and one of them is a grade two stakes winner.

He is also one of the buyers who canceled his purchase of one of my horses, which is why I'm at this damn auction.

"Glad to hear it."

He shifts his weight and glances around the crowd, clearly worried about who is watching the two of us. I'm starting to wonder if he regrets coming over to talk to me. "Listen, I wanted to reach out and see how you're doing. I know you're having a bit of an issue."

"You can say that."

"Yeah, I'm sorry."

"Can I ask why?"

Desmond sighs heavily. "It's nothing personal. I've loved the horses I've bought, won a lot of money too, but you know, there's been a lot of talk lately."

That's news to me. I haven't heard anything. In fact, it's why I'm so fucking confused as to what's going on. Hopefully he'll give me some answers. "Really? About what?"

His eyes widen for a second. "You...well, the whole thing about Travis."

I wonder if he knows where the fuck he is. So far, we've found absolutely nothing about where he is or where we went. All of the leads have been dead ends. I don't want to play my hand because this is the first I'm hearing anything about Travis or people talking. So, I shake my head. "I'm not sure what you mean."

"It's been going around, the whole scandal that he was doping horses when he was at Longwood Ranch...you haven't heard?"

Longwood Ranch is where he was working before he came to work for me. That's an absolute lie. There's no way that Travis would do that, he loves his horses. Yes, he's tough, but doping? No. I don't believe it. But, if that's the rumor, it would explain why Travis disappeared. Those kinds of allegations ruin lives. "I hadn't heard any of it."

"Yeah, apparently that's why he was fired from there."

I shake my head because that's a boldfaced lie. "He wasn't fired. I approached him and he came over, pissing Owen off in the process."

"That's...not what Owen is saying. He found proof that Travis was doping his horses, he fired him, and then you hired him—which is what a few owners are concerned that he was doing to theirs. Which is why no one wants to work with you guys."

Fucking hell. "That's bullshit," I tell him. "Plus, if that was the case, why is Owen saying this now? Why not when I hired him?"

Desmond shrugs. "Maybe he didn't want the rumors to fall on him and ruin his business, fuck if I know."

I need to set the record straight right now. "Travis was not doping my horses or any of the ones we boarded. I have them tested regularly."

"I'm just saying. I'm sorry I had to back out, but I can't be mixed up in a scandal, I'm sure you understand."

I get it, but there is no fucking scandal. If all of this is going on because Owen Perry wanted to run his mouth and spew a bunch of lies, I'm going to beat his fucking ass. I knew he would be a dick when I asked Travis to leave there, but I didn't think he'd try to ruin my entire operation.

He's known to be ruthless but not vengeful.

"I wish you would've talked to me. I could've shown you test results, veterinary records, and whatever documents you needed. I assure you, Travis might have been a tough trainer, but he wasn't doping the horses on my ranch or on Owen's."

If I can find Travis, I could prove this isn't true or at least discuss it. However, I don't know this for an absolute fact. Hell, even if he told me he wasn't, I can't be one hundred percent sure. The only thing I do know is that Everett would've caught signs of it.

"I'm sorry about that, but I've known Owen for twenty years and I have no reason to believe he's lying," Desmond says with a sigh. "I wish you the best, Killian. I truly do. Your horses were always top quality and I'll let a few of the guys know what you said here. Maybe it would be beneficial to have Travis also say something."

Yeah, it definitely would be, but I can't exactly tell him that Travis has gone missing right around when everyone started to pull out of their contracts.

"Thanks, Desmond," I say, extending my hand again.

He shakes it. "Of course, good luck."

Yeah, I'm going to need it.

I grab my phone and send a text to my contact at Cole Securities to get some answers.

> **Me:** I'm going to need an update. I think I found out what's been going on. We need to find Travis.
>
> **Liam:** I'll be in Ember Falls next week with some information. We are tracking down a lead and it'll take a little more time to verify if it's Travis.

Good. At least we're finally going in the right direction.

CHAPTER 15
TESSA

THE AUCTION WAS A BUST.

Killian came back home and was only able to sell two horses, but at such a terrible rate that it's clear that we're going to have to use plan B. Thankfully, I already had it in the works. He also informed me of the conversation he had about the rumors of Travis doping the horses here. All of it has forced me to change gears.

Tonight, we have our first bachelorette party. They rented the guest house that Travis used to live in as well as a two-hour trail ride out to the falls, a campfire setup, and a second trail ride tomorrow.

I just haven't broken the news to Killian yet.

I spoke with Brynlee, and she and I agreed that since he was resistant to any and all of my ideas, I needed to step in and do what my job is. Which is to get some income flowing, and this was the easiest and most viable option.

Now, I'm out in the front porch area of the guest house, stringing up some lights and decorations so that they can have a fun place to hang out after their ride and take pictures.

Gary walks over. "Tessa, I have the four horses chosen. When do you want me to saddle them?"

"The girls should be here in about an hour, so maybe two hours from now? I think we'll let them settle in, eat for a bit, and then we'll do the horseback ride before they start drinking."

He chuckles. "That's a good plan. And you want me to lead them out there?"

I nod. "You know how to get to the falls—I would probably get lost."

Since I've only been out there once, it's definitely not a good idea for me to be in charge.

"And Killian wants me to wear these?" He lifts up the pink shirt and baseball hat that says "Buck Wild."

The lovely little embroidery shop in town was able to make me a few things this afternoon. It's going to go over—terribly, but I don't care.

"Yup," I lie.

He glances over at the main house and sighs. "The shit I have to do on this ranch."

Gary walks off, and I go back to it. The maid of honor for the party asked if I could decorate with pinks and beiges in a very taste-ful way. No streamers or dick-shaped stemware, which was a shame if you ask me, but probably for the best because if Killian saw it, he might kill me.

It's still a possibility anyway, but maybe this way, there's less of a chance. I did let the bridal party know there'd be no outside people allowed, meaning no male strippers since everyone has to be buzzed in through the gate.

Another hurdle I felt was eliminated.

I have my music going as I continue to do my best decorating skills with the budget I have.

"Tessa?" I hear Killian's voice, which has a very strong echo of frustration in it.

Well, here goes nothing.

"Over here!" I call out with all the charm and joy I can muster.

I can do this with a smile and keep my spirit up.

"What the hell is going on?" Killian asks, looking around at the very tasteful decorations, if I say so myself.

"What do you mean?"

His eyes narrow. "What is this?" He picks up the pink cowboy boot cups I ordered.

I look around the deck that has pink and beige accents and the lights strung on the string poles that he's now pointing at. "Decorations."

"And what are you decorating for?" he asks, arms crossed over his broad chest.

"A party." I smile broader, climbing up on the ladder. "Can you help me reach this spot?"

He grumbles. "Tessa, what party are you having and why is Gary wearing a pink hat that says: 'Buck Wild'?"

"Oh, that's the name of the new division that does bachelorettes, birthdays, and women-run events. Our first gig is tonight."

"I said no to that." The warning in his voice should worry me, but it's too late to turn back now and, really, there are no other options available.

I sigh, ready for the fight I knew was coming. "Yes, I heard that, but you brought me here to make you money, right? Well, in order to accomplish that, I have to actually do something that will…make money. You didn't do great at the auction, and this is a guaranteed flat fee. Gary is on board to take the girls out to the falls, let them have a little trot, and come back here where they can drink, eat, and have fun. Do you know how much this little outing is going to make you in revenue?"

His jaw clenches, and I take that as a no.

"It's three thousand dollars. In one night. Now, I know that's nowhere near what you would make on a horse, but it's something. We need supplementation." I grab the hat that I had made for him, kiss his cheek, and put it on his head. "Here, now, can you help me reach up there please?"

I'm not sure if Killian is going to do it, but he grumbles and then reaches to the spot I couldn't get, putting the string light on the pole. "This is…absolutely ridiculous."

"No, what's ridiculous is hoping that somehow, this is just going to fix itself. It's been almost two weeks and you're losing money and sales. So, we're going to stop the bleeding and this is just one way."

He pulls the hat off, looking at it. "Buck Wild, really?"

I grin. "I was between that and Lady Lopers. I figured Buck Wild is a little more open ended. We can have bachelor parties too with that name."

He rolls his eyes and looks heavenward. "Deliver me."

"I'd rather you just trust me and let me do my job. I know you were very strongly against the kids' parties, so I didn't do that. And the rodeo is going to take a few weeks to organize, but I'm already on top of that."

Killian shakes his head, sighing heavily. "I can't believe this is the situation I'm in."

"Well, now we have a place to start fixing the rumors. We know they're being spread by your rival farm that you coaxed his best trainer from. Owen probably lost a ton of money after that, so we're going to work on repairing your reputation. I think having Everett pull all the horses' records and showing that there is no history of doping is the first step. Next, we'll work on getting you into more auctions as we do what we can to quell the rumors so you can keep selling and hopefully getting new boarding clients. Then, hopefully, we'll find Travis and get some answers there. For now, we are going to get cash flow going."

I hate this for him. I can see the worry growing with each day that passes. He wants this to be over, but we're nowhere near that yet. There's damage that's being done and I need to work on fixing it.

When I spoke with Brynlee about it, I expressed that I thought bringing people, even if it's just in the form of parties, onto the property would go a long way. It shows that Killian isn't afraid of people seeing his facilities. Word of mouth is what got him here—now we need to do something to get people to refute the rumors.

I move to him, and he lifts his gaze to me. "I'm going to keep doing what I can to make this work. I have money from my other business, and it'll keep me afloat here, but at some point, if we're not bringing in real income, I'll have to make some tough choices."

"I understand."

"If I ever heard that Travis was harming the horses…"

"I know," I say, truly meaning it. He would never allow it.

"I knew he trained them hard, but he backed off when he needed to."

I give him a sad smile, my hand moving to his scruffy cheek. "You'll get through this. I'm right by your side. We'll show the people in the town how wrong they were."

He sighs and takes his baseball hat, slipping it on backward, causing me to smile widely.

Killian looks ridiculously hot with that hat on. The pink corduroy not doing a thing to dampen it. "I'm not walking around town with a hat that says Buck Wild on it."

I lift up on my toes and kiss him effortlessly. "Maybe you can wear it tonight."

He pulls me against him, rocking his hips forward. "Maybe you'll show me just how buck wild you can be while you ride me."

"I guess we'll see."

He kisses me, his tongue sliding against my lips. "Oh, we definitely will."

And that's a promise I don't mind making.

———

I'm on top, riding him just like I promised.

His hands are on my hips, digging into the flesh, and I love it.

Killian's gaze doesn't move from mine.

It's the most intense sexual experience I've ever had.

The way he looks at me is almost too much.

My heart is pounding and not just from exertion, but from the emotions that are stirring inside of me. All of the fear, self-doubt, and worry doesn't exist when I'm with him. It's a safety, a sense of security, like he'd tear down the world for me.

I know that's absolutely ridiculous. We've only known each other a short time and it's very surface level, but no matter how much I tell myself these things, my heart isn't falling in line.

No, instead, it's running away with this idea that we could be more than this.

Killian is already taking pieces of my heart, and I'm not sure I'll be able to stop him from seizing the entire thing.

"Be with me, Tessa. Right here," Killian says, snapping my thoughts back to the moment.

And just like that, he freaking makes my point. How did he know?

How can he see inside my mind? It makes no sense.

Instead of allowing my overthinking brain to take back over, I do as he says. My hand moves to his chest, and I hold myself up, riding him at a different angle.

"I'm close," I whisper as my body is tense.

His fingers tighten and he stops me. "Not yet. Stay still."

I shake my head, hating him right now. "I need to move."

"I know what you need." He lifts me just a bit and bucks up, filling me while his thumb plays with my clit. "I'll give it to you," Killian promises. "I want you to come like this. Sit up straight."

I somehow push myself upright. "Now what?"

"Feel it. Feel all of me inside you. Look at us," he says, his eyes moving to where his dick is thrusting inside me. "Do you see that?"

I glance down at the erotic scene, how his cock is slick with my wetness as he rocks my hips, pushing it deeper inside of me. "Yes," I groan as my orgasm teeters on the edge.

"Who is inside of you?"

I moan. "You."

"That's right. Who is making you feel good?"

My head drops back, my hair brushing against my lower back. "You."

"Who's going to make you come?"

I gasp as he slams his hips up, and the pressure from his thumb increases. "God, you!"

He keeps going, relentlessly thrusting deeper and deeper. It's the most incredible sex I never dreamed possible. Killian drives me higher, continuing to give me more pleasure than my body can handle.

I lose myself, cresting over the precipice and drowning in ecstasy.

Killian follows me shortly after, and we lie here, both struggling for breath.

As much as the sex part is fantastic, I equally like this. Being in his arms, feeling as though nothing can harm me when I'm like this.

He pushes my hair back and I lift my chin to look at him. "That was pretty fantastic."

"I agree."

I grin. "Are you still mad at me?"

"For what?"

"The bachelorette party."

He chuckles softly. "No, angel. I'm not mad. I don't like it, but I understand the business side of it, and you're right. It's money and I can't be picky."

I raise one brow. "So you'll do kids' birthday parties?"

"Not a fucking chance."

I laugh and kiss him softly. "Fine, I won't push on that."

"I appreciate it." I start to roll to the left, but he stops me. "I'm not ready to let you go."

My heart inflates so large I fear it might burst. He's so sweet on top of being bossy. Each layer of Killian is a mystery. He's smart, funny, caring, dominant, but willing to give in, and I know there's so much more to uncover.

But at what cost?

Sure, there could be something terrible under there that will, once again, prove that men leave. He might have some deep, dark secret that could ruin my life. But, on the other hand, he might just turn out to be the best man in the world. I've seen that tender side of him, the one that makes me food, that ensured I had a place to sleep, even when he knew it would make things difficult for us both. If my instincts are correct, and all I'll unmask is a wonderful man I can't have, why do it?

There's no reason other than to make me feel even worse about myself than I already do.

No.

I'll keep my mouth shut about all my feelings and my heart locked firmly against opening up.

As if sensing the direction of my thoughts, he runs his finger down the slope of my nose. "What's going on inside that beautiful mind of yours?"

I should be as honest with him as he's promised to be with me. To tell him that I'm building a small wall around my very fragile heart so he can't touch it, but that sounds ridiculous, so I won't be doing that.

Instead, I latch on to the thought that there actually is something actionable I need to do. "I'm thinking that as much as I enjoy lying on your very sculpted and perfect body, I need to get dressed and go check on the bachelorette party. Gary is due back in about an hour, and the girls wanted to have their party items all ready to go when they returned from the ride."

He sighs heavily. "And you're the host?"

"Well, I didn't think you were going to want to do it."

"You think right since I had no intention of starting a new company, let alone one that caters to girls gone wild."

"Buck wild—get it right," I correct him. The low growl from his chest should be a warning, but I don't heed it. "Now, I'll go handle the party and you go do whatever it is you need to do to prepare for the auction this week. When we're done, I get to pick the movie and maybe we can get frisky before it's done."

"Then by all means…"

Killian allows me to roll off him, and I saunter into the bathroom to get dressed. Right before I get to the door I turn back and smile when I see him watching me.

Yeah, I'm definitely going to start building that wall…

CHAPTER 16
KILLIAN

"HERE IS THE INFORMATION WE HAVE SO FAR." LIAM, ONE OF THE lead case managers for Cole Securities places a folder on the dining room table, and Tessa reaches her hand out to rest on my thigh like she knows I might need the support.

I lower my hand to take her fingers in mine and squeeze before opening the folder.

At this time, Cole Securities hasn't been able to locate Travis. However, they show a money trail that would make it appear like he's gone somewhere out of the country. There's a plane ticket, a hotel reservation, and car rental in three different places. One of them is the Caymans, which…of course it is.

The other one is in Europe and the third in South America.

None of it really makes sense because it's not clear if he went to any of these. There are notes on the side that basically sum up the same conclusion that I have—nothing is adding up.

"What does any of this mean?" I ask.

"There's a summary on the last page, but basically, we've ruled out him going to the Cayman Islands. I have two very good friends who are there that would absolutely have confirmed his arrival. It doesn't show that Travis ever boarded that flight and they were able to say with certainty he isn't there."

"How would they know?"

Liam clears his throat. "They'd know."

That answers nothing. "Okay, let's go with that then—what about the other two flights?"

"The Europe one is pretty easy to confirm. The agency we communicate with has been digging and have no records of him ever arriving," Liam explains and then points to the third page. "My guess is that if he did leave the country, which we can't find any flight record that has him listed, it was to South America."

"So you think he's in South America?" Tessa asks.

Liam smiles at her. "I think it's possible. I do have an asset in that location. I've reached out, but as you can imagine, communication is difficult at times. I'm working on verifying with one of my coworker's contacts, but my gut says he's not there either."

Tessa and I share a look and then I return my gaze to Liam. "No?"

"I think he's still local. I think when someone works this hard at misdirection, they're usually hiding in plain sight. Do you have any information on Travis's past? Anything he ever mentioned in passing that would be a good place to start?" Liam asks.

I think back on anything he ever said, and I can't remember even having conversations like that. We didn't talk about our lives. It was all very much about business and visions for the future.

"I really don't know," I admit.

"Did he talk about how he got started?"

Tessa speaks up. "When I did some research on him, I found that he started in Kentucky. He comes from a racing family. His father started his love of horses. However, both of his parents passed away when he was nineteen, which is how he ended up working on a ranch with another pretty famous trainer."

I stare at her, a little shocked. "You researched him?"

"Of course I did. I get why you didn't. He was already well-known in the racing world, but I was looking into his past so I could use it if I needed to." She shrugs.

I could kiss her right now. To know she cares this much means the world to me.

Liam clears his throat, causing me to look away from Tessa.

"Right." I turn to him. "I didn't do any of that."

He nods once. "I get it. We'll start there. If I can build his backstory more, then I can find possible places where he'd be laying low. What I don't understand is why he'd just take off like that. Do you think there's any legitimacy to the rumors?"

"No, I test my horses regularly. One of my closest friends is a veterinarian. The only thing Everett has ever said was that Travis tended to work the horses too hard at times, but he never found anything that would indicate he was doping them."

I even asked him again the other day, to which he emphatically said he didn't believe Travis did. The signs of a horse being given performance-enhancing drugs were not visible, and he did routine blood work to make sure. Nothing ever showed as abnormal.

"All right. Give me about a week, and either I'll have Travis in hand, or we'll discuss the next step."

Tessa and I stand and we each shake Liam's hand. "Thank you."

"Of course, I'll be in touch."

Liam smiles at Tessa. "I have to tell you something."

Her eyes widen. "Me?"

"Yes. I wanted to mention it before, but I wasn't sure it was appropriate."

I'm very confused about what the hell Liam would want to tell her that isn't appropriate.

However, the look on Tessa's face shows she's just as lost as I am. Thankfully, I keep my emotions in check and don't say anything that would make me look like an asshole.

"I'm not sure…"

"You know my daughter."

Okay, well, that makes me feel marginally less homicidal.

Tessa tilts her head. "I do? I…I don't know who that is."

"Aarabelle."

Aarabelle, like the publicist that was supposed to be here instead of Tessa?

She laughs softly. "Really? Wow, that's such a small world."

"It is, anyway, she's said a lot of great things about you, and I just wanted to let you know that in case I don't see you again."

Tessa grins. "I appreciate that. I love Aara. She's so sweet and I've learned so much from her."

"I'm glad." Liam looks to me again. "Mr. Thorn, I'll call you if I know something sooner."

"I look forward to it."

Liam leaves, and Tessa is sitting at the table, reading through the folder he gave us. I move behind her, brushing her hair back and staring over her shoulder.

"The information isn't going to change, you know?"

She looks up at me from the side. "I know, but…sometimes we see things differently after the initial time. I was just hoping."

I was hoping for a little time with her. The last few days we've both been busy. She's been at Penelope's every day as the new website is launching tomorrow. I've been working with the horses and preparing for the auction. As well as trying to do some damage control by making calls to different people and explaining some of the situation.

While we've fallen asleep together, usually after watching a terrible slapstick comedy that she finds absolutely hilarious until she passes out in the middle, forcing me to watch it with more eye-rolls than I can count, I miss her.

I need a little time with her so I can get a grip on my emotions.

"How about we get out of here?" I ask, not really having a plan but knowing I don't want to waste this little time we have.

"And go where?"

"Let's go for a ride."

Tessa smiles broadly. "Okay. Wait here and let me go change."

She rushes up to her room and a few minutes later she comes down in those tight jeans I fucking love, a T-shirt, and that stupid pink hat.

I laugh. "Really?"

"I thought I should at least be supportive of the new business." Tessa loops her arm through mine. "Did you forget yours?"

"I did. Completely slipped my mind," I tease.

She takes hers off and puts it on my head. "Here. You can borrow mine."

I chuckle. "Thanks."

"Happy to help."

We make our way to the barn, saddle up the horses, and head out.

The sun is just starting to fall, casting the skies in purples, pinks, and still a few blues. I want to bring her back to my favorite part of the land. Where we can just be away from it all.

Tessa follows and pulls alongside me when I stop and we both dismount. We walk hand in hand over to the small clearing where the grass is low enough I can put the blanket out.

We sit, her back against my front, enjoying the silence and just being together.

After a while, Tessa speaks. "I'm glad we came here."

"I used to ride out here all the time. It's been a while."

I can feel her stare on me. "Why did you stop?"

My sister isn't a topic I talk about with anyone. Even my friends. However, with Tessa, it's almost too easy and I find myself saying words that I've never admitted to anyone else.

"Losing Alicia was difficult in so many ways. I felt as though I failed her and the promise I made to my parents. They died when I was in college and I vowed to take care of her, to make sure she was happy, which I think I did in a way." At least I tried. "This was her favorite place. She would saddle up Midnight and come out here anytime she wanted to just escape the hell she was in. Even when riding was painful—physically—she did it."

Tessa looks up at me from the side. "You're a great brother and man."

"I hope so." My eyes meet Tessa's and a moment of silent understanding passes between us. It's as though she can see right through me. "I wanted to give her peace."

"You did, Killian. I may not have met your sister, but I know that if my brother did all this for me, I would cherish it. It would be the most precious gift that anyone could've given me."

I swallow and turn my gaze back out to the mountain range. "And what gift would you ask for?"

Tessa falls silent, and I wait for her to tell me.

"A way to make a difference," she finally says before turning back to me. "I'd love to have a place I could open, a place for girls who were struggling like me. When I went to that camp, it saved me in so many ways. I'd want to give other young girls the same opportunity."

"Why can't you?"

She laughs. "Money. Land. Life. All of the things that matter. Besides, I can't open a horse camp in New York City, not really any real estate options for that, and I really don't want to go back to Indiana."

"I would agree with you there, but those aren't the only places you could live."

Her sigh cuts through me as it's filled with resignation and sadness. She sits up and turns to face me. "I can't, Killian. My family is complicated, and I have to take care of them as much as I can. I'm new at my job, I make enough to live and help out. It leaves very little extra funds to buy horses, land, staff, building out a camp, all of that. It's not that easy and I know that things aren't supposed to be. I'm not naive that way, but it would be pretty much impossible for me to achieve it at this point in my life."

"I don't think it's impossible. Difficult, absolutely, and maybe it's not the right time, but don't give up on something you want."

She shakes her head. "I wish it were that simple."

"Did the camp you went to close?"

"Yes, about two years ago. The costs were high and…a lot of the staff tried to save it, but they ran on a lot of donations that dried up. Most of the girls who went there were from single-income homes, so there weren't a lot of discretionary funds to send your daughter to a camp like that. The upkeep was also astronomical, as you know, feeding, housing, medical care, and all the other things with the horses alone were high costs. Then you had to feed the campers, house them, and insurance…it was a lot. I did a bunch of fundraisers to try to help through the years, but it was a drop in the bucket and couldn't make a meaningful difference."

I wish she saw her strength the way I do. Not everyone would work so hard to benefit others. She wasn't going to gain anything by keeping the camp open. Her life was already forged, she was working or going to school, but to give another girl, even one more, a chance to have a better life, she sacrificed her time.

I cup her cheek. "I bet you made a big of difference for the girls who got to go there because of your efforts."

She tilts her head and rests her hand against mine. "Just like you did for your sister by giving her a place to be safe."

I walked right into that one.

I smile. "I see your point."

"Good."

"Do you see mine?"

She drops her hand and turns to move back into my arms. "I do, but right now, I just want to enjoy your safe place for a bit."

I'd let her enjoy anything she wants.

I tighten my grip, holding her close, wishing we could have more, have everything.

Tessa makes me feel more than I've ever felt before. She makes me want things that I haven't thought about in forever.

Forever.

That word.

That promise of things I can't have because this is all we'll have.

A blip in time, one that will make us someday sit back and think of the fun we had, but it had to end.

Like a fucking song that breaks your heart at the end.

"You can use as much time as you like." I kiss her temple and rest my head against hers, giving her a safe place, even if it can't last.

CHAPTER 17
TESSA

I'M LYING ON MY BED AS MY PHONE RINGS AND DREAD FILLS ME when I see the name.

I've tried to avoid my mother. I've done a fairly good job of it, keeping it to mostly texts and explaining how busy I am, but it seems my avoidance isn't going to hold up since this is the third call today.

I steel myself, knowing that the tirade will surely come, and swipe the phone. "Hi, Mom."

"Tessa? Is that you?"

Let the gaslighting and manipulation begin.

"Yes, I'm very sorry I missed your calls earlier."

"Oh, I just didn't know if you had my number still. I haven't heard your voice in weeks."

My eyes close, and I start to count in my head, hoping it'll calm me. It does slightly. Although, for as high as I'd need to get, it would take the rest of the day to fully erase my feelings toward her.

"How are you feeling?" I change the topic. There's no way to appease her—might as well let her complain.

"Terrible," she says, letting out a heavy sigh. "The water heater broke, or at least I think it did. Reece said it was fine, but your brother is lazy at best. I think you're going to need to replace it or have someone come out who can fix it, and not with duct tape and bubble gum."

I want to laugh because of course I need to do it.

"I'm sorry that's happening, Mom, but I've sent all that I can this month."

"What do you want me to do then?"

Get off your ass and go back to work.

I don't say it because, that would be a horrific argument that we would never recover from.

"You're going to have to let Reece do his best."

My brother may not help financially, but he's incredibly handy and does fix most of the issues she has.

"I gave you everything you have in this world," she starts in. "I gave you food, money, love, and anything you needed, you had. Even with all the pain I've been in since my accident. I've never let you and your brother suffer for it."

I wish I could've recorded snippets of my life that rebukes all of this, but it would do no good. Even when Reece and I have told her our truth about our childhood, somehow it turns into us lying or just being cruel.

The only way to deal with her is either to accept that this is the way it'll always be or cut her off completely. While I wish I could be strong enough for the second option, I'm not.

She's my mother. She tried. I truly believe that my mother loves me the only way she knows how, and I will never be able to just walk away and let her starve or be on the streets.

"I know that, Mom, which is why I do whatever I can to help you. I'm sorry the water heater is acting up. I'll call Reece and ask him to come again to work on it. As soon as I get back to New York, I'll do what I can to send some extra money."

"You will?" she asks with a sniff.

"Yes."

My roommate, Brianna, has a lot of contacts and her one friend owns a bar. Occasionally, he lets me bartend, which always gives me some extra cash. I'll reach out when I get back so I can try to help her a little more.

Mom coughs softly. "Thank you, Tessa. It's not easy for any of us. With you traveling now, it's even worse."

Yes, it is—for me.

Speaking of work…

"I'll call you when I'm back in New York, okay? I have to finish up a project I'm working on now that I need to show the owner tonight," I partially lie.

"All right, darling. I love you so much."

If only I could laugh. "I love you too, Mom. We'll talk soon."

"Goodbye, my sweet girl."

I hang up, staring at the phone and wishing that I could've not taken that call.

Wanting to put that ugliness behind me, I go back to my laptop and the project that actually is giving me joy and a sense of accomplishment. I've been working all day on the rodeo, which is going to be fabulous. I have the food vendors lined up, and a company is going to bring all the fencing, bleachers, as well as some other things she said we needed in terms of rodeo equipment.

Prior to the auction, we are going to host a few horse owners to come tour the facilities and meet with the staff.

At this point, we can do nothing about the rumors other than prove them wrong.

I'm sitting on the bed, looking over the flyer I made, tweaking the font a little when something slides under my door.

I jump a little. After the whole bug thing, I'm not exactly keen on things moving. Then I see it's an envelope.

Weird.

I get up, pad over to get it, and smile when I see my name written across the front.

I open it and there, in Killian's handwriting, are two lines.

I'll pick you up at seven for a night out.
Dress warm.

K

What in the world?

I rush to the door and open it, but there's no one there. The stupid smile on my face grows wider when I reread it.

Then, that smile disappears when I see the clock.

Shit. I have less than an hour.

I don't have a lot of options for clothing, and I have no idea where we're going. Could be another horse ride, camping—hell, I have no idea.

I grab my jeans, a one-shoulder shirt, and a cardigan, laying them out.

It's cute. It's workable. It has layers.

That's the best I can do.

Next, I head into the bathroom, pulling my hair out of the bun I tossed it in, and run a straightener through, getting any bumps out. Then I do the best makeup I can before I'm getting dressed and rushing out the door.

"Killian?" I call out his name, but he doesn't answer.

I check my phone to see if he called…but no, he didn't.

I walk into the kitchen, expecting to see him there, only to find it empty.

"Killian?" I call out again as I walk into his office.

I glance at my watch, which shows it's seven, which is when he said to meet him.

There's no movement outside on the back deck.

So weird.

As I make my way back toward the front of the house, the doorbell rings.

Uhh, how the hell did anyone get through the gate?

Since I have no idea where Killian is, I might as well open it.

When I pull it back, my eyes widen because there, in a pair of olive-green dress pants, ivory polo, and cream-colored cowboy hat, stands Killian. He fills out every inch of that shirt, the sleeves looking like they could tear right off if he flexes his muscles. His green eyes are soft, as he removes his hat and then from behind his back, he produces a bouquet of flowers, extending them to me.

"These are for you."

I smile, butterflies taking flight in my belly. "What is this?" I ask as I take the peonies that are so beautiful.

"Flowers."

"I know that," I say with a laugh. "You're on the wrong side of your door."

He puts that sexy hat back on his head. "I believe it's customary for the man to ring the doorbell of his date."

A date? He's taking me on a date.

My first date.

My throat goes dry, and not just because he looks incredible, but because this is the sweetest thing anyone has ever done. Killian is giving me a moment that I so wanted to share with him.

Dear God, this man is going to wreck me in every way.

"We're going on a date?" I ask, even though he basically told me that.

"We are."

I smile so wide my cheeks ache. "Okay. A date."

He extends his elbow. "Shall we?"

My hand rests in the crook of his arm as he walks me to the car. I've seen his truck, but this is a cute little convertible that has never been in the driveway before. The top is up, thankfully, since my hair is down and the last thing I want to look is windblown.

He opens my door and all of this is like a dream.

I know that sounds stupid, but it's…surreal.

This man, who is just supposed to be a casual fling, is doing something that no one else has done for me before.

I watch as he walks around the front, trying to calm my racing heart and frantic mind.

"You really didn't have to do this," I say once he's settled in the driver's seat, placing his hat on the backseat, not even knowing what we're doing.

"I know I didn't *have* to do it."

I sigh. "I just mean that…"

He leans in, giving me a sweet kiss, silencing my objection. Once I'm effectively dazed by his sweetness, he speaks. "I'm not doing anything that I don't want to do. Tonight, I want to go out for dinner with a beautiful woman. I want to take her somewhere that I love and then, maybe at the end of the night, she'll let me walk her to her door and kiss her goodnight. We don't *have* to do anything, but I really hope she wants to."

I reach my hand out, cupping his face. "I want it more than anything."

Killian brings my hand to his lips, kissing my palm, and I melt. "Then let's go on our date."

The drive is quiet, and he holds my hand the entire time. We see each other all day so there's not much small talk, but he still asks me about the plans for the rodeo, and I tell him about my very exhausting call with my mother earlier.

"I just don't understand her. Nothing is ever enough," I complain. "I sent her what I could and she still wasn't happy."

He squeezes my hand. "I'm sorry. What if you were to stop sending her anything?"

I can't even imagine. Well, I can, but there's no chance of it. "She'd probably lose her house. I don't know."

"It's not your job to take care of everyone. You know that, right?"

Isn't it? My job is literally taking care of people. Throughout my life, that's what's been expected of me and I've just done it.

Even if I hate it.

"Maybe so, but I can't let my mother and brother be homeless."

"Yeah," he agrees. "I wouldn't be able to either."

He definitely wouldn't.

He couldn't even handle the idea of me being in that room above the store. Killian and I are a lot alike. Every morning when I come downstairs, he has a yogurt ready for me or sometimes it's a fancy omelet. I know he likes to cook, but it's more than that. He's always making sure that I'm taken care of and am fed. Then, when we're together at night, he doesn't stop until I've orgasmed before taking his own.

We both put others' needs before our own.

It's what I like the most about him. He cares.

"I think you like to take care of people too."

He glances over at me before returning to the road. "You do, huh?"

"Yes. You wouldn't let someone go hungry any more than I could. You give to your friends, the community, your family. It's probably why I'm so drawn to you."

"I knew you liked me," he jokes.

He's not wrong. "I think we knew I did."

"Oh? Do tell me all the things you like…"

I laugh. "You're such a dork."

Killian chuckles. "I know I like to do things for you."

"Like this date."

"I want you to know exactly how a man should treat you, Tessa. You should have someone ease your burdens. He should be worthy of coming to pick you up, bringing you flowers, and spending time with you. If that man can't be me, then I want you to at least have tonight to measure it against. If he doesn't do these things, he doesn't deserve you."

My chest tightens as a dizzy sensation passes through me at the thought.

I want it to be him.

I want this person who picks me up, who treats me right, who makes me feel safe to be him, but it can't be.

I need my job and there's nothing in Ember Falls that I could do and still help support my family.

Instead of letting the sadness of that reality ruin the night, I push it to the back of my mind and focus on the now, on what I do have—tonight.

I clear my throat, hoping I can say something flippant so he doesn't see the riot of emotions he stirred. "I'll be sure to keep that in mind."

"Good."

We pull up to what seems to be a small wood cabin with a big sign out front that just says: *Marge.*

"What is this place?" I ask, reading it again.

"This is the best restaurant in the area or at least that's what the guys said."

"I see, we're trusting them, huh?"

He chuckles. "For this we are because if it goes bad, I'll kill them. I should warn you, because the guys warned me—the owner serves whatever she wants, so don't get too excited about anything on the menu."

"Okay then."

I go to open my door and he reaches his arm out. "What are you doing?"

"Opening my door?"

I'm not sure why he's confused by this since I do it all the time.

Killian huffs. "We're on a date. Stay put."

He gets out and comes around to my door before I can say anything. He opens it and extends his hand, helping me out of the low little sports car.

"Thank you," I say, feeling incredibly special, which I guess is his entire point.

The inside of the restaurant matches the outer with a rustic feel and exposed wood logs. It's cozy and very cute.

A short woman comes around the front. "You must be Killian!" She comes to him, grabbing his cheeks and pinching. "Hello, dear. I'm Auntie Marge. I own this place and I got a call from not just one, but two of my favorite people."

Killian steps back, looking a little confused, but also has a small smile. "I'm going to guess Miles and Everett called?"

She scoffs. "Those two aren't my favorite. No, no, I got a call from Violet and Penelope. I mean, the two idiots called first, and I know better than to take either of them at their word, so I spoke to the women." Marge turns to me. "You know, men don't exactly make the best decisions, at least those two don't. You are lovely."

I blush and smile broadly. "Thank you. This is a beautiful restaurant. I'm guessing it's named after you?"

She shrugs. "It wasn't supposed to be. My husband and I wanted a name fitting and classy, but we couldn't agree. He's a little hardheaded and stupid so we just put up a sign that said my first name. It stuck, despite how ridiculous it is. But regardless of the name, the food will be wonderful. I can promise you that. Now, Everett said this is your first date?"

I nod. "It is."

"Wonderful. Come, come, this way."

Killian shakes his head with a smile and places his hand on the small of my back, leading me to the table.

Marge seats us in the back where it's secluded. The restaurant only has two other couples there, but I appreciate that it's a little quieter. "Thank you," Killian says to Marge as he pulls my chair out for me.

"Oh," she sighs, clutching her hands to her chest. "You're a gentleman. Nothing like those other fools." Then Marge turns her attention to me. "You should keep this one."

I wish I could.

She heads off, informing us she'll bring the wine and then our first course.

"So, we have dinner and then what?" I ask, smiling warmly as he takes my hands in his.

"You'll have to wait and see."

"Now I'm intrigued."

Killian leans in. "You should be."

He's so cute. Not only in the attractive way, but in his heart. "You're really going to make any man that comes after this work for it, huh?"

"Damn right."

"Is this what you'd do if we weren't just having casual sex?"

I don't know why I just asked that. It's stupid. No matter what his answer is, the facts remain that we are not dating. We're having a lot of sex, working through his company's issues, and then I'll be on my way back to New York.

His thumb brushes the top of my hand. "If we were dating, and not just *having casual sex*—as you call it—we would be doing this. I'd take you out on horseback rides, which we've done now. We'd definitely do dinners, movie nights—"

"Which we do now," I say.

He chuckles. "I guess we do."

As much as I want to guard my heart and keep it locked away, with Killian, it's as though I can't.

Before I met him, there wasn't a chance in hell anyone could get this close to me. I dated a guy, which is a generous description for what we did, in college for two months and I don't think he even knew I had a brother. I definitely didn't disclose personal information about my parents.

With Killian, it just comes out. As though I know that my heart is safe and he won't break it.

Although, I think I'll be the one who breaks it when I have to leave Ember Falls.

It's nights like this that will cause the ache in my chest. He's giving me things that I will never be able to forget.

"Killian," I say his name softly.

His green eyes find mine in the candlelight. "Yes?"

"Thank you for being my first real date."

He releases my hand, moving it to my face, before pulling me gently across the table while leaning in. His lips are soft, sweet, and tender. I catalog every second, the way it feels. The warmth of his lips, the callus on his thumb that grazes my cheek just a little, the smell of his cologne—a little leather, a little woodsy, and a note of musk. All of it is him. All of it I will hold on to.

Too soon, he pulls away, his hand still resting on my cheek. "Thank you for being the one who came to Ember Falls."

Marge clears her throat and smiles knowingly as she places our first course down, and I do whatever I can to focus on the food and not on the man who is taking my heart bit by bit.

"Where in the world are we?" I ask as we pull up to a barn in the middle of nowhere. "Am I about to end up on one of those true crime podcasts?"

He huffs a laugh. "If you keep it up, maybe."

"Great. I should've at least told my best friend where I was."

"You don't even know where you are," Killian reminds me.

I pull out my phone and notice there's no service. Well, if I am going to die, hopefully it's painless.

Although…I've been in his house the past two weeks and I haven't died, so I'm going to guess this isn't anything nefarious.

Killian pushes a button on the mirror, and the convertible top drops down. He gets out, goes to the back, and pops the trunk, taking something out before coming to open my door.

"What are we doing?"

"You'll see. Here, climb in the back."

Oh, maybe we're going to have backseat sex.

He gets in after me, draping a blanket over us that he must've taken from the trunk and opening a bag. "Pick your poison."

I smile. "What is that?"

"Snacks."

"Oh? For what?"

Just as I ask, a light comes from behind us, and a rectangle of light illuminates the side of the barn where a movie will play.

I gasp and sit up. "Oh my God, we're at a drive-in?"

Now that I look around, it's clear that's what this is. To the left is an area where there must've been a food stand, a swing set—minus the swings—and an old ticket booth.

"We are. This is my friend's farm and it used to be the biggest make-out spot in the area."

"You took me to a make-out spot? Hoping for something?"

He grins. "Always. I'm happy to let you take advantage of me."

I laugh. "I bet you are, but I'm pretty sure I'm the sweet, innocent girl who is going to be corrupted by the hot guy who knows how to kiss."

Not that I'm complaining one bit about that.

He grins and wiggles his brows. "Are you corruptible?"

"Maybe."

"I sure hope you are."

I'm pretty sure he knows there's very little I wouldn't let him do to me, but since this is a first date, I'm going to play hard to get.

Well, kind of.

"I guess we'll have to find out. However, I just have to tell you, this is pretty much a surefire way to win me over. Dinner and a drive-in is perfect."

"I know you love movies, and I thought this would add a little bit of fun to it. We are not watching one of your terrible movies, this one is a classic."

This adds so much to it.

He opens his bag of popcorn and puts a bag of M&Ms inside it—his movie snack of choice—and I grab the Sno-Caps that I can't ever resist. They remind me of my grandma, she always had a bowl of nonpareils sitting on the kitchen counter when I came over.

"What are we watching?" I ask as I pop one in my mouth. He picked the last movie, which was a terrible karate movie. Yes, I usually fall asleep in the middle no matter who picks it, but in that one I was out in thirty minutes.

He grins broadly.

Oh boy.

"I decided we needed to watch something that has more meaning."

I eye him warily. "Meaning what?"

"This is a movie that my father loved. He always made me watch it with him, so it's special to me."

Then I definitely want to watch it. I want to share things that are important to him and the fact he picked it has me really excited. "I can't wait to see it."

"Remember, I was a famous football player," he says with a smirk.

"How could I ever forget? You're so famous that people haven't even heard of you."

He pinches me. "I'll have you know I have been mentioned on television—twice."

I clutch my hands against my chest. "Oh, dear me, how lucky I am to be in your presence."

He never talks about his football career, but he has photos in his office that I see every day. He was superhot then too. Although, I think he's aged like a fine wine that has only gotten better with time.

"Just…you know, keep that in mind when it starts up. There are a lot of similarities for me."

He lifts his arm, draping it behind me, and I snuggle into him, resting my head on his chest as the movie cues up. This is one of those moments that I know I'll never forget. The way he smells, like fresh air and cologne. The sound of his heartbeat in perfect sync with mine. How even against his hard chest, I feel comfortable and safe.

Every part of tonight is perfect.

The title stretches across the screen: *Rudy*.

Killian holds me to him as we watch the story of a college athlete whose only goal is to play football for his team. He works harder than anyone I've ever seen. In a lot of ways, I see myself in him. The inability to give up, no matter how many times you're told no.

I often catch Killian repeating lines to the movie and I have to stop the silly grin on my face.

I watch it with him, but a part of me can't help but be lost in my own movie. The one I'm currently the star in. Handsome man comes into a girl's life, giving her things that she never dreamed of, and she prays she can hold on to him, knowing it can't last.

The ending isn't what I want, but the middle, the meat of the story, is pretty fucking perfect.

I drape my arm around his middle and sigh as the credits start, and I look up to see Killian turning his head, wiping at his eyes.

"Are you crying?" I ask, surprise ringing in my voice.

"No," he says quickly and clears his throat.

"You are!" I say with a gasp.

"It's the dirt. It got in my eye."

I fight back a laugh, but I can't stop it. "Awww, that's so cute. You're crying over a football movie. Are you a little in your feels?"

Killian sighs heavily. "No, but how are you not emotional at that ending?"

I purse my lips. "It was uplifting and really sweet. However, I'm not crying or…I mean, I didn't get dirt in my eyes."

He ignores the last part. "It's more than that. The cinematic magic that happens when his dream comes true. All of that work, all the people telling him it would never happen, I've seen it firsthand, and so many just give up, but not him. He fought for what he wanted."

Hearing Killian so passionate about it has made me like him even more. I push up and throw a leg over his lap, straddling him, my hands going behind his neck as he holds my hips. "I can see why you feel that way."

"Can you?"

"You're fighting now, and I promise, when you turn all of this around—overcome all the business drama—I'll have your friends come carry you around and chant your name."

Killian groans. "Anyway, I wasn't crying."

"Of course not, baby."

I lift my hand, running my fingers through his hair. My emotions are bubbling to the top, but it has nothing to do with the movie and everything to do with Killian. "I will never forget this night."

He adjusts a little, bringing me closer to him. "I won't either."

"You'll never understand just how much this has meant to me. I'm pretty sure there's not a man alive who can ever live up to this."

"Maybe that was my plan."

I lean in, pressing my lips to his, but to my surprise, Killian pulls back. "Not tonight."

I blink. "What?"

"It's our first date, and you should really make me work for it."

"I think you're now on overtime."

He chuckles. "No, angel, tonight we're going to do this right."

I run my hands down to rest on his chest and sigh. "All right, what's next?"

"Next, I take you home."

That's fine by me because he happens to sleep where I do.

Killian helps me out of the car and packs the basket up before putting the convertible top back up. We make the fifteen-minute drive back to his house holding hands the entire time.

Once again, he opens my door and then walks me upstairs to my bedroom door. I lean against the wall. Shyness rushes over me because I really want to ask him to come inside, but I don't want to be rejected again. It's dumb since I know he wouldn't be doing it because he doesn't want me, that much is clear, but because he wants me to know how it all feels for the first time.

I glance down at his feet before looking into his eyes. "I had the most amazing night."

He rests his weight on one arm that is placed beside my head. "I did too."

"Am I supposed to ask you to come in?"

He shakes his head. "You're not."

"Killian..."

"Tessa..."

I roll my eyes but smile. "All right then. Goodnight."

"Goodnight."

I press my hands to his solid chest and slowly bring them up to his shoulders. The moment is charged, full of a promise of what's to come. He doesn't move, allowing me to make the choice, and really, there is no choice.

I want to kiss him more than I want to breathe.

The anticipation builds, and I close my eyes, leaning into him. Like the brush of a butterfly's wings, my lips touch his before his hands wrap around my waist, holding me tightly. The kiss moves to being just a little more before I open my mouth and Killian takes charge. He kisses me gently, as if I'm so precious, he doesn't want to break me.

I love it.

And I want more of it.

As if he can sense that it's going to get hot and heavy, he pulls back.

It wasn't a long kiss, but it has my heart racing and desire swimming between us.

With a rough voice he says again. "Goodnight, Tessa. Lock the door."

He forces himself to take a step back and then turns, but when he's halfway down the stairs I rush toward him. "Killian?" He stops and glances at me. "The door won't be locked, in case you're roaming the halls tonight."

My smile widens when I hear his groan, and then I head into my room, flopping on the bed. I kick my feet like a total dork, because this was the best night of my life.

I hear the ping of my phone, hoping it's him, but the text is from Meredith.

> **Meredith:** How are things?
> **Me:** I think I might be falling in love.
> **Meredith:** That's...wow, you? Are you okay?
> **Me:** He took me on a date tonight. Dinner, a movie, then a kiss at my door. Mer, how do I stop myself from falling?

There's a pause and I wait for some kind of words of wisdom from my best friend.

> **Meredith:** You can't. I tried with Jake and we saw how that turned out.
> **Me:** That's what I was afraid of.
> **Meredith:** Just know that even if the fall ends with pain, you'll survive, and you can always cry on my shoulder.

Yeah, I just wish I could avoid the breaking.

CHAPTER 18
KILLIAN

"A RODEO?" EVERETT ASKS, HANDING ME A BEER AS WE SIT ON Hazel's porch.

"I need to bring people onto the ranch, let them see that all the rumors are lies."

He shrugs. "I guess, but...a rodeo?"

"Tessa thinks it's the best way to get other types of horse people there, not just race breeders. Plus the rodeo will turn a rather large profit if it goes to plan. The fuck do I know?" I say, exhaustion setting in.

We've been at Hazel's all day for the second weekend in a row. She has more projects going on than I could ever imagine doing. Her primary bathroom is completely gutted, and she has to use the hall one until we finish it. The kitchen is stripped pretty much down to the studs, and she decided she wanted to remove a wall last time we were here. Thankfully, Everett put a stop to that idea—for now.

"I've learned after falling in love with Violet that there's very little we won't do for the women in our lives. I debated getting a goat again last week." He takes a long drink from the bottle.

I want to comment on the love part because that doesn't apply here. We both know that this can't go anywhere, so I don't need to worry about that.

Or more like I choose to live in denial that I could very easily love her.

Instead of saying any of that, I focus on the second part of what he said.

"A goat?"

"Don't ask."

I grin. "Well, she thinks the rodeo will help put us back on the right track and it'll give the town a boost too."

"She's right about that. All anyone who comes into the clinic talks about is how great it's going to be. I think you might have single-handedly saved the pizza parlor too by having them supply the food."

At least I can feel good about that, I guess.

We have two major food vendors—the pizzeria and the bar, which will be offering barbeque options.

Hazel will also be there with coffee and baked goods.

All in all, it'll be good for my friends as well.

"I know I'm a transplant Ember Falls resident, but I do love this town and I'm glad they're all excited."

He claps me on the back. "You're a good man, Killian Thorn."

"I appreciate that."

"Before I forget, Violet asked if you and Tessa wanted to come over for dinner."

I pause, absorbing that. "I can ask her, but we're not together. You know that, right?"

"Sure you're not."

"We're not."

Maybe if I say it enough, I'll actually believe it.

"So, you just took her to Marge's for...what?" Everett asks.

I took her for a date because she deserved to have one. I have no idea when she goes back to New York if she'll meet someone or stay single. Giving her that night was what I needed to do.

I had to know that, at least once, a man put her above his own selfish wants.

"Dinner."

He laughs as he brings the bottle to his mouth. "Sure. Whatever you say. Just like Lachlan wasn't in love with Ainsley and their relationship wasn't serious. Then there's Miles and Penelope who absolutely weren't together, it was just friendship. Or take me and Violet. We had no plans of being anything, since she was going through her divorce. That didn't pan out—thank God."

All of those situations were different. Lachlan had feelings for Ainsley, whether he ever wanted to admit it or not. Penelope had a lot of baggage and was just scared, but she always knew she and Miles had something. Everett had been in love with Violet since they were kids. Of course they were full of shit.

Tessa and I don't have that.

We had a one-night stand, discovered we have incredible chemistry, and now we're…casual, even if I think about her all the fucking time.

"We're different. Tessa lives in New York. I'm going back to Boston soon because I can't afford to lose two businesses. I took her to dinner because we have to eat."

Everett shakes his head. "All right. I believe you."

He doesn't.

He takes out his phone and starts to type, then my phone buzzes.

Everett: Killian is in love with Tessa and living in denial. Just wanted to let the group know so when he's heartbroken, I can say I told you so.

I glare at him. "Asshole."

Miles: No shit he loves her. He took her to see Marge.
Lachlan: Did you tell him it's easier to just accept it now? Causes a lot less stress.
Me: Shut up. All of you. As I told this idiot, I'm not in love. I like her, sure, but that's it.

Other than the fact that I can't stop thinking of her and spend every night with her.

The night of the date, I did lock myself in my room. It was the worst night of sleep I've had since she arrived, but I was serious when I said I wanted her to experience a real date.

If I'm completely honest, I also wanted it for us.

Jesus. Maybe I should start lying to myself a little more.

Everett: I wonder when he realizes that he does love her, if it'll be too late.

Lachlan: Ainsley said...yup.

Miles: Penny said the same.

Me: Tell them they're wrong.

Lachlan: What do we get when we're right? We should place bets. Fifty bucks says Killian fucks it up and realizes the truth four days after she leaves.

Everett: I say two.

I roll my eyes. "You know I'm right here."

"That's what makes this even more fun," Everett says with a laugh.

Miles: I think it'll take him longer. He's that old and broody type. So, I'm going with a week. After that, he'll be sweating, walking around, thinking maybe he's just sick, but it'll be heartbreak.

Me: That's never going to happen.

Everett: You might be right. Well, if that does happen we can at least make fun of him for something else other than just being old.

Thankfully, Hazel pulls up, stopping at least Everett continuing to egg the group on.

"Thank God," I say softly.

"Great. She's going to yell at us about something or add another project on."

"*You.* She's going to yell at you."

"No shit." Hazel opens the door, and Everett speaks quickly. "Hazel, how are you? Killian and I are done with the kitchen demo and we were just helping ourselves to the extra beer you had in the fridge. Didn't want it to go bad."

She laughs softly. "You're such a humanitarian, Ev. Truly, I don't know how anyone around here could survive without your generosity and help."

"You took away my free coffee, so I've opted for beer."

Hazel turns to me. "Thank you for being here, Killian. I know you're busy and dealing with so much. I truly appreciate it."

"Of course," I say, happy she's not yelling at me.

"What the fuck?" Everett cuts in. "You're thanking *him*? I'm the one who's doing all the damn work. Killian just stands there with a hammer wondering if he can bang anything that's not his publicist."

"Watch it," I warn.

"Sorry, bro. She makes me hostile."

Hazel tilts her head to the side. "I would thank you, but…you know, I'd rather not."

Everett scoffs. "Fine. See how you do when I stop coming by."

"You forget, Everett Finnegan, I'm not afraid to call Violet," Hazel warns.

This is going to get ugly if I don't step in. "Is there anything we can do before we take off to help make this next week easier for you? I know it's hard to live through construction."

She smiles. "Thank you, but I don't know. At this point, I'm just hoping we can get the kitchen done first."

That was not the original plan. She said she wanted the bathroom done first before she decided she wanted to knock down the wall in the living room to make it an open floor plan.

"Uhh." Everett lifts his hand like he's in school. "That's not what you said."

"It's what I meant," Hazel says as though that should make any sense.

"Right, but that's not what you said. So, we've been working on the bathroom, like you…said."

Hazel sighs heavily. "Is it done?"

"No, what the fuck do I look like, Bob the Builder? I don't have a crew. I have Killian, who—" he leans in, talking out of the side of his mouth "—isn't all that handy, if you know what I mean."

"I'm happy to leave," I offer.

"Ignore him," Hazel says quickly. "I'm pretty sure you know more than him."

"Considering I helped flip houses in Boston, I would say I do."

Hazel takes the beer from Everett, downing the rest before handing him the empty bottle. "Can you maybe switch gears to the kitchen? Remove that wall."

Everett rubs his hand down his face. "We can't remove the wall, Hazel. Not until we have someone check if it's loadbearing. Not to mention, I think a water line runs through it. The last thing we want to do is cut that."

"You think? You don't know," she retorts.

Everett looks to me. "Any help?"

I shake my head. "Sorry, I can't. I need to get going, though—good luck!" I wave a hand up and head to my car, back to the house, and to Tessa, who I am not in love with.

CHAPTER 19
TESSA

"I'm so glad you could come meet me," Meredith says as we're walking through the outlet stores about two hours away from Ember Falls.

Killian is working with Everett, and I needed a break from planning the rodeo.

"Me too. You need a dress for what now?"

She sighs heavily. "Jake has some corporate party to go to. Usually I just wear my tried and true black dress, but he said I needed something a little fancier."

"Too bad we aren't in New York. We could find a million options."

Meredith smiles. "Do you love it there?"

"I do, but...you know, it's totally different from where I grew up."

"Yeah, I can imagine. Speaking of, how are things with your family?"

My mother has been very quiet since our last call. A part of me wonders if she's respecting my boundaries, but that would be both hilarious and a first. She believes that because she's my mother, it entitles her to whatever she needs. I owe her—you know, for breathing.

"Right now things are good. She asked for more money and I

promised I'd send it when I get back to New York. I'm sure she's behaving so she gets it."

She shakes her head. "You know that's absolutely ridiculous, right?"

"I do."

However, I can't just leave her to fend for herself either. It's a never-ending loop of guilt and a lifetime of manipulation that doesn't have an end.

Meredith loops her arm in mine. "I just hope one day you'll be able to stand up for yourself when it comes to her."

"Me too," I say with a nervous laugh. "I think I'm getting better, though."

In the past, I would stay on the phone with her as she berated me. I allowed the abuse to continue without speaking up. Now, I choose to converse with her less and less. I focus on myself a lot more, giving her what I can because I do hate the hell she's in after her accident.

"Yeah?"

I nod. "It's not like it was in college. I don't stress to the point of making myself sick. I've also come to understand why she is the way she is."

Meredith glances over at me, surprise on her face. "What do you mean?"

"She had terrible parents. My grandmother was obsessed with herself, and she neglected my mother. She was a wonderful grandmother, but I think a lot of that was to atone for the hell she put Mom through. Her father worked fourteen-hour days, and that left very little time for anything with his kids. Then, she met my father, and we all know how that went. She was eighteen, and I honestly believe she did her best."

"That's very mature of you."

I laugh. "Therapy. A *lot* of therapy. What about you and your dad?"

Meredith falls silent for a moment and then sighs. "It's better. I wish my mother was alive because there are a million questions I would ask, but I can't now. I'm accepting my situation, and I love my dad, but I worry about him a lot. Which makes Jake worry about me. It's a fun circle."

"Why do you worry about your dad?"

She exhales deeply. "He's angry too. He was lied to. He thought I was his daughter, biologically. Now he looks at me differently, although he says he doesn't. I think he's just feeling betrayed and is worried I'll want to know my real father more."

"Do you?"

"I don't know," she admits. "But, I don't really want to think about it either."

I can get on board with that. "Well, today we can pretend we are both happy and well-adjusted."

The two of us giggle and she pats my arm. "I like that plan. Speaking of happiness and making good choices, how are things with the client?"

I was really hoping I could avoid this conversation, but I should've known better. "Honestly?"

"Do we lie to each other?" Meredith asks.

"No, we don't." However, I'm getting really good at lying to myself since I keep saying how this is casual and I'm not falling in love with him. I keep my gaze down, not wanting to look at her when I confess this part. "I'm worried," I admit.

"About what? Did he hurt you?"

The concern in her voice has me speaking quickly. "No, no, the opposite."

"Okay..."

"I like him, Mer. I really do. I told you that we went on a date but it was so sweet. He slipped under my door with instructions, and... the whole night was perfect." Even him crying at the end of the movie. "Everything he did, it was to make me feel special."

"You *are* special, Tessa."

For the first twenty years of my life, I never felt that way. I was sad, alone, always working and pushing myself to be whatever others needed. My mother needed a friend who she could complain to, so I was that. My brother needed a mother to take care of him, so I was that. My friends needed someone who they could treat like shit and take it, and I was really good at being that.

Then I met Meredith.

She didn't treat me like shit. She didn't require or demand anything of me. I was who I was with her, and she accepted it.

I didn't know that a friendship could be that.

She's also the first person who ever made sure I knew how special I was.

I let out a long sigh, still struggling to believe the words most of the time. "You know that I struggle with my self-worth."

"Yes, but it seems like this guy sees what I see. So, what's his name, I'd like to do the proper bestie stalking and make sure there's no skeletons in his closet we need to know about."

I snort a laugh. "Absolutely not. You know he's a client and there's no way I'm giving you any information about him."

My job is to fix his image, not give any hint of scandal to it.

"Who the hell am I going to tell?"

"Doesn't matter, just know that part of my job is to investigate them so I've done my due diligence on his background."

"Okay, but this is my favorite thing to do," Meredith complains.

I smile. "And that's what worries me."

"You're no fun. You know I'll find out his name and everything else when I meet him."

That is never going to happen. "Mer, that's…not possible. What we have…it can't last. I'm going to go back to New York."

We stop outside of one of the storefronts, and she turns to face me. "No matter where you go, if it works out or it fails miserably, life is about living. It's not about guarding yourself and hoping for the best. When we started dating, Jake lived in Virginia and I was in Georgia. I didn't think it was going to work out. I sure as hell didn't want to move here after college, but for him, I made it work. I'm not saying this guy is worth it, only you can decide that, but you deserve to be happy." She presses her hand to my cheek. "If he makes you happy, then fight to hold on to it for as long as you can."

"I'm really impressed with how things are going, Tessa," Brynlee says on our conference call. "Killian said you've been an incredible help and offered some real solutions. How did he feel about Buck Wild being started?"

I force a smile. "He was reluctant at first, but he eventually relented."

And then we had sex…a lot of it.

Since our date, I've somehow lost the ability to compartmentalize the fact that I'm here for work. It's as if my brain stopped remembering that little part of our arrangement, but right now, it's very apparent that I'm here for Anchor Light, and I need to remember that.

I'm talking about the ranch, that we haven't heard anything from Liam after we informed him about the rumors, and the plans regarding the rodeo.

I haven't felt uncomfortable about what Killian and I were doing—until now.

When I'm looking at my bosses and Aarabelle, feeling as though they can see it in my eyes, I hate myself a little.

"Well, whatever you're doing with him, keep it up. He's happy, even though we don't see how all the pieces fit together yet. I'm glad things are going so well there."

God, I want to crawl under my desk right now. "Thank you, Brynlee."

"What about the new rebranding launch with Penelope?" she

asks, and thankfully we're able to spend the next twenty minutes not even saying Killian's name as I go into detail about Penelope's new launch.

It really was a success.

We rebranded the website and created a new social media campaign that went better than I hoped. Penelope and the owner, Nicole, are happy and want to have me stay on as their publicist.

My first client that I signed due to my hard work.

At least I can feel good about the work I'm doing with her.

"How much longer do you think you'll need to stay in Ember Falls?" Aarabelle asks.

"I'm not sure. Right now, both of the clients are here, so it's been good to be physically close. I'm working with Kill—Mr. Thorn on the rodeo we're hosting next week, so I'd like to at least see that through," I explain.

Brynlee nods. "I agree. I want you to stay as long as you can. Killian Thorn's other company is my number one account and while we're doing this as an extension of that contract, I want him happy. Okay, that's all I have. I want to get off this call before my husband realizes I am not in bed and really working. Anything else you guys have for me?"

I laugh and so does Aarabelle. "Not on my end."

"Me neither," Aarabelle says.

"Call if you need anything and keep up the good work."

We hang up, and I sit here for a second.

My heart and head are fighting about the entire situation.

Killian doesn't ever treat me as though I work for him. He's so damn sweet, and we laugh a lot. All of our time together we're able to keep our emotions and work separate in a way that doesn't make it feel wrong.

When we're in his office, we're very hands off. We go through whatever issues we have and then formulate a plan. In the kitchen and the bedroom—well, that's a different story.

I sigh, running my hands through my hair, when there's a knock on the door.

I turn to see him standing there, shirt off, sweat casting a gleam over his absolutely stunning body.

Remember that war I was having—I picked a side.

The one that has him removing those basketball shorts and seeing if I can make him sweat in other ways.

"Enjoying the view?" he teases.

"Very much."

Killian chuckles. "I like my scenery as well."

I'm wearing a button-up shirt but no pants. I didn't need to be fully dressed for the video call, and now I'm seeing other benefits.

I stand, looking down at my outfit and smirk. "You do, huh?"

"I do."

"Even though I'm not wearing any pants?"

"That's my favorite part." His husky voice drops a little lower. "I like you pants-less."

"I bet you do."

He grins. "Are you done working?"

"Maybe."

Killian steps deeper into my room. "Do you need a break?"

I pull my lower lip between my teeth, watching his green eyes fill with desire. "What kind of break did you have in mind?" I ask.

My heart is pounding as he stalks into the room, getting closer in very slow, measured steps. "What kind of break do you want, angel?"

Oh, I know exactly what I want—him.

He stops, raising one brow, and I remain quiet, loving the game we play.

"Maybe you don't want this then," Killian says, taking two steps back.

"No, I do want it."

"How much? Because I'm not convinced."

I feel a shiver run through me as his heated gaze roams over me.

Killian moves back further, retreating when that's the last thing I want.

He leans against the wall now, putting way too much distance between us.

"Very much."

The air in the room crackles with desire. God, just him looking at me has me desperate for him.

"Stand," he commands, and the timbre in his voice has my heart accelerating.

He's going to make me work for this—in the best possible way.

CHAPTER 20
KILLIAN

SOMEONE TAPS ME ON MY LEFT SHOULDER AND I TURN, BUT NO ONE is there. Then I feel it on the right, and when I turn, I'm floored at who's standing before me.

It's my best friend. "Nathaniel? What the fuck are you doing here?" I ask as I clasp his hand and pull him in for a hug. "You didn't tell me you were coming."

He laughs. "I know, and yet here I am."

I shake my head, completely shocked. "What...why?"

"Dude, you've been here for over a month. I was worried that someone kidnapped you and was holding you hostage."

"No," I sigh heavily. "Just doing what I can to save this place."

Nathaniel smiles and clasps my shoulder. "Wow, this is something," he says as he looks around the setup as the rodeo is in full swing. The grandstands are packed with people from the area, lines are long for food, and the entire arena is buzzing. "I honestly never knew rodeos were such a thing. There isn't anything like this where I grew up or ever lived."

I clear my throat. "We really wanted it to be something everyone in the town would remember."

And by we, I mean Tessa.

She's worked tirelessly. Every detail has been planned and then executed to perfection, despite any obstacles.

This morning I found her sitting in a corner telling herself some affirmations and stating how she was going to put all the good vibes out.

An hour later, we found out that there was an issue with one of the trucks that was bringing the animals in, and I watched her flip a switch and go into crisis-management mode.

I've never been more grateful for her innate attention to detail because she quickly made a few calls and the issue was solved.

"I don't think anyone will forget this, Killian. Good idea."

"It was Tessa's," I tell him.

"Oh! The girl you told me about, our publicist, right?"

Yeah, I didn't tell him everything, and I don't plan to. "Yes, she's from Anchor Light."

"Good, I'm glad that's working out and we hired them for things like this. They've been working on some PR with me as well. We're donating and doing some charity things. I didn't want to bother you with it while you've had your hands full," he explains and then looks down at the bull rider who is in the chute with one hand raised. "Is that...safe?"

"Probably not, but it's also why I'm not in there."

He laughs once. "Holy shit, they're just going to open the door?"

"Yup."

The bull rider nods a few times and then is released, his body swaying with the bucking bull as he works to get him off, but the rider holds on...until he doesn't.

"Damn, well, that was entertaining." Nathaniel says with a chuckle. "So, you're good here? You look good."

I'm only good because of the woman who came here to help. "I am."

"Here I thought I was going to come down here and save the day."

Of course he did. I roll my eyes and chuckle. "You're the one who usually fucks things up."

"This is true, but..."

Tessa comes over, a huge smile on her face. "Hey, Killian." She looks to Nathaniel beside me, and her eyes widen in recognition. "Are you Nathaniel? I saw your photo in the office."

I chuckle softly. "Tessa, meet my business partner and longtime friend, Nathaniel."

He extends his hand. "Tessa, nice to meet you. I've heard all good things."

She returns the gesture and dips her head a little. "Thank you, but it's been all Killian. I'm just here to help. I hate to interrupt…"

"No, no, please don't let me hold you up. I'm going to watch this for a bit and then take off. I was in the area for a meeting and saw the ranch wasn't too far, thought I'd pop in and see if I could help, but it seems he's in good hands."

Leave it to Nathaniel to lay it on thick. I sigh heavily. "Yeah, yeah. Find me before you take off."

"Of course. Do you mind if I head into the house to change?"

"My house is your house," I say.

He smiles again, bows slightly to Tessa. "A pleasure, Tessa."

"It was all mine," she says with her hand on her chest.

Nathaniel melts into the crowd, and I turn to her. "I had no idea he was coming."

"It's nice he did, right?"

I nod. "Yeah, he's been worried about me."

"I think we all need good people in our lives. My college roommate is still my best friend. Those friendships stand the test of time." She sighs and then continues, "I came over because there's a buyer asking for you, said he knows you. He's standing over to my right—don't look!"

She scolds me when I glance over.

"Sorry."

"His name is Drake, so if you don't remember him—lie. I've strategically placed people to help with any situation. I suggest taking him out to the barn if he doesn't ask."

"You really thought of everything."

Her eyes brighten. "Of course I did. That's my job. Now, you go do yours."

So far today I've met with a few buyers that were repeat buyers. Pete came by first thing to apologize for pulling out of the sale. We talked a bit but I got pulled away. It's been interesting putting faces to some of the names I've been staring at for weeks as we tried to uncover what happened with Travis.

Tessa and I walk over, and Drake perks up. I instantly remember him so I don't have to fake anything. He bought quite a few horses from me and we discussed using one of my mares with his stud. We shake hands, exchange pleasantries, and Tessa excuses herself to deal with some kind of cattle emergency.

"Would you like to see the barn?" I ask as Drake mentions the horses that are available.

"I'd love to. You know, this rodeo idea was a great idea," he says with a chuckle. "Gave us all a chance to see for ourselves, huh?"

I could deny it, but Drake is one of those guys who just likes utter honesty. "That was also the goal. Although, not the entire reason. I hoped other horse buyers and breeders in the area would see the truth that I have never and would never harm or do anything to my horses."

He claps me on the back. "I didn't believe it, but the rumors seemed pretty damning."

"I understand." We walk toward two of the horses he had looked at in the auction, and Everett is standing just to the side—as though I conjured him.

I didn't. This is all part of Tessa's plan.

"Killian," Everett says and then turns to Drake. "Good to see you."

"Dr. Finnegan, I didn't realize you were here," Drake says with a hint of confusion.

"I'm here all the time to check on the horses."

"I see," Drake says slowly. "You're the vet for Ivy Thorn?"

Everett laughs as though it's funny to even ask. "Of course I am, Drake. I'm in Ember Falls and Killian knows I take care of all the animals here as if they were my own."

"Yes, it's why you're also my vet."

Everett nods. "I'm glad you agree. Anyway, I came down because I wanted to make sure all the excitement wasn't causing stress, but everyone is doing great. It was the right move to keep them in this barn as opposed to closer where the noise could've spooked any of them."

Another reason why Tessa is a fucking genius.

"We always put the animals first," I say.

"Dr. Finnegan," Drake cuts in. "What do you think of the rumors?"

Everett looks to me and then back to Drake. "They're complete bullshit."

Drake laughs. "How do you know that?"

"Because I'm here all the time. I check on them, do blood work. I also know Killian and I knew Travis—no one was doping these horses. If it was happening, it was after the sale and not on this property," Everett says with such finality, it's honestly more than I could've hoped for.

He's a good friend. A bit of an asshole, but he's the guy you want beside you in a fight. He's not going to back down, and he's not afraid to throw a punch.

Drake is quiet, looking over at the black thoroughbred in the stall. "So you think Travis's disappearance is…what?"

"I have no idea, and I really don't care. As soon as Killian learned he left, he called me, and we did everything to make sure the animals were okay."

"I see," Drake says. "So, you'd buy a horse from him?"

I wait, knowing that Everett would never screw me, but still, a part of me hesitates.

"In a heartbeat. In fact, if I were a racehorse guy, this is the one I'd bet on," he points to the horse in front of us.

"Why is that?"

Everett goes over the physical attributes as well as the spirit he's seen. He details where his strengths are and then how he thinks with the right trainer, his weaknesses could be worked out.

Drake and I discuss more about the horse, and before I know it, he makes an offer.

For way more than I expected.

"You've got a deal," I say, extending my hand. "We'll send the paperwork to you tomorrow."

Drake shakes my hand. "I'm going to make a lot of money with this horse."

"I think you will too."

And he's right. This was one of my top options. Everything Everett said is right. He's got a great build and he really loves to run.

Drake leaves a few minutes later, stating he'd like to see some of the bull riding still on the program, and I stay back with Everett.

Once he's gone, I exhale for what feels like the first time in weeks.

"I can't believe that," I say, leaning against the stall door. "Do you want a job as a salesman?"

Everett snorts. "You can't afford me."

"Probably not," I agree.

Right now, I can't afford much, but with the last few sales—and the bachelorette parties—this place might just be okay.

Might.

Of course the cost of the rodeo cuts into a lot of these profits, but we're selling horses again. If we can sell more after and get some people to board with us, then…it'll have all been worth it.

"How has the rodeo gone so far?" he asks.

I push off the door and jerk my head toward where it's still going on. "Good. It should be done pretty soon."

"I'm glad. You seem to be smiling, which is something you haven't done much lately, other than when you're with Tessa."

Of course he's going to bring her up. He's like a dog with a bone.

"I smile plenty."

"Sure you do. So, how many horses did you sell today?"

"Three."

"This is a good start for you, man," Everett says as we start to walk out of the barn. "I think word of mouth and the fact that Drake is aware the rumors were crap is going to accomplish more than anything you could've on your own."

He's right.

"It was Tessa's idea," I admit.

"What was?"

I laugh, thinking about how she was so strategic in certain parts of this whole event. I didn't see it at the time, and I also didn't have the time to invest in planning the rodeo.

I've been busy trying to make sales as well as help Gary with running the farm. Without Travis, and having to let go of one of my ranch hands, it's been me picking up the slack, exercising the animals as well as doing other chores.

"She thought it would be a good idea to have other ranchers come. Not just guys who have bought from me before, but local breeders who would be able to see the ranch, know the conditions, and be at least able to speak to what they've seen." She was right. "I didn't think they'd come."

Everett scoffs. "Please, for them to get a chance to see your operation up close and be able to gossip? That's their favorite thing. Also, they all hate Owen at Longwood Ranch, so they will love proving he's a fucking liar."

That makes sense. Still, I didn't think it would be a good idea. I didn't want a bunch of assholes who have spread the rumors to be able to come here and make my life hell.

I was wrong.

"Hopefully it works."

"I think it already has. You got a few horses sold, and I'm pretty sure more will come."

"Yeah," I say with a grin. "I hope you're right."

"Keep listening to Tessa, and maybe you'll get out of this mess for good. When does she head back?"

Soon. Way too fucking soon. When I last spoke to Brynlee, she told me that Tessa would stay on until the rodeo and now that's over.

Well, almost.

"And that's the end of our evening, folks. Thanks for coming out to the rodeo here on Ivy Thorn Ranch. We hope you had a good night, don't forget to check out the vendors and we'll see you again soon!" The announcer says and a loud round of applause fills the air.

I turn to Everett. "She was staying until this was over."

Something like sympathy flashes across his face. "I see."

"See what?"

"She's going to leave," he says. "I just…hope that you guys are at least honest with each other before she goes."

"We are honest," I say quickly.

"Oh? Is that what we're calling it? Okay then." Everett slaps me on the back. "In that case, I need to find my wife."

I raise one brow. "She hasn't made that mistake yet."

"We're practically married. We're living together and having a baby," he grumbles. "At least I'm deeply in touch with my feelings, I'm not living in denial."

I roll my eyes. "Shouldn't you be getting home to Violet? I'm sure she's anxiously awaiting your arrival."

Violet is about eight months pregnant and pretty much over everything.

"I should. Anyway, this has been fun. I'll see you in a few days?"

I nod. "I'll see you at practice. Thanks again, Everett."

"Of course. Remember, we're best friends."

Right. "How could I forget?" I tease.

We shake hands and I make the rest of the walk, having to dodge the crowd of people heading to their cars.

It takes me about fifteen minutes to get into the arena, dreading the amount of work that's going to be required to break down everything.

When I enter the arena, I'm...shocked.

What the hell?

Literally, twenty minutes ago, there was a ring, chutes, corrals, and bleachers. Now, half of it is broken down and being taken out by the massive amount of workers there.

There, in the middle of what was the rodeo, is Tessa. She's pointing and directing everything. "You, right there—hi, how are you? Thank you so much, can you please move that fence there so the machine can get in here?" she asks, her beautiful smile causing the young man to nod quickly. "Thank you."

He grabs the section of fence that was sitting on the ground and brings it to the side. She continues to give orders, and I watch her in amazement.

She looks as though she's done this her whole life.

Tessa's eyes meet mine, and she graces me with that smile. Only this one is warmer. She waves. I wave back and then she ducks her head.

"Killian? Can you help me with some of this?" Hazel asks, appearing at my side and pulling me away from staring at Tessa.

"Of course."

Hazel and I work on her booth, taking everything down, packing it away in a very specific order—one that I wasn't aware of, but apparently should've known.

She huffs.

I laugh.

We then get it done.

"Anything else?" I ask.

"Do you want some coffee? I have a feeling you're going to be out here for the night."

I chuckle. "I'm sure. I'd love some."

Hazel goes into her car, grabs a thermos, and pours me a cup.

Seriously, she makes the best coffee I've ever had. I don't know what it is, but she truly has a gift. "This is perfect," I say.

"I'm glad you like it. Hey, would you mind grabbing my purse and laptop that I left in the main house? I'm so sorry. I just need to finish loading the car and it's a bit like Tetris, so…it's better if I do it."

"Sure thing."

I walk across the property, and if I thought Tessa was brilliant before, now it's confirmed. The entire arena is almost cleared out. The rodeo is broken down, all that's left are a few of the vendors who clearly don't have Tessa orchestrating things.

Once I find the purse and laptop, I make my way back so I can give them to Hazel. By the time I come within earshot, she's talking to someone new.

"Seriously, Tessa, this has been absolutely amazing. You are truly amazing. To have put all this on, to have brought the town together, just…wow," Hazel says, and I stop before I get close enough that they can see me.

It makes me happy that Tessa is going to hear about how great this was from someone else.

Too few people let this woman know just how incredible she is.

"Thanks, but truly I didn't do anything."

Hazel scoffs. "Please! You did all of this. Everyone here was so impressed. None more than me, though, I have to tell you. Which leads me to my next question for you."

"Oh?" Tessa asks with a hint of confusion.

"I was wondering…are you taking on new clients? I think Prose & Perk could really expand a bit if I had the right person to help me with this stuff. I didn't even think about doing any kind of event like this, but I made so much money today. Not to mention all the people who said they will come by now because of the coffee. It was a great way to get some exposure."

I watch as Tessa's eyes brighten. "Are you serious?"

"Yes, I don't know what your costs are, but I'd love to talk about it. I really wish you could stay in Ember Falls, but I know that's just my wishful thinking."

Mine too. I want her to stay here—with me.

The thought hits me so hard that I clutch my chest.

"I wish I could too," Tessa admits. "I mean, you know, because... all of my clients are here."

Although, in her voice, I hear something else. A longing. One that I feel in my heart.

"Not because of any other reason?" Hazel nudges her.

"He's also my client."

"He is, but...why can't you stay? Do you like it here?"

Tessa nods quickly. "I do. I love Ember Falls. It's such a great town and, I could see myself here, but...my job is in New York. I can't imagine that Brynlee or Thea would let me just move here."

"Think of all the travel you'll save on," Hazel says with a laugh.

I watch as Tessa shakes her head, seeming to search for something to say and then settles on, "I wish. For several reasons."

Hazel reaches her hand out, resting it on her shoulder. "If one of those reasons happens to be the owner of this ranch, I think it's a good one."

"Even if I could, I can't." Tessa laughs and then tucks her hair behind her ear. "I know how that certain owner feels and...you know, I wouldn't want to just assume."

"I don't think you know anything," Hazel informs her and then grabs one of the boxes, putting it in the car. "Let me ask you this then, if you had permission from your boss and Killian wanted you to stay, would you?"

I wait, my heart pounding against my chest, not realizing how much I want the answer to this. How badly I want more days and nights with her. Not understanding that while we've been telling ourselves this is casual, and my attempts to make that be the case, it hasn't been.

She's more.

So much more.

But I want her to live her life, chase her dreams, and not be some guy in another state who holds her back.

I want to be the man who makes her dreams come true, not robs her of them.

Tessa smiles. "Yes. There's nothing I would want more than to stay."

Her answer takes me by surprise. I thought she wanted to go back to New York and live the life she's worked so hard for, but this…this changes everything.

If she wants to stay, even if there's just a chance of it, then I need to show her that I never want her to leave.

CHAPTER 21
TESSA

I'M LYING ON THE BED LIKE A FISH. JUST SPRAWLED OUT—BEAT.

Today was the best and most exhausting day I've ever had.

Everything went great, and for that, I'm so happy, but I need to sleep for a week.

Killian is still at the arena, finishing up a few things while I came here to grab a sweatshirt, but somehow ended up flopping on the bed and am now unable to move.

As great as things went, my mind hasn't stopped for a moment. It was planning, executing, breaking down, admitting my feelings for Killian are so much more than I ever thought they would be, and I want to stay in Ember Falls, realizing that's never going to happen.

All of it, on top of the physical stress, has me just wanting to sleep and forget this ever happened.

Stupid, stupid, stupid is what I am.

Why did I let myself think about a future?

I know better. I'm a smart woman. I'm aware of the limitations regarding our "casual relationship." They all amount to one thing: *do not get attached.*

And I royally fucked that up by falling head over ass right in love.

Although, to my credit, I didn't push that. He did. He took me out on a date. He made me fall in love with this place. He gave me more than I ever knew was possible, so really, I should blame him.

I sigh because I can't. I saw this coming and instead of jumping off the train tracks as the locomotive barreled forward, I stayed put and said: *Hi train, just hit me, it's fine, I want to be a pancake at the end.*

My phone dings with a text.

Killian: Where are you?
Me: In bed. I don't know how I got here, but I'm pretty sure my body has given up.

Just like my heart has on resisting you.
I slap my palm to my forehead.
Stupid, stupid, stupid, Tessa.

Killian: Don't move.

At least that is a command I can obey. My limbs have decided they're going to stay like this unless something infuses them with energy since I'm all tapped out.

A few minutes later, there's a soft knock on my door. "Come in," I say.

I hear Killian's deep chuckle. "Well now, don't you look comfortable."

I push myself up onto my elbows, looking at him and ignoring the one part of my body that doesn't ever seem to be too tired for him.

"I don't know about comfortable."

He enters further, kicking the door closed with his foot. "Poor angel. Are you tired?"

I flop to my back. "Very."

I feel the mattress lower as he climbs on. "That's too bad. I really wanted to show you my appreciation."

That perks me up a little. "You do?"

"I do."

"For what?" I ask. "You know, so I know exactly what I'm being thanked for."

Killian grins as he now leans over me. "Many, many things."

I wrap my arms around his neck, my fingers playing with the ends of his hair. "I think I need specifics."

"You do, huh?"

I nod. "Just one, maybe."

Killian leans his face close. "How about just because I want you? Because you make me happy? Because you make me smile? Because…I really fucking like you."

My heart pounds against my ribs, and those reasons make me want—more. That word whispers through me, demanding to be heard, and I work hard not to read into what he says.

However, my heart does a bad job at listening.

I run my fingers against his collarbone, our eyes connected. "I like you too."

He leans down and presses his lips to mine. "Good. Now," he says, getting off the bed, and I sit up straight, wondering what the hell has him pulling away. "I want to thank you, give you a night you won't forget." Killian extends his hand and I take it, allowing him to help me up. "Will you do as I ask?"

I'd do just about anything. "Yes."

He pushes my hair back and smiles. "Good. I'm really glad you said that."

He steps back again, and the loss of his heat is felt everywhere.

"Now what?" I ask, my voice trembling.

"Take off your shirt."

I start to work at each one but he cuts in. "Slowly."

The last thing that I want is to slow down, but if I don't do as he says, he might leave and that would be the worst possible thing. I take my time with each button, sliding my fingers down the fabric until I reach the next one. "Like this?" I ask.

"Yes, just like that."

"I think you should do this for me," I challenge. It's his hands I want on me.

"You want me to undress you?" he asks, as he's casually leaning against the dresser.

I nod. *So very much.*

"Then get on your knees and crawl to me."

Oh. My. God.

I shouldn't be turned on by this. Every part of me should be screaming in protest at the idea of crawling to him, but instead, I'm hotter than I've ever been.

Keeping my eyes on his, I slowly sink to the floor, the cool wood floors are like ice against my overheated body. I do as he says, on my hands and knees, coming to him, wanting so badly for him to touch me.

When I reach him, his erection is tenting his pants. He extends his hand and helps me to my feet. Then he cups my face, bringing his lips to mine in a searing kiss. I hold on to his neck, arching my body into his.

I love how he kisses me. So deeply, so possessively, and I let him claim me each time.

The minty remnants of his gum linger on his tongue, sliding against mine. We kiss and kiss and I could do this forever.

Killian's hands move down my neck, to my breasts, where he squeezes and rubs his thumbs against my nipples through the fabric.

Every nerve ending comes alive, and my mind is screaming for more. He rips my shirt open, buttons scattering to the floor.

I kiss him harder, pouring all my desire into the touch. Killian responds by pulling my bra down, making my breasts pop up, and then pinching my nipples. He breaks the kiss, moving his mouth down my neck, his tongue leaving a hot trail in its wake.

"You taste like honey," he says against my neck. "So sweet. So fucking addicting."

My fingers move to his hair as I lean back, allowing him more access to my skin. "Killian," I sigh his name when he moves his tongue to my breast, but avoids the nipple.

"As sweet as you are here, you're even sweeter here." His hand goes to my core, and he rubs against my jeans.

"Please, take them off."

He releases me from the confines of my clothes—my shirt, bra, and then pants and underwear are off. I stand here naked before him.

Killian's eyes flash with desire and then his hand returns to my clit before he fingers me. One long, deep stroke that has me gasping. "I love your cunt."

I groan. "Take it."

"Oh, I plan to. I'm going to lick you, finger you, fuck you, and you're going to let me, aren't you?"

"Yes," I agree without pause.

"Do you want my cock, Tessa?" he murmurs against my ear and then slides his finger out before slamming it back in.

"Yes!"

"I know, angel. I can feel you tightening around me, wanting more." He fists his hand in my hair, pulling it back, and I gasp. "You like this, baby? You like when I'm rough with you?"

"I like it every way with you." The admission falls too easily from my mouth.

That answer though, while revealing more than I planned, sends him over. He pulls his hand from inside of me and releases my hair, letting me go so quickly that I would've fallen if he didn't have such a good grip on me.

He walks us to the bed, placing me down before going to his clothes. He tears his shirt off then his pants are next.

I go to sit up but he's already naked and climbing on the bed. "I know I said I wanted to lick your pussy, but I need you. I can't...fuck, Tessa, I can't wait."

I love that he's out of control. "I can't either. Please, I want you inside of me."

He kisses me again. This time, it's not frantic. It's slow and measured. I can feel how hard he's fighting the urge to just plunge deep.

My fingers drift up his back, and he groans into my mouth.

The kiss softens more. It's tender, and my chest grows tight.

This moment, this kiss, it's so much more.

He pulls my leg up and my hips cradle him. I need him.

I can't wait.

I need him right now.

"Killian, please," I beg as he shifts.

"Condom," he murmurs but I grab him, not letting him move.

"I'm on the pill. I've been tested."

He stares down at me. "I've been tested as well. You're sure?"

I want to feel him, all of him. "Are you?"

"To have nothing between us? I'm sure."

His dick presses right at my entrance, and I whimper. It feels so damn good. He did this to me before, teasing me with his cock, and I've thought of how good he felt without a condom.

Maybe this is stupid.

No, I know it is, but I don't care.

I have never felt so safe, so cherished as I do with him.

"Tessa," his voice cracks as he pushes deeper. "Fuck, you…it's… you're perfect."

Only with him.

Killian thrusts his hips forward until they slam against mine and I nearly cry in ecstasy.

He pushes up onto his hands, staring down at me. "You feel so good."

I inhale harshly. "Please."

"Please what?"

Please make love to me. Please don't make me say it. Please God make my heart stop feeling this way.

Instead of saying any of that, I rest my hand on his cheek. "Take my thoughts away."

He moves then, in and out, slow and steady. As though there's nothing but time for this. I don't know how long he makes love to me because all I see is him. My orgasm hits me so hard, so suddenly that I cry out over and over. One minute it was building and then, watching him watch me sent me spiraling.

This is not sex.

This isn't just two people who can't seem to control their sexual attraction.

This is a joining. Two people who are saying more with their bodies than they can with their mouths.

Because I can't put words to this.

It will shatter my very carefully constructed understanding of what we're doing. So I lift myself up, holding on to him so I can't see his beautiful face, think about this change. I wrap my legs around his hips, ensuring that he can't see the stupid tears that are filling my gaze.

Killian isn't for keeping or loving and yet—my heart is becoming his a little more each day.

I look forward to being around him, our horse rides, the movie nights, the way he kisses my neck when I wash dishes after he cooks for us.

I want to stay here with him.

I want a life like this, one that we build together.

He has stolen my heart, and if I leave, it'll break me.

"Tessa, angel, I'm close. Do you want me to stop?"

I hold him tighter. If this is all I can have, I want all the memories I can get to torture myself. "No, please."

I release my hold around his neck, wanting to watch him. Killian takes my hands, pulling them over my head with our fingers entwined.

I watch him as he stares down at me, his hips bucking, and then he practically roars his release. The sound cuts through me, and he collapses on top of me.

He struggles to catch his breath, still buried deep. "That was incredible," he says between breaths.

"It was."

"Let me clean you up," Killian says as he pulls out and heads into my bathroom.

I lie here, waiting for a towel, questioning my life choices.

He returns and I head into the bathroom to finish.

What am I thinking? I can't do this. I can't make love to him. There is no love to be had.

This was a huge mistake. I have to rebuild that wall that was made of straw and use some freaking bricks this time.

Once I have my plan firmly in place, I exit the bathroom, ready to see him getting dressed so I can go to bed.

Instead of finding that, he's in the bed, arm outstretched.

"Come here," Killian requests.

I shouldn't.

I should kick him out and put that damn wall up.

However, like a dumbass, I go to him and curl up on his chest.

Killian runs his fingertips up and down my back, and I count the ways I'm screwing up.

One, I'm falling for him.

Two, I'm sleeping with him when I should've never done it in the first place.

Three, I'm lying on his chest even knowing that one and two are important.

Four, I'm still not moving.

The list could really go on and on because the mistakes are piling up.

I lift my head and rest it on my hand that sits on his chest. Maybe I can talk myself out of this. I can say something about what I'm feeling, scare him off, and then that could be that. The rodeo is over. I should go back to New York anyway. This can be the shove I need.

He cups my cheek, his green eyes assessing. "What are you thinking?"

I'm not going to answer that honestly. "That you're incredible in bed."

Killian smirks. "Only in bed?"

"You're not bad out of it."

"I'll take that as a compliment."

I smile. "You should."

"You're not bad in or out of bed either. Actually, you're pretty spectacular."

We fall silent, the moment settling around us. I do my best not to let my mind wander about how much I'll miss this. How we solved a lot of issues today and I'll need to leave soon. Financially things are back on track, he's working with Gary who will help with the breeding program, and as for Travis, well, that's Cole Securities' job. My job was to manage the PR crisis, which I did as much as I think I can.

Killian kisses the top of my head, pulling me closer to him. "Tessa?"

"Yes?"

His hand moves up and down my arm. "I was thinking… I know the rodeo is over and the farm is on the right track, but maybe… maybe…you could…stay?"

My body locks up. I feel panic starting to rise. "Stay?"

He shifts, and I'm forced to lift my head to look at him. "I'm just saying that things still aren't fixed here. Not completely. I really think you should hang around a while longer."

"For work?"

"For work…and because I want you to."

"Killian," his name comes out as a breath. "You're the one…"

"I know that I set the rules—although, I think we both did. I'm just saying that I don't want you to think that I don't want you here." I shake my head and he continues on. "Don't make any decisions now or even really think about it, just know the desire is there—on my end."

As though I can think of anything else other than what he just said.

He wants me to stay.

It's what I want, but it's all too…messy.

I can't just give up my job, my life, in the hopes that this is going to work out somehow. I have to think about all my responsibilities. If I were to give up my job, who is going to take care of things?

Then, my heart thinks about what I'm going to give up when I leave him.

The fact that in a few short weeks, he's shown me what love can be like and that was with us both holding back.

If I let him love me, let myself love him, what could that look like?

Killian brushes my lips with his thumb. "Hey?"

I blink. "Hey."

He chuckles. "What's on your mind?"

"How old are you?" I blurt out the first thing I can think of. He said something about getting to know him, so I'm going to choose a basic question that won't rock the boat.

Safe is my goal for the rest of the night.

Killian's eyes widen for a second before his deep laugh shakes the bed. "My age? That's what you want to know, why?"

"I don't know, I just…we've talked about childhood trauma, but I don't know the basics. Like, how old are you? What's your birthday? Favorite color? Those are things most people get to learn before they have sex. We skipped all that and have veered into a little bit of a dangerous territory, so let's go to the safer topics."

"All right then. I'm forty-four. My birthday is January 27, and blue is my favorite color."

It's weird, but knowing that makes this feel a little more normal. "Forty-four, huh?"

I knew he was older, but I thought maybe late thirties.

"I'm afraid to ask your age based on the look on your face."

"It's not terrible. I just didn't guess right. You do not look forty-four."

His body *definitely* did not age.

"And what about you? Who is Tessa Rivers?"

I let out a long breath. "I'm twenty-five. My birthday is August 9, and my favorite color is green." It was orange my entire life, but as I've stared into his green eyes over the last three or so weeks, I've found a new color I adore.

He chuckles once. "Twenty-five? God. I feel ancient."

"It's not that bad."

"It is when I have a daughter your age."

Okay, when he puts it that way, I guess it is that bad.

"I didn't know you had kids—you said you weren't married."

"I've never been. I didn't find out about her until a few years ago," he explains and pushes my hair behind my ear. "She did one of those online DNA tests online to check for medical conditions and it matched that I was her father."

That's exactly how Meredith found out when she did her test a while back.

"Wow, and you never knew about her?"

"No. I met her mom in high school, but she left Colorado and moved to Georgia, not knowing she was pregnant. I had a scholarship to play football in Oregon, so I left right after graduation. She met someone and told him she was pregnant with his kid and he raised her. She had no idea he wasn't even her dad until she got the results back."

My brows furrow the more he speaks and my mind spins because his story is too similar to one I know all too well. Meredith is from Georgia, and her mother moved there in high school, but... it couldn't be.

Right?

There's no way this can be the same because, surely, the universe wouldn't hate me this much.

Cautiously, I ask the next question that will put all of this to rest. "When did you learn this?"

"Two years ago, I think. She actually lives not too far from me, which is ironic since neither of us is from Virginia."

My stomach sinks, and I feel lightheaded. It can't be. What would the odds be?

Oh God. I might die.

Right now.

My heart might literally give out.

I sit up and put some distance between him and I. "Killian, what's your daughter's name?"

Please don't say Meredith. Please don't say Meredith.

"Meredith."

My heart threatens to give out as I leap out of bed, holding a pillow in front of me to cover myself. "Oh my God. Is her last name Scarpello?"

He sits up, his eyes widening. "How do you…?"

I let out the loudest burst of air, and I swear I might start hyperventilating. "Oh my God. Oh my God. This can't be happening. Meredith Scarpello is your *daughter*? Meredith, who is married to a guy named Jake, and they live like an hour from here?" I ask, praying that maybe, just maybe, there is a God who doesn't want me to throw myself off a cliff.

"Yes? Tessa, how do you know this?"

I let out a cry. "We are so fucked! And not the kind of fucking we just did. Oh my God. I'm going to have to tell my *best friend* that I've been sleeping with her *dad*!"

CHAPTER 22
TESSA

I CAN'T BREATHE.

I can't think.

"I can't believe this!" I scream as I start to pace.

Killian Thorn is Meredith's freaking father.

Like, really, Universe? Really? You really needed to fuck me this way? Literally!

"Tessa, I need you to…"

"To what?" I fairly shriek. "Calm down? *Don't* tell me to calm down. We knew we shouldn't do this weeks ago. It was bad enough you were my client, but no, I had to defy the universe. It said, *you shouldn't be together,* but instead, we did this—a lot. We said, *screw you, universe,* and now look at what we did."

Killian shakes his head. "Okay, yes, we made a mistake, but we didn't defy anything."

I turn to stare at him, naked in my bed. So gloriously handsome and…my best friend's father.

"We sure as hell did. We spat in the face of fate. We were told: don't do this. We knew the rules that we were breaking. How in the ever-loving hell am I going to look at her ever again?" Then the next part hits me. "*My God, she talked me into this!*"

Just the other day I was telling her how much I liked him, how special he made me feel. This just gets worse and worse.

"What? You talked to her about us?" Killian finally seems to catch on to the absolute shitshow this is.

"Yes! She's my best friend. I told her about the amazing sex, the fantastic date, the way you make me feel. To her! I'm a horrible person. That's all there is to this."

"When did you talk to her?"

Too many times, that's for sure. She's going to kill me. I may give her the tools to do it. I mean, talk about a betrayal of friendship. It's not her ex, but it's her damn dad.

Sure, she doesn't know him all that well, and she's never told me his name. I had asked once but she was so distraught and she just kept saying it didn't matter, so I didn't know, but still.

I'm going to throw up.

Killian looks to me, waiting for an answer to his question.

Not that it matters.

"The first time was when I went to see her. Remember that Saturday after your Ultimate Frisbee thing? I drove out to see my best friend from college. That's Meredith, and she was the one who said I should throw caution to the wind and give in. Well, I bet she didn't anticipate *this* outcome."

Lord knows I didn't.

"Tessa, we don't have to say anything to Meredith. She and I… we don't even really know each other. She has her father. Yes, I'm her biological father and sure, it's a little weird, but what we're doing has nothing to do with her."

I stop moving.

No more pacing.

No, I'm just staring at him.

Wondering what in the hell he's thinking.

I wait for him to come to his senses.

He doesn't.

I stare, blinking several times. "You're kidding, right? I can't lie to her. She's like one of the only friends I have." I throw the pillow at him, maybe it'll knock some sense into him. "We have to tell her! We can't keep it from her, and we're not doing it again anyway…"

"And what are you going to tell her?" Killian asks, his voice full of frustration.

I throw my hands up and realize I'm fucking naked.

I groan, grabbing the pillow again and sitting on the edge of the bed. This is truly the worst freaking thing. I can't believe that he's her dad. Sure, he's not like close with her, but still, that's not going to matter and there's no way I can keep this from her.

She would never forgive me and I would never forgive myself.

So, there's only one thing I can tell her…

"The truth," I say with a long sigh. "I can't believe this is happening."

"I don't think you should make any decisions tonight."

Killian watches me, his beautiful green eyes filled with so much emotion. I can see him grappling with all of this, and suddenly, I realize that this isn't just about me.

"Oh God, I'm so sorry. This is going to…she's going to be upset with you too."

He shakes his head, moving toward me, but I pull back. Killian freezes, closing his eyes and then exhaling deeply. "I'm not worried about Meredith. Not right now. I'm worried about you, about us."

My heart literally aches at that.

In one moment, everything has changed. There can't be an *us* anymore. If he doesn't want me to tell her, then we can never share another moment like this ever again. We will have to have a strictly professional relationship.

Even after telling myself all of that, I reach for him, wanting just one more second of contact. Just one more damn time I can be close to him, but I stop myself. "I can't do this, Killian. We can never be together again. You understand that, right?"

He shakes his head and rubs the bridge of his nose. "No, I don't understand. I think, right now, this is overwhelming and neither of us is making rational decisions."

I laugh at that. "There is no rational, Killian! You and I have made too many mistakes and we're being punished."

I wait for the voice of reason. For the smart, pragmatic man I know who is going to say something about how this will all work out, but he stays silent.

The two of us wait, watching the other, and my heart is breaking. We both know the truth—this can't work now. We can't possibly carry on a relationship. All of this was doomed from the start, our decisions damned us to hell.

Killian must see something in my eyes. He nods. "I understand." His voice is raw and angry. "I'll stay in the guest house so you can have your space and I don't make you uncomfortable."

"What? No! I'll go stay there. I should've probably stayed there to begin with, but we were hoping Travis was coming back."

"I'd rather go and let you have the house," he says.

I can feel the moisture building in my eyes, hating all of this so much. We weren't supposed to end like this. I still had a few more days before I had to leave. More time where I could be happy. I didn't even have time to fully enjoy what we had.

I knew it was coming, but not so soon.

"How did this happen?" I ask the window, not wanting him to see the tears in my eyes.

"I don't know."

I feel him leave the bed. He walks to his discarded clothes, pulling his shorts on before returning and sinking onto the edge of the bed. His head is hanging low, forearms resting on his knees, and he's just staring at the floor.

He looks so sad and it breaks me, causing me to throw away all the reasons I had not to touch him.

I reach out, resting my hand on his back before moving it up to his shoulder. "I'm sorry."

"What the hell are you sorry for?" he asks quickly, glancing at me from over his shoulder.

I pull my hand back, forcing myself to put a little distance between us.

There are so many things I did wrong.

Things I should've been smarter about. I may have been ranting about pissing off the universe, but it's true.

We broke the rules.

We knew that being together was stupid, but I didn't care. I wanted him. I wanted whatever we could have. I convinced myself that none of it mattered, that we were adults and we'd just walk away at the end.

I should've never let it get this far, and the worst part is that now I know him.

I know the beautiful man he is, deep inside. I know what this entire place means to him and I've let him down.

"All of it. I should've left after we had sex the first time. I should've done the right thing, brought another publicist down here. I compromised everything for you, Killian. If you lose this farm, it's on me."

Killian gets to his feet so fast it stuns me. His voice is stern and there's a fire in his eyes that wasn't there before. "Listen to me, this is not on you. Not even a little. I did this. I asked you to stay. I wanted you to stay. Fuck, I still want you to stay. You did nothing wrong. Jesus, Tessa. You don't see it? You don't see how the only reason I'm still fighting is because of you?"

I rear back, my throat tight as I try to process what he's saying. "What?"

He takes a step closer. "I love this place, I always have, but the reason I'm doing all of this is for you. I want you to see how fucking special you are. I would've...I don't know...sold the fucking farm by now. Yes, it means something to me, but I would've let it go. I'm holding on because you care. You've convinced me to keep caring. You've fought and so I'm beside you, fighting as well. You have pushed and shown me that it's possible, not easy, but we could do it.

I wouldn't have done some bachelorette girl's thing. I would've sold the horses, sold the farm, and gone back to Boston by now." Killian extends his hand slowly, grazing my cheek. "I'm fighting because you've made me believe we could. I understand why you're upset, but don't for one minute think it's just about the farm for me. It's much more. So much more."

His hand drops and then walks out of my room, taking my heart with him.

CHAPTER 23
KILLIAN

I'M SO FUCKING TIRED. THE LAST FEW WEEKS HAVE TAKEN YEARS off my life, but Tessa was the bright spot, slowly giving me hope that it wasn't going to be all doom and gloom.

Well, that's gone.

All of it's gone.

I don't know what the hell I'm going to do. I can keep fighting to save this place or just let it go and…move back to Boston, away from all of this shit.

Even though I love Ember Falls.

It's where I want to be, why I keep coming back, and what I brought Anchor Light here to save.

Only, it seems now I've lost something else.

"Hit me again, Max," I say, as the bartender starts to walk away.

"You've had a lot, Killian. Are you sure you want another one?"

"Are you my babysitter or bartender?" I ask.

I don't need anyone else fucking telling me what to do.

He nods once. "All right then."

I rest my head on my hand, staring out at the people enjoying their lives. How nice for them. I wonder what that's like.

All I have is a failing business and a woman I can't have.

Not that I could have her before I found out she's my daughter's best friend, but now I really can't.

Like, no chance.

Zero.

Not even a kiss.

Max returns with another glass of whiskey, and I take it like a shot. Why not? Maybe it'll hit faster and I can pretend my life isn't a big pile of shit.

"Pretty sure you're supposed to sip that," a feminine voice says from beside me. Only it's not the voice of the woman I want to talk to—it's Hazel's.

I put the glass down, looking at her from the side. "I'll take that under advisement."

She sits beside me. "You just had a great night. What the hell are you doing here?"

"Wallowing."

"Clearly. And you're not doing it all that well."

Good to know I can't even drink right. At least when I fuck up, I do it spectacularly.

"What do you want, Hazel?" I ask, a little rudely, but I don't have the emotional bandwidth to give a shit.

She lifts her hand, and Max comes over. "Can I get a glass of Pinot and a water for our friend here?"

"I didn't ask for water."

Hazel grins. "And yet you're going to get one."

I sigh heavily. "Do you mind? I really just want to be alone. I'm clearly not in the mood to socialize."

Maybe I can avoid being a complete dick to her if I'm just honest.

"What I've learned in all my years of taking care of Everett Finnegan when he was drunk is that the last thing you should be is alone when you're like this. So, I'll just sit here and if you want to talk, we can or we can just be quiet."

Quiet it is. I have nothing to say because all it will do is make things so much fucking worse.

Max brings over her wine and my water. "I'd like another shot."

He eyes me, looks to Hazel, which pisses me off, and then grabs the bottle, pouring me a shot. "I think after this you should...you know, go easy."

I should do a lot of things, but right now, the only reason I'm not losing my mind is because I'm starting to feel numb. Not numb enough, of course. No, I would need an entire bottle to erase all the pain I'm in right now.

Just when I let myself hope.

Just when I opened myself up and told her I wanted her to stay, I'm reminded why I don't do relationships.

Because they always fall the fuck apart.

"Why do they fall apart?" Hazel asks and I jerk my head back.

"What?"

"You said you were reminded why you don't do relationships..."

"I didn't mean to say that out loud."

She grins. "Yes, which is the beauty of getting smashed: you say and do dumb shit. So, I'm going to assume something happened with Tessa, which is why you're here, wallowing in your whiskey."

"I'm not talking about it," I say, going for my glass but realizing it's empty.

Great.

Hazel laughs softly, leaning back in her seat and crossing her legs. "You know, I've always really liked you, Killian. Out of all the guys, you're the most levelheaded, honest, and you've been patient. There are so many women in this town who have tried to turn your head, but you've let them all down easy. Trust me, it didn't go unnoticed, even by them. There's something about a man who can be kind even when saying something you don't want to hear."

"I had no intention of dating."

"Until Tessa," she finishes.

"We weren't supposed to be dating either."

She gives me one of those smiles. "Some women come into your life and smack you upside the head. We've seen it three times now.

Ainsley wrecked Lachlan's world, or…gave him the world. Then Penelope completely upended Miles's life, which has been the best thing for him. Violet has turned Everett into a totally different man, and now you seem to have had the same thing happen to you."

I scoff. "I have not."

"No? So, what has you sitting in the bar tonight?"

"Maybe it's the fact that I'm not like the other three? Maybe it's because they have something I can't have."

Hazel shrugs. "Maybe."

I blink. "What the hell does that mean?"

I know I'm shitfaced, but I think she agreed with me. Why would she agree? Why can't I have it? Oh, yeah, because Tessa is going to leave—and she and my daughter are friends.

That's why.

"It doesn't mean anything," Hazel says and then looks to the door. "Ahh, finally."

I glance over, praying to God she didn't call Tessa, but it's worse. She called Everett.

I groan and drop my head on the bar. "I was told I was needed because there was a belligerent drunk who needed a ride?"

"Fuck off."

"I see it's you. Well, this is new."

Hazel hops off the chair. "My work here is done. Good luck getting him home." She leans in and kisses my cheek. "Tell her how you feel, Killian. I bet she feels the same."

If only it was that simple. "I did," I tell her, but when I look over at Hazel, she's already gone.

Huh. She was right here.

I look around, swearing that…did she disappear?

"You did what?" Everett asks.

Seriously, where the hell did Hazel go? "Is she a witch?"

"Hazel? Probably."

"That would explain so much," I say aloud.

He laughs. "Come on, let's get you home."

I pay Max, or at least I throw down a bunch of money, half of which Everett grabs back, shoving it in my jacket pocket.

I drape my arm around his neck and stumble my way to his truck.

He climbs in, and I lean my head against the window. "I swear, if you puke, you're buying me a new truck."

I give him a thumbs up. "Do you know what?"

"I don't."

"I have a kid," I tell him.

"Yes, I know."

"She's twenty-five."

Everett laughs once. "You've told us."

"Did you know she's a girl?"

"That must've slipped right past my notice," Everett informs me.

"I'm glad I could let you know."

My words are starting to come out slower and I can't feel my lips.

Thank God.

Now I won't remember the way they felt against Tessa's. Maybe next my body can go numb too. That would be really nice.

I lift my arm to wipe my face, but end up slapping myself.

Fuck. That hurt.

"Dude, close your eyes and just...don't hit yourself," Everett releases a heavy sigh.

"Everything is spinning," I say with a groan. "The world. The car. My life. All of it just...going."

Everett is quiet for a second. "That's sort of how it goes. I'm going to take a guess and say that this is because something happened with Tessa after we all left."

I turn my head to face him. "Yup. It did."

"You'll figure it out—when you're sober."

"Sobriety changes nothing."

Unless it can change reality. Although, I think that is what happens when you're drinking, so, if that's true, then I should keep drinking.

I think I have whiskey at home.

Whiskey is good, and if I drink enough, I can have a whole new reality.

That would be ideal.

Everett chuckles. "You can't drink yourself into a new life. If anything, you're going to spend tomorrow wishing you didn't try it. Trust me. I know that all too well."

"Yes, well, fuck off," I mutter. Then I close my eyes, resting my face on the cool glass, trying to keep my stomach from releasing its contents along with the thoughts in my mind.

All of it rolls around, bouncing with each bump.

I broke all my rules for her and now, I broke both of our fucking hearts.

CHAPTER 24
TESSA

I'm pacing at the front entry, waiting to see headlights.

I got a call from Hazel that she was at the bar and Killian was not doing well. Then fifteen minutes later, I got a text that Everett was driving him home and was going to need help getting him in the house.

The foyer brightens as the truck pulls up. I head outside as Everett is climbing out. "Hey," he says.

"Hey, Hazel said you'd need help?"

He nods. "He's passed out. Maybe between the two of us we can get him inside."

Great. "Let's try." Killian is snoring in the front seat, face plastered against the side of the window. "If you open that door, he's going to just flop out," I warn.

"That's half the fun," Everett jokes, or at least I think he's joking.

Thankfully, Killian stays passed out. Everett climbs in the front and I watch from the window as his beautiful green eyes open after Everett slaps his cheeks a bit.

"Tessa, my angel."

Oh boy.

I open the door carefully. "Hey there. Do you think you can walk inside?"

"Your bed or mine?"

I snort a laugh. "Yours."

"Just like our first night," he slurs. "The sex was great then." I glance at Everett who is just grinning. "The way your mouth was when you were on your—"

"Stop talking," I say quickly, putting my hand over his mouth. "Let's get you inside. You need to sleep this off."

"Only with you, baby."

This time Everett laughs. "This is so much better than the shit he was saying with me."

I'm sure it is.

I loop my arm around Killian, and he slides out of the truck, resting against the side with his head back. "I'm drunk."

"Yes, you are."

His eyes open and he looks at me. "It's your fault."

"I'm sure it is."

"You made me like you."

I laugh once. "Ditto, buddy."

He lifts his arms, drapes them around my neck. "I like you, and I wanted to keep you."

"No more talking, Killian."

"Please, keep going," Everett encourages. "I'm pretty sure I just won the bet."

I have no idea what bet he's talking about, but he's supposed to be helping me. Instead, I have a very drunk, very heavy man hanging on me as I try to walk us inside. "Some help, please?"

Everett comes around and throws Killian's other arm over his shoulder, taking some of the weight. Killian turns his head to his friend. "I don't get to keep her, Ev."

I roll my eyes. He's a very chatty drunk.

"We usually have to fight for them, my friend," Everett informs him.

"Can't fight. Can't talk. Can't have her."

"Can't stop talking," I say as we finally get him in the front door.

He turns to me. "I'm being quiet."

"You're really not. Come on, a few more steps and then you can be in bed."

"But not with you, angel," Killian says almost as though he's singing. "I can't have you again, can I?"

I'm not even going to dignify this with a response. Mostly because his friend looks like he's enjoying this way too much. I have no idea if he told them that I'm not just his publicist, I'm also best friends with his daughter, and I don't plan to offer up that information.

We finally make it into the living room, only a few stumbles along the way. I open his bedroom door, and then we get him to the bed. Everett pretty much drops him and then lets out a laugh. "Well, I gotta go. As much as I would love to hear what the hell brought him so low, Violet sent me a text that she's not feeling well."

"Thank you for driving him."

"Of course. Listen, for what it's worth, he really likes you."

"I like him too," I admit.

"Then, whatever the hell had him going to get drunk, you guys should find a way to work through it. Trust me, losing someone you could've had a future with never gets easier."

Killian lifts a hand. "Preach!"

"Oh for fuck's sake," I mutter.

Everett laughs and then winks at me. "Goodnight, Tessa."

"Goodnight."

He heads out, and I look down at the drunk hot mess in front of me. I could leave him like this, but he's going to hate himself enough in the morning as it is. I sigh and make my way over, staring down at him. "You reek of alcohol."

He opens one eye. "I tried to drink the memories away."

"Did it work?"

"Nope."

I grin. "Let me take your shoes off and get you to bed."

He doesn't fight me as I remove each shoe, tossing them into his closet. Then I try to grab his legs to get him under the covers, but he's like a damn boulder. He groans and finally I'm able to shift him enough.

Next he needs a bottle of water and if I can get him to choke down some medicine, that would be ideal. I head into the kitchen, grabbing it and the Tylenol, then come back in. He's lying there, eyes closed, and I debate waking him.

He looks so…sad.

I sit on the bed and run my fingers through his hair. "Killian?"

He groans my name. "Tessa."

I smile, even though right now, it doesn't feel like there's much to smile about, but even in his drunken stupor, he's thinking of me.

Not that it changes a damn thing.

"Killian, wake up, you need to take this."

His eyes slowly open. "You're here."

"Yes, and you're drunk. Here, drink some water."

"Tessa," he sighs my name. "Don't leave me."

"I'm not leaving you. I'm just saying you need to drink some water."

He shakes his head. "No, I mean, after the water. Stay."

The tightening in my chest makes it hard to breathe. "Please, take the water and the medicine."

"Only if you promise."

Great, now this is a freaking negotiation. "Okay, fine, I'll stay if you drink this."

He grins and then leans up, taking the water. I watch as he gulps it down, then throws the pills back and swallows those. "Now, come here."

"What?"

"You promised you'd stay."

"Yes, and I'm going to stay in my room."

"No."

"Yes."

Killian somehow moves quickly, hooking his arm around my hip and throwing me, *yes*, throwing me over onto the bed.

I squeak and then try to move, but he has a good hold of me, pulling me closer and locking his legs around mine.

"Killian!"

"I need you," he confesses.

I stop squirming and look into his eyes. "What?"

"I need you, Tessa. Tonight. I need tonight. I need to hold you. Please." There is a deep ache in his voice, and I feel it in my heart.

A deep sigh escapes, and I feel the fight start to leave me. "Just to sleep," I tell him—and really myself more than anything. "Because I'm worried about leaving you this drunk and alone."

People have had really bad things happen. He could fall, he could choke, there are a million things, right?

It would be irresponsible of me to leave him.

"Just to sleep," he agrees.

The lights are bright as hell, and before I can say anything, he tells the home smart system to turn all the lights off and set the alarm.

Apparently he's not too drunk to do that or haul me around.

I shift my body, and he loosens his hold around me a little. My head rests on his arm and we're facing each other.

"Sleep, angel," he tells me.

I wish I could, but my mind is running in circles. Worse than when he left. Now, I think about all the things he said. How he keeps asking me to stay. How *I* really fucking want to stay.

All of this is too much, and yet not enough.

He moves his hand slowly up my back, stopping between my shoulder blades, and his head lowers, until his forehead is resting against mine.

It feels so damn good being close to him.

My palm sits on his chest, and the pounding of his heart is in time with mine. His breathing evens out, and I relax a touch since he's asleep. "I wish this could be my life," I confess so softly as not to wake him. "After today, I was ready to think it was possible." He doesn't move and I continue on, "I hate that it's not."

Killian moves, and I freeze, hoping he didn't hear any of that.

His eyes slowly flutter open and he stares at me. "It could be. You just have to want to fight for it."

On the second to last word, his eyes close again, and he lets out a snore.

I stay awake for most of the night as I contemplate what he said and what I can even do.

———————————

When I woke up, Killian was gone.

I was alone in his bed, exhausted, emotionally drained, and confused as hell.

He not only left the bed, he left the farm.

Gary said he had a meeting with the guys from Cole Securities. It was important, and he was gone without giving much more information.

I tried to call him, to find out what the hell the update was, but it went straight to voicemail.

Instead of sitting around, I decided that I needed to do something. Something that would help me make a decision about what I want regarding staying here or going back to New York—and also face the truth that I already know what I want.

So, I'm standing at Meredith's door with a bottle of tequila and a whole lot of fear.

I lift my hand to knock, but the door opens and she's there. "I was wondering what the hell you were doing out here."

I lift the bottle. "We need to talk."

She stares at our tried and true truth serum and sighs. "Well, this is going to be bad."

That it is. "I just think certain talks require certain things."

Meredith takes a step back. "Come on then. We only drink this when we are in pain or know we're about to be."

"Can it be both?"

Her eyes widen. "That'll be new for us, but I'm sure it's possible."

Jake comes down the stairs, reading something on his phone. "Oh, hey, Tessa. I didn't know you were coming over."

"I didn't either."

He looks at the bottle. "Oh fuck."

Meredith and I both laugh. Too many times Jake found us drunk as hell, crying or laughing beyond hysterics.

She walks over to her husband and kisses his cheek. "You look scared."

"I am scared. If you have tequila, it means the two of you are about to be out of control and I have to, somehow, handle you."

"I think you've done a great job so far."

He eyes her warily. "I'm not so sure of that. Remember that tomorrow we have breakfast with my boss, okay?"

She nods. "I promise I won't get too drunk."

I don't know if that's a promise she can keep. Once I tell her this, she's really going to want to wash down the memories, but I don't say anything.

Who knows? Maybe Meredith won't care? It could happen. It's highly unlikely, but still, a girl can hope.

That leads me to my second worry, what if she does react great and tells me she doesn't really care about any of it. Then what? Do I go to Killian, talk to him about how I'm feeling? I'm not sure that anything he said when he was drunk is what he really feels. Lord knows my father lied when he drank.

There's only one way to find out, and it starts with talking to my best friend.

We go into the living room, and she grabs two shot glasses, placing them in front of us while I pull the top off and then pour.

My thinking is to just get it out there. Rip the Band-Aid off quickly and efficiently. The less time I sit and make us both stew, the better it'll be.

So, we both lift our glass, clink them, and I say, "May we survive this conversation with smiles on our faces in the end."

Meredith laughs and then we take the shot, slamming the glasses down.

She looks to me, and with a pit the size of a boulder in my stomach, I blurt it out. "I'm in love with the guy I've been with for the last few weeks."

"That's what we needed tequila for?" she asks. "Jesus, I thought this was going to be bad."

I wish.

I shake my head and pour us another shot.

Once they're both down and we've had two shots in us, I tell her the rest. "No, the man I'm in love with and have been sleeping with is named Killian Thorn."

The blood drains from her face, and her jaw drops.

This is it.

This is going to be the moment where I lose my very best friend.

Not that either of us had any idea, which is why I quickly move to explain the rest. "I didn't know. I didn't know who he was. It wasn't until last night after we…" I skip what we were doing, although I'm sure she can figure it out "…that he mentioned he had a daughter my age. He started talking about how he came to find out about her, and I swear, Mer, I swear, I didn't know." She keeps opening and closing her mouth, before pouring herself another shot, taking it quickly. "I've ended it. I mean, there's no way I can ever do that again, and I'm here because I'm begging you for your forgiveness."

"What?" she asks quickly. "Why the hell do you need my forgiveness?"

"Did you miss the part where I said I've slept with your father?"

She covers her face with her hands. "Don't say that ever again, please. I beg of you. Call him Killian."

"Sorry." I choke on the word.

She sits back on the couch, her face full of disbelief and confusion.

I can only imagine how she feels. The entire drive up here, I tried to put myself in her place, to hear her say those words about my father, which—eww, but still.

Every scenario came back to me feeling angry or extremely grossed out.

Meredith looks at me. "You love him?"

I nod once.

"I'm not going to lie and say I'm completely okay right now, mostly because it just is...weird."

"I know," I say, hating myself for needing to have this conversation. "I didn't want to lie to you. I knew, as soon as I found out, that I needed to come tell you. He and I are over. I'm going to go back to New York and start my life over," I admit. Tears start to fill my vision as I think of leaving and never seeing him again. "I can't be with...I can't do that."

She pours us both a shot this time and nudges it toward me. "Take that, please."

We both take another shot, and she lets out a deep huff.

"I'm going to be honest. I don't really know what to say right now."

"I'm sorry."

"Sure, we don't really have a relationship and we've only met and talked a few times, but...you're my best friend, you know? And he *is* technically my father."

I nod, feeling despair fill me. I hate that this is the end of my relationship with Killian. I hate that it all happened this way. That more than just my career stands to be ruined by our bad decisions—it could ruin their relationship as well.

Meredith will have to handle knowing her biological father slept with her best friend. It's strange. It's impossible to wrap your mind around, and I just pray our friendship can endure this awkwardness.

"Please, you don't have to explain yourself. I understand." I start to stand, wanting to leave so I don't make things worse.

She shifts forward, gripping my hand. Meredith's eyes are a storm of emotions. I can see her trying to grapple with each one. Finally she sighs. "Tessa, I'm not mad or upset. You and Killian didn't do anything wrong. I'm just not sure how to feel. All of this is really freaking weird and I just need a few days to sort of wrap my head around it. He's not my dad, it's not like he raised me or even knows me, but…do you get what I mean?"

"In a way, yes, but I want you to know that I'm not going to do anything you're not okay with."

"I want to be clear, you don't need my permission."

I may not need it in her eyes, but I need it for me. "Meredith, I may love him, but I love you more. So, whenever you're ready to talk about it, I'll be here."

And really, there's nothing else to say. If she's not okay with it, then there's nothing else to do but walk away and try to move on.

CHAPTER 25
KILLIAN

I'M SITTING AT THE RESTAURANT WHERE LIAM ASKED ME TO MEET him, about halfway between the both of us in some town in Virginia, and my mind is a damn mess.

I have a killer headache.

I don't remember half of last night, and I'm wondering if that's for the best since when I woke in my bed, Tessa was beside me, on top of the covers, her head buried in the crook of my arm.

I rolled over, downed the water that she must've put there, and then saw I had three missed calls from Liam. Now I'm here, wanting to know what had him adamant we needed to meet immediately and in person.

The fact that I haven't heard a word from Tessa has me on edge.

When I woke up this morning, I knew that no matter what, I was ready to fight for her.

Her entire life, people have let her walk away or walked away from her, I'm not doing that.

Not when I love her.

Yes, I *love* her.

No matter how hard I fought against it, I fucking love her. I would do anything for her and now I need to prove it.

I know I said I would let her go, but I can't.

Not when I know the life we can have together.

Letting her go isn't an option.

I let Gary know where I was going, and to inform her, so I just hope that happened and she isn't packing her shit before we can talk about what *we* want. Not about what Meredith wants. Not about Tessa's job, but about what we actually want.

We can sort out the issues later.

I want her to stay, or hell, I'll sell the fucking ranch and move to New York if that's what it takes.

I'm not letting her go. Not ever.

The door opens, and Liam spots me, walking toward the booth, a messenger bag slung over his shoulder. I get up, we shake hands, and he motions for me to sit.

"Thanks for meeting me here."

"I'm not sure I had a choice," I joke as we settle into the booth.

He shrugs. "I thought this was something better done in person and quickly."

"Neither of those gives me a comforting feeling."

"This won't either. I'll be honest. I've learned a lot, but I'm not sure what it all means, so I'm going to let you see the information and hopefully you can shed some light on possible explanations. Then you can make some choices on what to do next." Liam pulls out a folder from his messenger bag and places it down on the table between us. "I followed the one lead I thought was the most credible as to where Travis could be in the States. It was tricky at first because either he's really smart or he has really smart people helping him. But I did end up finding him after a little bit more digging. Open it and let me know if that's him."

I open the file and see a photo of Travis. His hair is grown out, and he's attempting to grow a beard, but it looks a little ridiculous. However, it's very clearly him in the photo. "It is."

"He was last seen in Maryland at a casino." Liam points to the second photo. "I tracked him there two days ago. He behaved very... strangely. Most people don't look over their shoulder every thirty seconds, but Travis did. I sat next to him at the tables so I could observe him closely. I'm usually able to get a pretty decent conversation out of most people. He was so tight-lipped it was really remarkable. I won't lie, I was half impressed."

What does any of that have to do with me?

"You think he was worried someone was following him?" I ask.

"It would make sense. Did Travis steal money from you?"

"We haven't been able to find a few payments, but two of the sellers said they never sent anything. The thing I lost mostly from Travis were the sales that were promised."

Liam nods. "So he wasn't worried about you coming after him?"

"He could be, but at this point, he's been gone for weeks. The damage to my ranch has already been done. If it's about money, maybe he stole it from someone else. Maybe he crossed another rancher and is trying to win money so he can keep up with the debt. I really don't think he'd be worried about me finding him. Even if I did, I just want to know what the fuck happened—not hurt him."

All I wanted were answers to why he forged my signature and where the fuck he went. We had a business together, and to just take off? It's bullshit.

"People who don't want anyone to be able to remember seeing them behave a certain way. Short answers, nondescript clothing, looking around, and after about five minutes, he got up, went to a new game. Again, he didn't want me to be able to recognize him. It's what we're trained to do. Hide in plain sight."

"Are you saying he's undercover?" I ask.

Liam shakes his head. "No, but he's hiding. I was able to get into his hotel room and look around. All of his belongings were packed in a bag, ready to grab. He used an alias as well. He's running from something or someone."

I can't even begin to imagine he'd run from Owen. Sure, he's a prick, but he's not terrifying. Travis worked for me already and was making a ton of money. None of this adds up or makes sense.

I pinch the bridge of my nose, my head still pounding. "Is there something else that has you questioning all of this?"

"Maybe. Does the name Antonio Gibrelli mean anything to you?"

I think about it for a second, but it's not ringing any bells. "No."

"Do you know this man?"

He flips the page again, and I see someone I recognize. He was one of the first people to pull out of the deal we had with his horse we were boarding and training. He also had two more thoroughbreds he was purchasing—canceled both of those contracts as well. "Yes, that's James Gardiner."

"What about this guy?" He shows me another photo of a man, dressed in a suit, his black hair pushed to the side. It honestly could be anyone, but I don't recognize him.

I shake my head. "No, I don't think so."

I also have a raging hangover and this is causing the ache to become a throb in my skull. This might not have been the best time to make really bad decisions.

I chug the glass of water in front of me and point to the photo. "Who is that?"

"That's Gibrelli's son. He's the second in command of their organization."

"Okay, what the fuck are we talking about?" I ask, frustration at not understanding why I'm having to look at all these people's photos starting to take hold.

Liam turns to the next page, and there's a photo of three guys and Travis standing between them.

"Do you think Travis is mixed up with them?"

"Yes, and I think there's a lot more to this. Gibrelli's son also purchased a horse from you, only he did it under one of his dummy holdings, which happens to be the name Andrew Bennett."

That name I recognize. "He bought six horses, two canceled contracts."

"He also had three horses boarded and being trained by Travis."

"That aren't at my ranch anymore," I finish.

Liam goes to the next page. "This guy is Pete McMahon, he's one of their enforcers."

"Enforcers for what?"

"Organized crime."

My eyes widen as understanding hits me. He was at the ranch yesterday for the rodeo. I remember him. There are certain people who just have a presence and he was one of them. Strolled right up to me, extended his hand, asked a bunch of questions about Travis, ironically. Told me how he was hoping to finally meet the illustrious trainer who has done so much good for the racing world and asked where he was.

It seemed strange to me because everyone pretty much is aware Travis left, and the rumors surrounding his disappearance. When he asked me, I was taken aback and thankfully got pulled away by Tessa when another buyer came around. Still, I remember thinking it was strange.

I glance up at Liam, trying to put the pieces together. "This guy was at my ranch yesterday."

"You're sure?"

"Absolutely." I explain the entire meeting with the guy and all that he said. Liam listens and takes a few notes. We discuss the entire rodeo, the people who were there, anything I remembered that maybe felt a little strange.

There really wasn't anything that stood out other than him fishing about Travis.

Liam rubs his chin. "I think we have a bigger problem than your trainer taking off out of the blue. There's a connection with a pretty big crime ring here. There are a hundred possibilities, but... something is off."

This is a nightmare.

Here I was, thinking this was about a doping scandal that didn't exist and now we're talking about a fucking crime ring?

I can't believe this.

All I want to do right now is rush home, pack, grab Tessa, and let the damn ranch fall apart.

However, that's not going to make the situation go away, so I need help dealing with all this.

"What's the next step?" I ask. If there's an issue, I want it found before anything else happens.

I was just getting the ranch back on track. The sales yesterday, two new boarding clients, and Tessa booking six more parties. All of those were movement in the right direction. The last thing I need is something else to derail it.

Liam stands, throwing a twenty down. "For the next step, I'm going to collect Travis and we're going to figure out what exactly he's been up to. Keep your phone close—I'll call as soon as I have him."

———

I pull up to the house. Tessa's car isn't here, and panic sets in that she left, for good.

Fuck. She's probably halfway back to New York by now.

Not that I'd blame her. I was a fucking mess last night, and God only knows what I said or how the hell she ended up in bed beside me.

I really only remember talking to Hazel at the bar, then Everett coming and taking me home. After getting in the car, my memory is very fuzzy.

I have no desire to walk in this house. I don't want to face an empty bedroom, a slept-in bed, and no Tessa.

I need her. Hell, I miss her already. As soon as I hear from Liam, I'll be in the car on my way getting her back, to proving I'm the right man for her.

However, when I walk into the living room, Tessa is sitting on the couch, one leg pulled up, her arm wrapped around it.

"Hi."

I blink, my heart starting to beat again at the sight of her beautiful face. "Hey."

"How are you feeling?" she asks.

I'm not sure how to answer that, but honesty is probably a good place to start. "A bit...foolish."

"Why?"

I move to the sectional and sit opposite her. "Well, last night was not normal for me. I don't drink like that—ever."

I've never had a great tolerance. I probably should've heeded Max's advice on when to stop, which would've been after the first, but I just wanted to be numb. It felt so good to get out of my own head for just a little.

Tessa tilts her head. "Do you remember much?"

Shit. I must have embarrassed myself.

"I don't," I confess. "By the way, where is your car?"

"That's a shame you don't remember. You were pretty talkative." Her smirk is playful, and now I'm really scared.

"Fuck. What did I say?"

She shrugs. "Doesn't matter. Where did you go today?"

Right, that would be good information for her to have as well. "I went to meet with Liam. Where is your car? When I got here, I thought you'd left."

"What did Liam say?"

Why is she avoiding my question? "Tessa, where's your car?"

"I got a ride here from a friend, well, from her husband. I went to see her and brought a bottle of tequila so we had a few shots. Even though I'm not close to tipsy, I didn't want to add DUI onto my list of crimes since coming to Ember Falls."

Her.

I know where she went. My heart is pounding and I'm both nervous and angry at her because I can guess who the "she" is that she went to see.

"You saw Meredith?"

Tessa sits back, bringing her other leg up and wrapping both arms around her legs. "I did, but I'd like to hear what Liam said before we talk about it."

"Fuck Liam. I want to know what happened with Meredith. You…I would've gone with you. You didn't need to do this today. We could've talked, come up with a plan. You didn't have to face all of this alone, I would've been at your side!" I lean forward, coming closer to her.

Right then my phone rings, but I don't care. I need to tell her how I feel before she tells me that Meredith doesn't want her best friend with her father.

I know that she told me to let her go last night, but I can't. I can't just let her walk away. In the month that I've had Tessa in my life, it's been the best possible time I've ever had. She makes me so fucking happy. Everything about her gives me joy. She lights up any room she enters.

I see what life could be, what we could have.

Yes, we'll have obstacles, like our age, where we both live, and my daughter, but we can find a way. I won't let her go.

"That's sweet and all, but I thought this was the best way to handle it."

I shake my head. "No, it's not."

"It's not?"

"No!" I get to my feet, feeling all the frustrations fill my entire body. "I care about you, Tessa. More than I should. More than I ever thought possible. You make…everything in my life make sense. You're smart, beautiful, caring, and I'm sorry, I don't care what anyone says, we belong together."

The phone is ringing, but I ignore it. She's more important than anything else.

Her arms fall away from her legs, and she rises. "I can't. Not without her being okay with it."

"I understand that she's your best friend, but do you not understand this isn't about anyone else? It's about us. You belong with me."

"It doesn't matter what we want, Killian. She's your daughter! Your freaking daughter and my best friend. How do we navigate that, huh? Do you lose her? Lose any chance of knowing your daughter and son-in-law? What about when they have kids? Are you going to be okay with never knowing them? No, you're not. Because you're an amazing man. She didn't say she's against it, just that she needs some time, but we need to be realistic."

I want to fucking scream. "I can't lose you."

"I don't want to lose you either, but you and I can't pretend this isn't an issue."

"I'm not willing to give up on this, Tessa. I…" I hold the words back. This isn't a time to say it and score points. This has to be on her terms.

"You what?"

The phone rings again. I look down at it, grateful for the interruption so I don't put my foot further in my mouth.

"Are you going to answer that?" she asks.

"It can wait. I'd like to know what happened. Did she get upset?"

Tessa sighs and shakes her head. "That's the worst part—she wasn't. She just needs to kind of wrap her head around it. She wasn't mad. She said neither of us have anything to be sorry for, but can you imagine how she must feel?"

It would be great if I could lie to her, tell her I wouldn't care if it was me, but I can't do that. If the roles were reversed and Nathaniel was sleeping with my mother, I'd fucking lose it.

"Tessa," I say her name with exhaustion. I've been up half the night, I'm hungover, my head is pounding, and after my meeting with Liam, I don't know what end is up. I have to sit tight while I wait for him to tell me if Travis somehow involved me in some organized crime scandal.

The phone rings again, and we both stop to glance at it, but before I can move to answer, there's a loud pounding on the door. Several voices are screaming and lights fill the windows. Before either of us can move, the front door smashes open. I quickly move in front of her, shielding her from whoever is breaking in.

She screams, and through the front door come at least ten men in black, shields over their faces and guns pointed.

"FBI! On your knees! Get on the ground!" they yell, and then I'm shoved to the floor, my arms are pulled behind my back, and I watch, helpless, as they do the same to Tessa. This is so much worse than I ever imagined.

CHAPTER 26
TESSA

"Where are you taking him? What's going on?" I'm sitting on the bench outside of the front door trying to get an answer as agent after agent walk in and out of the house.

Killian is in the back of a car, handcuffed, and God only knows what the hell is going on. I'm so confused and...I'm trying to keep it together, but this is absolutely terrifying.

Finally, one answers me. "Ma'am, we need you to stay calm. I'll see if someone can come speak to you, but I need you to stay seated."

I rub my wrists where the metal handcuffs were just a few minutes ago.

They brought us both outside and started questioning me over and over. Asking if I knew these random people I'd never heard of. Finally, a female agent came over, and I explained who I was. I must've said the right things because I was suddenly no longer being detained, but I'm forced to stay out here while they search the house.

I watch as box after box gets carried out and placed in the back of SUVs.

None of this makes any sense.

I don't understand what is going on. Is this all over Travis? Did something happen to him and now Killian is caught in the cross-hairs? Is there more to this? I try to think about all the paperwork we found, the signatures that didn't match, but that seems a little minor for a freaking FBI investigation. Why would they give a shit about a horse breeder whose sales fell through?

My mind grasps for any kind of conclusion I can find that will explain this, but I can't.

I have no information. I can't form any kind of plan. This is going to be a PR disaster. All the hard work we've done over the last few weeks is going to disappear the moment any kind of story breaks about Killian.

Killian.

My chest grows tight as I remember his face, him telling me it'll be okay, trying to shield me as they entered the house. The way he pushed me behind him, and then when we were both on the floor, his face, the ultimate devastation I saw in his eyes, broke my heart.

He doesn't deserve this.

None of it. He's done nothing wrong. I've been with him every day, and I would've seen *something*.

An agent heads toward me, and as I look at his face, recognition dawns on me.

I know him. He was here—at the rodeo.

He talked to me, told me he was interested in buying a few horses, and I even brought him to Killian.

Drake. That's his name.

What the fuck? He's an FBI agent.

The man stops in front of me, giving me an awkward smile. "Hello, Ms. Rivers. I'm Special Agent Drake Halsey. We met at the rodeo."

"Yes, I remember. I don't remember you saying you were an FBI agent, though."

"No, I wouldn't have."

"Can someone please explain what the hell is going on?"

He sits beside me and hands me a glass of water. "We have an arrest warrant for Killian and a search warrant for the residence. He will be brought in on the arrest warrant, and once we finish executing the search warrant, you'll be able to go back inside."

"What about Killian? What is he being arrested for?"

He gives me a kind look. "I'm sorry, but he's an adult and I can't tell you any information. However, at this time, we do not believe you're involved and you are not being detained."

That answers nothing.

I'm back in the house, standing here, feeling lost and confused. Killian's gone. They took him—somewhere. I was only told that he's being held and has to see the judge on Monday.

Two fucking days from now.

Two days where he's going to be God knows where while I have no information.

The house is wrecked. Things were moved, left strewn around, and I sink into the couch and put my face in my hands.

I have to do something.

I have to get help, but, of course, I don't have my car.

On the counter are Killian's keys. I grab them and rush out. I need to find Everett or Miles or Lachlan. They'll know who to call, a lawyer or someone.

On the ride, I make a phone call I'm not sure I should.

"Hey!" Meredith answers.

"Mer," I say her name and my resolve crumbles. I cry. Tears pour from my eyes and thankfully I've reached the center of town so I can pull over.

"Tessa? What's wrong? Why are you crying? Did he react badly?"

I sob, full-on shaking sobs. My chest heaves as the last few hours crash through me. Wave after wave of the fear, sorrow, terror, and pain of watching the car drive off with Killian takes me under.

Each breath is painful, and I hear Meredith through the phone, but I can't answer. "Oh my God, what is wrong? Where are you? Tessa! Jake—help!"

Then Jake is on the line. "Tessa, I need you to take a deep breath." I try but it's impossible. As I inhale, I almost choke on it.

"No, Tessa, listen to my voice. Make a fist and rub your chest in circles. Can you do that?"

I can't answer verbally, but I nod, even though he can't see it.

I do as he says, making deep circles against my chest. I can feel my body starting to respond, and my breaths must even out a bit because his voice is low and soothing. "Good. Keep doing that. Slowly. When you can, take a deep breath in and hold it for three." My hand continues the motion, and then I inhale deeply and count.

One.

Two.

Three.

"Good, now let it out for three."

I exhale.

One.

Two.

Three.

"Again," he says. We do that four more times. "Tessa, can you tell me where you are?"

"I'm i-in Ember F-Falls. The FBI came and took Killian. I don't kn-now what's happening." I choke out, stuttering on certain words.

"The FBI?" Meredith this time. "Are you okay?"

"They stormed the house," I explain and then feel the panic rise again. I do another round of deep breathing. "I don't know why. They wouldn't tell me anything. They took him."

"Where, Tessa?" Jake asks.

I've always prided myself on being calm in the face of crisis. Right now, I'm not able to call on that. Tears keep falling, and I know I need to get it together. Me sitting here sobbing on the side of Main Street isn't going to help Killian.

I wipe my nose and let out a cleansing breath.

"All the agent would tell me is that he'll be taken to the county police station where he'll stay until Monday. I'm guessing they'll take him somewhere else after that. I heard another agent say something about federal charges and seeing a judge? Maybe."

Meredith gasps, and Jake consoles her softly and then speaks to me. "Okay, we're coming there. Are you staying at Killian's?"

"Yes."

"Where are you now?"

"I'm going to find his friends. They're like family to him, and they'll maybe know what to do."

"All right, Tessa. Stay in Ember Falls—we'll be there as soon as we can."

The call disconnects, and I wipe my tears away and exit the car.

I'm praying Everett is here or at least one of the group. If not, Hazel is the best shot I have.

I pull the door open to Prose & Perk. The bell chimes, and Hazel pops out from the back.

"Tessa! Hey!" Then she sees me. Her big blue eyes widen and she flips up the countertop. "What happened? Are you okay?"

I shake my head and spill out all the information I have. She rubs my back as I tell her everything I remember. "I need Everett or someone. I need help. I have to help him."

"Of course. I'm texting the guys now, and we'll get this figured out."

Hazel's phone rings and she answers, explaining a brief summary of what I told them and instructs whoever is on the other end to get here and get the others.

"They're on their way."

I let out a shaky breath and remind myself that part of the reason I'm here is to help. I was sent to fix any issues with Ivy Thorn, and now I need to do that. I can cry and feel all the feelings later. Right now, Killian needs me to do my job as well.

"I need to call my boss," I explain. "We have to manage this from a PR stance as well. Killian doesn't need any of this, and I don't think for one minute that he's involved in any of it anyway. I spent weeks pouring over paperwork, creating lists and trying to find whatever Travis was up to. I know Killian. I know that sounds nuts since we only just met but…"

Hazel lifts her hand. "It doesn't sound crazy. It sounds like love. You do know Killian, and I know him too. He's not a criminal, at least, there would need to be some pretty damning evidence to get me to believe it."

I head outside and call Brynlee, describing the events. I feel as though I'm going to have to tell this story a hundred more times, and I'm hoping by then I won't relive it as I recite it.

It's horrible and I've never been more scared in my life.

She instructs me to keep the information as guarded as possible. She's going to work on her end to get in touch with a lawyer her husband uses. I'm to sit tight and stay close to the phone.

I push open the door, and Hazel leads me to a table. She hands me a cup of tea and takes my hand. "Are you okay? That had to be scary."

"It was. Now it just all feels so…surreal. I don't know what's going on, and I'm worried about him on so many levels."

"I'm sure. I am too."

My eyes meet hers. "I don't want to lose him," I confess softly. "I know that sounds selfish and stupid, but I'm worried. I watched them cuff him, and I just had to lie there. He kept his eyes on mine, as though he was trying to tell me to stay calm and it's okay."

"I bet he was," she says, squeezing my hand. "Killian, whether he knows it or not, loves you—or at least has really strong feelings for you. I've never seen him as torn up as he was at the bar when he said he lost you."

I jerk back at her mentioning he loves me. It's too soon. He doesn't love me. He can't.

"He didn't lose me."

She smiles at that. "No, but he was worried he did. I'm going to assume you guys had a fight?"

I scoff. "I wish. We learned some information that neither of us was prepared for."

One of her dark brown brows rise. "Really?"

"It's not important."

The door chimes and in come Miles, Penelope, and Everett. They each see me and rush over, all talking at once.

Hazel stands. "Easy, she's been through hell too."

"He's going through worse," I say as I get to my feet. "I need all of your help to squash any rumors of the arrest."

"If it was spreading, one of us would've already heard," Everett says. "Where's Lachlan?"

"He's on his way," Miles says and then turns to me. "Did Killian say anything? Do you think he had a clue this was coming?"

I shake my head. "I don't think so. We were talking after we both had pretty interesting mornings..."

My God. I remember where he was before this. He was with Liam, and it was for something important—at least that's what Gary said.

"What?" Miles says quickly, but I turn to Penelope.

"Penny, your brother, he knows Liam, right?"

She nods. "Yes, they've been best friends forever. They work for the same company."

"Can you call him?"

"Sure. Liam or my brother?"

"Do you have Liam's number?"

"Yes," she answers quickly, pulling her phone out of her bag. She rattles off the number, and I quickly dial it.

He answers after the third ring. "Dempsey."

"Liam? This is Tessa and...we've had a situation with Killian."

"I'm sorry, I don't know a Killian."

My entire body slumps. I don't have time for this, but just as defeat washes over me, Penelope extends her hand for the phone and I give it to her.

"Liam, it's Penny. The FBI came, raided his house, and arrested him. Tell her whatever she needs to know." She hands the phone back to me.

"Penny?"

"No, it's Tessa."

He sighs. "I tried calling his phone, but no one picked up."

Liam was the one who was trying to get in touch with him. "We were talking…and…he didn't look."

"I'm on my way to Ember Falls. We have a lot to go over. Just… stay there."

I had no plans to go anywhere else. I need to help the man I love.

CHAPTER 27
KILLIAN

"What can you tell me about this man?" Special Agent Drake Halsey asks as he puts another photo down.

That was a fun little reveal. The man who came to buy horses, who I've met before, isn't a horse breeder like myself—he's an FBI agent who has been undercover to investigate my ranch.

For what?

I still don't know.

They aren't forthcoming with anything, insisting over and over that if I just cooperate, tell them what they want to know, the law will look favorably on me.

No matter how many times I explain that I don't know what the hell they're talking about, they keep going.

Hours I've been sitting here, looking at photos, answering when I do recognize someone and then explaining I've never before seen the next person they show me.

"I don't know who that is," I say with my hands clasped in front of me.

"No? He bought three horses from you six months ago. He paid almost $675,000 for one."

"I've never sold a horse for that much," I say quickly.

"Really?"

"Really."

He opens one of his many folders and pulls out a bill of sale. "Is that not your name there?"

I read it, but…that doesn't make any sense. "It is, but I didn't sell that horse."

He points to the signature. "Is that your name there?"

Not really. It looks close enough, but it's not mine. "I didn't sign that."

"You're telling me that it's forged? Is that what I'm understanding?"

"Yes. I'm telling you I didn't sign that paper. Someone else did or it's fake."

Special Agent Halsey nods, placing it back in the folder. "Funny how someone would just forge your name on a document that implicates you in a money-laundering scheme, isn't it? All of these, Mr. Thorn, were found in your office. Do you recognize them?"

Sure enough it's the pile that Tessa and I made that had the suspect signatures.

I'm so fucked.

"I do," I answer. "When my trainer went missing, I went through all the documents on the sales, trying to make sense of what the hell was going on. These were the ones where the numbers or the names didn't match."

"And what is Tessa's involvement in this?"

My head snaps up and anger fills me. No matter what the hell this is, I won't let them drag her into it. "She has nothing to do with anything."

"She was at your house," he says.

"Yes, she's my publicist and has been trying to help me fix the mess that Travis made."

"We're going to dig, Killian. You understand that. Surely, you've started to deduce the trouble you're in, and the sooner you stop trying to lead us in circles, the better this will go."

"You keep saying that," I say through gritted teeth. "I've cooperated. I've told you everything I know. Travis came to work for me, he handled the ranch while I was in Boston most of the time. Half of the documents you showed me that have my signature, I wasn't here to sign. How could I possibly have handled the sales if I wasn't even in Ember Falls? Travis and I had an arrangement and then he suddenly just left."

"And then you brought Tessa in?"

Each time he says her name, I want to lose it. "As my publicist."

"She's more than that, though, isn't she?"

She's everything.

I don't speak. I don't acknowledge the statement because I won't drag her into this. I have to protect her, and the less I say her name, the better. I have no idea if they took her in. If she's scared in a cell, waiting to see if the worst thing she did was fall for me.

I hate myself for having her even remotely tangled in it.

And if she's not arrested or being held, what does she think? Did they tell her I'm a monster who didn't know he was one? She probably hates me, and I can't even blame her. She had guns pointed at her head, was pushed to the floor, cuffed, and pulled out of that house like a fucking criminal.

"We haven't arrested her. If you're wondering."

My chest lightens slightly. "Thank you."

"For now, she's not a suspect, but we are still combing through things." He leans back, steepling his hands in front of himself. "See, here's the part that I can't make sense of. You and Travis were involved in this together, you claim you have nothing to do with it, Travis disappears, and you bring in Tessa to 'fix it,' as you said. All of it points to someone named Travis, but your name is on all the documents, so of course you had to do your part, right? You had to make sure the area sees you as a good guy, just a victim, while you were making money hand over fist. Your horses were selling at rates no one has ever seen, winning races, allowing the money to just keep flowing in. So did Travis catch on that something illegal was happening and go on the run? Did you force him out? Want a bigger piece of the pie?"

Dread starts to flow through my veins. This all looks bad for me. "None of that is true. Travis disappeared and the sales stopped, my boarding program collapsed, and I was left trying to pick up the pieces. I still am. Did you think of that?"

"I did," he agrees. There's a knock at the door, but Halsey continues. "Then I saw you at the rodeo. You had multiple people coming to see the horses, including this guy." He places a photo of Nathaniel down and stands. "And I know you know who that is."

Then he leaves, and I'm left staring at the photo, wondering what the fuck is going on.

———————

Special Agent Halsey doesn't return. Instead, another agent takes me back to the cell.

I'm lying here, staring up at the ceiling, trying to make sense out of anything.

Nothing so far has made any sense.

It's been hours of my mind going in a million circles.

Why the hell did Halsey show me Nathaniel's photo?

Of course I know who he is—he's my best fucking friend. The one who was there when I struggled in college. The man who stood next to me, hand on my shoulder when my sister died. The friend who became a brother when I found out I had a kid and missed her entire life, when I was struggling to figure out how to make it right. The guy who came all the way to Ember Falls to make sure I was okay and offer his help.

But that's not what the implication is.

I saw photo after photo of people who they wanted me to recognize as being part of whatever they're assuming I'm involved in.

The only reason they'd show me Nathaniel is if they think he's involved too.

CHAPTER 28
TESSA

ALL THE GUYS WENT BACK TO WORK OR HOME TO GIVE THE APPEAR-
ance of everything being status quo. We all agreed the best way to
protect Killian was to just pretend he went back to Boston suddenly.
Penelope came back to the ranch with me as I wasn't ready to be
here alone.

Thankfully, Killian lives far enough away from Ember Falls'
main drag that it offers some seclusion. Although, I'm not stupid
enough to believe no one saw the entire fleet of black SUVs swarm-
ing through town in the middle of the day.

"Here, you need to eat something," Penelope says as she hands
me a yogurt parfait that Killian made and was keeping in the fridge.

Do not cry, Tessa.

Stay strong. He needs you to keep it together.

"Thank you," I choke the words out as I take it from her.

Penelope doesn't try to fill the silence, and I appreciate it more
than she'll ever know. It allows me a few minutes to just be alone in
my thoughts. I eat, thinking about what type of crisis-management
plan I can create for when this breaks.

Of course, it all depends on what was seen.

"Tessa?" Penelope calls my name softly. "Liam is pulling in."

Finally. He clearly knows something, and I need any information I can get if I want Killian to be released.

We both stand up and head to the door, opening it as he arrives.

Liam is tall with dark hair, and he has a three-day beard coming in. He looks at Penny and smiles. "Pen."

"Liam, you've met Tessa."

He shakes my hand. "I have. It's good to see you again, Tessa." He then motions to come in. "May I?"

"Yes, sorry. Of course."

We head back into the living room and sit as he clears his throat. "I'm still working on getting the entire story from my contacts at the FBI, but this is what I know so far."

"I met with Killian this morning to let him know that I located Travis. He was seen with some members of a known crime organization up north. These men are involved in a lot of nasty things. Drugs, money laundering, among other things."

"Okay…" I say hesitantly. "What does this have to do with Killian being arrested?"

He lets out a long sigh. "The FBI arrested six other known members of this crime ring at the same time that Killian was arrested. I was at the casino where they arrested Travis as well as one of the ring's suspected hit men who happened to be there as well—I don't think it was to just check up on Travis. So, Killian being arrested proves one of two things. Either the FBI thinks Killian is involved in this crime ring or Travis is involved, which I believe he is, and he's done a good job implicating Killian. Which could mean Killian is set up to take the fall for all of it."

My heart sinks all the way to the pit of my stomach because this is the worst possible news and either option is terrible. "*No.* Killian didn't do anything."

Penelope rubs my back and looks to Liam. "Do you think he's involved?"

"I don't. Not even a little. I made a few calls, and I'm doing what I can to talk to my friends at the FBI. It's not going to change anything for a few days, but I'll turn everything I've found so far over to them. It may not accomplish anything, but I'll do what I can."

Staying strong no longer feels possible. He might go to jail, and I might lose him forever. I didn't get to tell him how I feel, how much he means to me, that I love him, that I want a life with him. We needed just a little more time to talk to Meredith and work it out. But instead, that chance was taken—he was taken.

I look into the eyes of my only hope to clear his name. "Do what you can, Liam. Please, bring him back to me."

He stands. "I'll do everything I can."

That's all I can ask for. I just hope that it's good enough.

"Jake reached out to one of his family friends who is a defense lawyer. He's done a few high-profile cases, and we're just waiting to hear from him," Meredith explains.

"Thank you. I know my boss did the same. Brynlee said the lawyer will come here in the next day or so to speak with me and then see what he could do about getting Killian released."

Meredith and Jake got here two hours ago and it has been such a huge comfort.

"We'll get him out of this, Tess," she says as we're both curled up on opposite ends of the couch.

Regardless of whether she knows Killian or not, he is still her father. He cares about her, and I know she cares for him too. It's hard to see her struggle over him being in jail for something he didn't do.

Well, *I* don't believe he did it.

I look over at her with a soft smile. "I should be the one comforting you."

She shrugs. "I have Jake for that."

He's been a force of nature from the moment he heard about

Killian's arrest, calling everyone, asking for information, and trying to work whatever angle he can.

"I just want him home." I look over at her, and she looks slightly uncomfortable. "I'm sorry, Mer."

Her eyes snap to mine. "For what?"

"This has to be really weird. I know you said you needed time, and it's only been like, what, twelve hours."

She shrugs. "Sure, it's a little strange, but at the same time…it's really sweet. If this was Jake, I'd be the same as you. Desperate to find a way to get him home. I know you told me you loved him, but now I get to kind of see it."

"I didn't even get to tell him," I confess.

"What?"

"I never told him how I feel."

Meredith pulls the blanket up and sips on her coffee. "I bet he knows. I mean, do you think he loves you?"

I do. Or at least I think he does, but it all feels so fast. "I hope he does."

She grins. "If he doesn't, he's an idiot—a big one. Considering I came from him and I'm pretty much a genius, I'll bet he knows that right now, you're moving heaven and Earth to get him out."

"I would do anything for him."

"Why don't you go to bed? It's already midnight, and you've had a really intense day. You need your rest so we can tackle this in the morning."

I can't sleep in a warm bed while he's in a cold jail cell.

Besides, I don't think I'll be able to close my eyes without hearing the door come off the hinges, the screaming, the guns. I don't think I'll be able to sleep without seeing the look in his eyes when they took him away.

I clear my throat. "I think I'll go check on the horses."

Meredith seems to know I need some space right now because she says, "Okay, I'll be here if you need me."

I nod and get up, wrapping my sweatshirt around me as I walk out into the cool summer night.

This day has been a storm that came in hard, then left only to return again. The thunder and lightning have clashed, causing everything to feel unsettled.

The only thing is, during the lull, luck seemed to be on our side. Everett and Miles both reached out to tell me there's been no talk in town about the arrest. Lachlan is at the firehouse for work and is also keeping an ear out.

Hazel texted that the only talk she's heard is about how amazing the rodeo was and how everyone hopes Killian hosts another one soon.

It may be a small victory, but I'll take it.

I push open the barn door and grab a few apples from the bucket that hangs on the inside of the door, putting them in my pocket. To think yesterday this place was full of people and life. There was a hope in the air that was contagious.

Little did I know that it wouldn't last.

Instead of replaying the shitstorm my day was, I walk in and smile when Midnight comes to the front of the stall.

"Hi, girl," I say, and she roots her head around, sniffing near my pocket. "I see how it is—apple first?"

She snuffs her head against my shoulder, and I smile. "All right, you can have the apple and then you'll let me pet you, huh?"

I pull one of the apples out, and she takes it gently. She really is a sweet horse. After she eats it, she stays put, allowing me to pet her.

I stand here with just the overhead barn lights on, and she rests her head on my shoulder, so I lean against her. I close my eyes, allowing this beautiful animal to comfort me and I hope I'm giving her the same.

While she doesn't know what happened, there was so much commotion here that Gary had a hard time getting some of the horses to calm down after the FBI whisked Killian away.

"You weren't one of the ones who was scared, were you?" I pet her neck, wishing she could talk. "We're going to fix this. There's a lawyer coming, and it'll be okay. We just have to have faith."

We stay like this, my head resting against hers for a few long minutes. As we do, my heart starts to find its staccato and my strength begins to build.

I meant what I said—it'll be okay. I just have to have faith. Otherwise, there's nothing to fight for.

Who knew I just needed a horse hug to feel like the world isn't ending?

CHAPTER 29
KILLIAN

"KILLIAN THORN?" THE U.S. MARSHAL CALLS FROM OUTSIDE THE holding cell as I'm waiting to be arraigned.

I come forward, and he extricates me, cuffing my wrists and ankles. "Too tight?" he asks.

"No, it's fine."

None of this is fine, but it is what it is. I spent the last two days in the police department, waiting for today. Hopefully I'll find out what the hell is going on and they'll grant me bail so I can return home to wait for the trial.

"All right, let's go."

I walk with him through a back hallway and into the courtroom.

The judge is sitting there behind the bench, and the Marshal points to where I have to go—beside a man in a dark gray suit.

"Your honor, I'm David Turner, standing in for Anthony DeCarolis who is representing Mr. Thorn. I was unable to meet Mr. DeCarolis's client prior to today's arraignment, so I would like to ask the courts for permission to speak to the client before we begin."

The judge looks irritated, but he nods once. "Clerk, pass the case, and we'll recall in five minutes. Deputy, bring them to the back room until we're ready."

The deputy grabs my elbow and brings me and my new lawyer I didn't know I had into the interview room.

"Can you please uncuff him?" my lawyer asks.

"Sure."

Once the deputy leaves us alone, David turns to me. "Anthony DeCarolis was hired by Brynlee and Crew Knight to represent you. He wasn't able to get here in time for court today, so he called me, and I came immediately. We're going to ask the judge not to arraign you until he gets here tomorrow."

"So I have to spend another night in jail?"

"Yes, but honestly, based on the charges, I'm going to assume the government will ask for you to be held. Right now, I need to know if you spoke with any agents and what was said."

I run through what I remember and what I said. "I don't understand any of this. I've gone through it all for the last forty-eight hours, and I know it involves Travis somehow, but I don't know how to prove it. Also, the last thing the agent showed me before he left was a photo of my business partner in Boston. None of it adds up. He and Travis met maybe two times in the years I've had the farm."

"So you're telling me you aren't involved in running a money-laundering operation for an organized crime ring by buying and selling horses with dirty money?"

What? Jesus Christ. This just keeps getting worse and worse.

"Of course not. I have nothing to do with it. I've never met any of these people. I don't even know someone in a fucking crime ring. Travis is the one who went to the auctions and set up the private buyers. So much of the paperwork we found recently that has my signature on it was either forged or I didn't know, maybe I did sign it, sometimes Travis would just bring papers in and I would sign."

"Anthony will be able to help with all of that, but for now, I just want to get you another day before we enter a plea."

"I swear to you, I had no part in any of it."

"That's what they all say, but I believe you. You have one of the top criminal defense lawyers in the country."

Before we can continue on, the U.S. Marshal reappears, cuffs me again, and we all head out to stand before the judge.

Only this time, the room isn't empty.

There, standing in the front row, is Tessa. Her long, brown hair is pulled to the side, but it's the worry in her eyes that has my heart ready to break.

Beside her is my daughter, holding Tessa's hand as she smiles softly at me.

God, the two women I never wanted to see me like this.

Tessa looks tired and scared, and it kills me that I can't go to her to comfort her. I walk past her, our eyes staying connected. Does she believe that I didn't have anything to do with this? Does she know I would've never put her in that danger? Those big blue eyes stare back into mine and I see the trust, hope, and resolve glimmering in hers. She knows.

Now, I have to stand here, my back to her, and pray the judge sees all of this is a huge mistake.

The clerk calls the case to order, and the prosecutor reads the charges. With each one named, my dwindling hope becomes zero.

The judge then looks at my stand-in lawyer. "Would you like to proceed with arraignment today?"

"No, we request the court to delay so he can meet with his lawyer tomorrow."

The gavel bangs. "Arraignment is set for tomorrow at 3:00 p.m."

I hear Tessa's quiet sob and turn to face her. "It's okay. It'll be okay."

She shakes her head, tears in her eyes. "I'll get you out soon."

I want to tell her she won't, not with the way things are looking. Instead, I force my lips into a smile and then nod.

The Marshal grabs my elbow. "Let's go."

As I'm taken away, back to my cell, I chance one last look at Tessa and find her with a hand resting over the heart that I'm breaking.

Last night was by far the worst.

Not that I've slept at all since being in jail, but last night all I could see was Tessa's face when I closed my eyes.

So I stopped trying. It's hard enough being in here, not knowing what the fuck is going on, but to see her tears, to know that I'm the reason she has dark circles under her eyes, I fucking hate it.

A police officer comes to my door. "Thorn. Your lawyer and the prosecutor are here."

I sit up, confused as to why the prosecutor is here too.

He unlocks the cell door. "Turn around. I need to cuff you and bring you to the interview room."

I do as he says, going through the motions I never thought I'd know in my life. I allow him to lead me into the room where Agent Halsey grilled me for what felt like an eternity. When I get inside, the officer uncuffs me and the prosecutor is sitting on one side and the man I'm assuming is my lawyer are sitting on the other.

The man stands. "Killian, I'm Anthony DeCarolis, I received a call about an hour ago from the prosecutor to meet here. There have been some developments in your case."

"I see," I say, walking over to sit beside him.

"Mr. Thorn, the FBI has brought forth some information regarding your involvement after two arrests were made this morning. We are going to be dropping all the charges against you," the prosecutor explains.

I blink in confusion. "All of them?"

This makes no sense. How are they suddenly coming to this conclusion?

"Yes, the details that have come to light fully exonerate you, and we have a written confession that explains exactly how the operation was being run."

"What exactly is this operation?" I ask.

She places her hands on the table. "How well do you know Travis Brown?"

"I would've said very well a few months ago, but right now I'm not sure I know him at all."

In fact, it feels like I don't know anyone anymore. The only people I trust right now are the Disc Jockeys, Tessa, and Meredith. I would've added Nathaniel to that, but they planted a seed of doubt at the end of their interrogation, although including his photo might have just been a mind game.

Hell, this entire thing feels like one.

"The reason we're dropping all charges is that at the same time that you were arrested, so were five other members of a suspected money-laundering scheme the FBI had been investigating. Upon Mr. Brown's arrest, he was offered an opportunity to help himself and he took it."

"You arrested Travis?" I ask. "Who are the other five members?"

"Each of the men whose photo you were shown is now in custody."

My jaw clenches. "Was one of them Nathaniel Richmond?"

"Yes."

I shake my head in disbelief. I thought I knew him. I trusted him, thought of him like a brother, and now I find out he was somehow mixed up in this? Maybe it was innocent, like mine, and this will be cleared up for him too. "What is his involvement?"

Anthony speaks before she does. "I'd like to see the paperwork showing you're dropping his charges before we go any further. Do we have that in writing?"

She reaches into the briefcase beside her and extricates a piece of paper. "Here you are."

He reads over it and then slides it in front of me. "You can sign it."

The prosecutor hands me a pen, and I read it over before I find myself in a situation like this again. Sure enough, it's stating that I'm being released, and all charges are dropped. I don't hesitate to scrawl my signature across the bottom.

"Okay, so here's what we've learned…"

CHAPTER 30
TESSA

I'M STANDING OUTSIDE THE POLICE STATION, WHICH IS WHERE Killian's lawyer told me to come immediately when he called me two hours ago. I was just getting out of the shower, mentally preparing myself for another day of seeing Killian in handcuffs and not being able to touch him, and now I'm here. Unsure of what the hell is happening, but hopeful it's good news.

Meredith and Jake were at Prose & Perk to get breakfast when I called to update them, and tell them that I'd call once I knew more.

My phone dings with a text.

Meredith: Anything yet?
Me: No, I'm waiting for the lawyer to come out.
Meredith: Keep me posted. I'm at the house now, waiting for you to tell us if we should head to the courthouse.
Me: I'll let you know as soon as I know anything.

I pace back and forth, biting my thumb. I turn to look at the door and when I do, my stomach drops.

Killian.

He's outside, without cuffs, and he's walking toward me.

He's...out?

Before I can even think, I take off, my feet moving so fast as I rush forward and crash into him.

His arms instantly wrap around me, holding me so tight it's hard to breathe, but I'll take it. This is the best reason in the world to struggle for air.

I'm in his arms.

I pull back, looking at him through blurry tears. "You're out?" I question, needing to hear the words.

"I'm out."

"For good?"

He chuckles softly, his hand moving to cup my face. "Yes, angel. All the charges have been dropped."

"How? Why? What happened? Thank God, but how?" I ask, my mind reeling. "David was brutally honest with us yesterday after court that things weren't looking good. He was pretty sure the judge was going to hold you without bail based on the severity of the charges."

He brushes his thumb against my cheek. "It didn't look good. I was prepared for today to be the last time I saw your face."

"What?"

Killian's green eyes are haunted and there's a pain beneath them that makes my stomach ache. I don't want him to be sad, not now.

"I didn't think I would ever get to do this again. To touch you, hold you. I wasn't even sure you'd be here ever again—not that I would've blamed you if you were already back in New York."

I blink a few times. "Of course I'd be here, you idiot—and not just because you pay me to protect your company. I'd be here because...I care."

I love him, and while our entire relationship is up in the air and this may end up being goodbye, I'd still be here right now.

"Tessa, I watched them storm the house and take you into custody. You should be livid that I put you in danger. You should hate me for what you went through. I...fuck, you were caught in the middle of this mess."

I shake my head. "*You* didn't do this. You didn't purposely make this happen. Yes, I was scared, and it's definitely not something I'd ever like to experience again, but the agents only held me while they searched the house. I was let go immediately after they were done, and then I went to work on getting you out. I knew you didn't have anything to do with this."

"I knew I didn't, but I didn't know how to prove it. Tessa, I... fuck, I'm so sorry."

I place my fingers over his lips. "You have nothing to be sorry for." I move my hands to his chest, resting them over his pounding heart. "How are you in front of me right now?"

He lets out a heavy breath, and his beautiful green eyes fill with a mix of anger and frustration. "I'm not even sure how to process everything right now." Killian takes my hands in his, brushing the top with his thumbs. "Can we just...go home? I want to get out of here, shower, and then I promise we can talk about everything."

As much as my desire to know everything is burning, I can only imagine what he's been through and how much he doesn't want to stand around here anymore.

I lift up on my toes and press a soft kiss to his lips. "Of course, we can."

As he rests his forehead against mine, my eyes close, and I just take this moment in.

My Killian is here. The charges were dropped and we're together. The sheer relief of it all is so intense, it's hard to keep it together, but he doesn't need a frantic woman on his hands right now.

I squeeze his hands and pull back.

"Ready?" he asks.

"Let's get you home, right where you belong."

We made the forty-minute drive home in silence, his hand in mine, and we didn't let go of each other the whole time.

It felt like no words would be adequate. We'd just glance over, smile, and then go back to looking at the road ahead. There is so much we still have to talk about, but right now, I don't want anything to ruin this.

We pull up to the house and he sits, car running, staring at the front door.

I sent a text to Meredith and the group chat I'm now in with his friends, letting them know that Killian was released and all charges have been dropped. I told them I'd let them know when, and if, he was up for visitors.

Everett and Miles came and replaced the decimated door the day of the arrest. It's not the same though. No longer is it the beautiful black door with windows up top. Instead, it's white and has two large windows in the center, now serving as a reminder of that horrible day.

"You got new doors on the house?"

His voice cuts through the long silence. "I did."

"That's good."

I look over after a prolonged silence. "Killian?"

He sighs heavily. "I spent four nights in that jail, wondering if I'd ever get out. Confused and trying to make sense of what was happening. I tried to put the puzzle together, but I couldn't. Now that I have all the pieces, I almost wish I didn't know the truth."

I let him talk, my heart pounding as I hear the sadness in his voice. Whatever information he learned has clearly upset him. "Do you want to talk about it?"

He shakes his head. "Not yet."

"Can I ask why?"

Killian's eyes find mine. "Because once I say it, it'll make it real. Not that it isn't now, but…it'll just be different."

"I understand," I say softly.

"Is Meredith here?"

I nod. "She's waiting inside. The guys all want to come over, but I asked them to give you some time."

He glances back out the window. "God, I'm sure we have a new PR nightmare on our hands."

"Ironically, we don't," I say, hoping that maybe the small sliver of good news will brighten his mood. "Because of the time the raid went down, no one caught wind of it. There was a small rumor floating about the appearance of all the SUVs, but Everett told them it was a dignitary passing through. So far, all of us have had our ears to the ground and haven't heard anything."

He scoffs. "That won't last long once the story of Travis's arrest breaks. It'll be all over the horse-breeding world, and I won't be able to escape it."

"Then we'll manage it," I promise.

I don't know how, exactly, but we'll find a way. We didn't get through all of this to not come out on the other side of this story.

"We already have interest in another horse and a few more weekends booked for Buck Wild. The town has been buzzing with the rodeo, so we could host another one and keep the focus there. Let me do my job in protecting you from this."

He turns to me. "And what about my job of protecting you? What about how *I* promised you things? I wanted to show you how a man treats a woman when he…" he trails off, and my heart skips a beat.

"When he what?"

"When he loves her," Killian says solemnly as he reaches his hand out, pushing my hair behind my ear. "I know that this is the absolute worst way and time to tell you how I feel. I know that we have everything stacked against us. But I also didn't want to spend another minute without telling you."

Tears fill my eyes. "Killian…"

"No, baby, let me say this and then we can go inside and deal with the fallout. I may not deserve you. I may never be worthy of you, but I love you so fucking much. I've never felt this way about anyone. I've never had someone take over every part of my heart, soul, and life. You make me so damn happy, but loving you means I want your happiness more than my own. It means that I'll walk away, even if it's the last thing I want. You told me you weren't comfortable without Meredith being okay with it, and I understand it. I'll give you what you need above my own desires. So, I love you Tessa Rivers. I love you despite the universe telling us we shouldn't. I love the way you smile, your laugh, your eyes, and your beautiful heart. If I can't have forever, then I'm glad we had the time we did."

A tear slips down my cheek. My throat grows tighter and I have so many things I want to say. "I don't want to lose you," I say quickly. "The last few days were impossible, and I never want to go through this again. I'm not sure I can survive losing you."

Killian brushes my tears away and smiles. "You will. You're so much stronger than you know." I shake my head, but before I can tell him he's wrong and that I love him too, the front door opens and Meredith and Jake come out. "Come on, let's go inside. We at least have tonight together."

"Wait, so they arrested everyone at the same time?" Meredith asks.

Killian and I came inside and said hello to Meredith and Jake before he excused himself to shower and change. Now, we're all sitting outside on the deck as he finally relays everything that happened.

"Yeah. The FBI took their suspects into custody. Me, even though I wasn't involved. Travis, two other guys I don't know about, and Nathaniel."

My eyes go wide, and I gasp. "Wait! Nathaniel? As in your *business partner* in Boston?"

Killian runs his hands through this thick hair. His voice is pained as he answers. "Yes, apparently, they moved as quickly as they did because Nathaniel was getting on a plane to leave the country and if they lost him, they'd lose everything else in their investigation. He betrayed me."

"You're telling me your best friend is responsible for this?" Meredith asks.

I inch closer to Killian, taking his hand in mine, wanting to offer him comfort. No wonder he's devastated. Not only did he go through absolute hell with the arrest, almost had his business go under, and possibly lost his farm, but he also lost his best friend.

That's why he's so willing to walk away from us.

He doesn't want me to suffer through that same thing.

I glance at Meredith, and she looks at me, then her father.

"Nathaniel was the head of this entire thing. He was using our properties in Boston to wash some of the money. He's been buying the properties with dirty money through various buyers who paid more for the houses than they should be worth. He started getting some heat on it and shifted to using my horses since no one pays attention to horse sales. Travis would set it up, Nathaniel would send one of the buyers to get the horse at some stupid price, and they kept doing it when he realized no one was on to them. But Travis got spooked by something Nathaniel said, I don't know exactly what yet, but that's when he took off. Apparently, the rumors that were fed by Nathaniel canceled all the legitimate sales we had, but the rest of them, they were all fronts for the crime ring."

I can't believe what he's saying. Nathaniel offered to help. To loan him the money he needed in order to get through this rough patch. He came here because he said he was worried. Now to find out that he was behind all of it has to be devastating for Killian.

All of it was lies and for what? Money? I hate all of it. I hate that he did this, and I hate him for almost ruining Killian's entire life.

"I don't even know what to say," I confess. "I can't believe it."

"Me neither. I've known Nathaniel for most of my life, and I never would've believed it, which I think the prosecutor knew, so they let me read Travis's full confession. He explained everything, how they did it, where they found the buyers, why they used them, and then how the horses that won just brought them more revenue. All of it was in there. The dates, times, names, properties where Travis would meet Nathaniel at in Boston when he told me he was going to check on a stud or a new mare. Everything was a fucking lie."

Jake scratches his cheek. "Jesus. And your name was tied to it all?"

"Yes, the paperwork that Tessa and I found with my signatures was really one of the most damning parts. Nathaniel and Travis were smart. They entwined me in it where they could and the fact that the whole scheme involved both of my business partners pretty much made me a prime suspect all along," Killian explains.

Meredith looks to me. "Don't ever make me an accomplice in your life of crime."

I chuckle. "I'll do my best."

Jake scoffs. "Please, she should be saying that to you. If either of you is going to be the troublemaker—it's not her."

"True," I say with a smile.

Killian clears his throat. "I'm going to grab some water. Does anyone need anything?"

We all shake our heads.

Killian then looks down at me longingly, and I do my best to stop the pang in my heart. All I want is to be close to him, touch him, confess my feelings, but I also know that if I do that, then it could mean he loses his daughter.

He needs his family, and I need him to have that. I just hope Meredith comes around soon and sees that I love him.

I watch him go inside, not able to take my gaze from him, my chest so tight it feels as though it might break.

"Tess, will you take a walk with me?" Meredith asks.

My eyes move to hers. "Now?"

She nods.

"Okay."

Jake gets to his feet. "I'll go get water or...you know, disappear so you two can talk."

Meredith leans in and kisses him quickly. "Thanks, babe."

She loops her arm through mine and we start to walk down toward the dock. I can hear the river moving, hitting the rocks and splashing up as it flows down from the falls that are much further down.

"How are you holding up?" she asks.

My brows furrow. "What do you mean?"

Meredith snorts. "Please. I know you better than that. You love him, he's home, and it's very clear he loves you too. But the two of you look like you're in pain."

Because we are in pain.

"I'm going back home in a few days."

She jerks her head back. "Why?"

Because I can't be close to him and not have him. And I can't have him until you decide.

I look away from her so she doesn't see the agony I'm in at the idea of leaving. "It's...I can't be here."

"But you love this place and you should be right here." She pauses for a moment. "You should be with Killian."

"What?" I ask, not sure I heard her right.

Meredith gives me a smile and pats my arm. "I've had the last few days to really see things for what they are. When I asked for some time after you told me about you and Killian, I pretty much already knew how I felt, I just wanted to be sure I didn't jump the gun and then let you be hurt later on. My opinion doesn't matter because your happiness is all I care about, but knowing you, you probably were waiting for it. I want you to be with the person you love, no matter who that is."

"You're sure? You mean that? You're okay with me and your... father?"

"I'm sure. Here's the thing, while Killian may be my biological father, I don't really know him. He's tried to be there, have a friendship of sorts, but I couldn't do it. I felt like I was betraying my dad. Killian is not him, you know? My dad is the guy who taught me to drive, took me fishing, sat at my graduations, changed my diapers, raised me since the moment he found out about me." Meredith runs her hand through her hair, which she does when she's nervous. "Killian is...a guy who I found online who's technically my biological father. You didn't do anything wrong and you definitely didn't know who he was, just like he would have no idea who you are to me."

I blink. "What are you saying? Spell it out completely. No room for interpretation."

Her head falls back, and she laughs at the sky. "I'm saying you should date Killian. I'm saying you and he should be happy. You should love him and he should get the privilege of loving you."

"Meredith, I don't want you to feel like you have to say this."

She smiles at me and takes my hand. "You're my best friend in the entire world, Tessa. I would never want you to be miserable. Look, I'm not saying this won't be a little strange, but I would rather experience a little discomfort than watch you hurt. I see the way he looks at you, and it's the same way Jake looks at me. All I've ever hoped for was that you'd find someone to love you that way. Every girl should know what that feels like, and I will be the absolute last person in the world to take that from you."

For the first time in the last four days, there isn't a boulder sitting on my chest.

She seems...okay with it.

Genuinely.

"You're sure?" I ask again, not allowing my hope to build into something I won't be able to control.

"Absolutely. Now go get your man."

CHAPTER 31
KILLIAN

I WALK OUT TO THE BARN, LOOKING FOR THE GIRLS, AND I SEE TESSA wiping at her eyes. Meredith is doing the same when they spot me.

"Hey," Tessa says, sniffling a little. "We were just coming to find you."

"You were?"

Meredith comes to me first. "Yeah, I wanted to tell you what I just told her."

"What did you tell her?" I ask, curious about what the hell has them in tears.

"I was saying how happy it makes me to know Tessa's found someone who sees how special she is. She deserves to have a man who truly cherishes her and will do whatever he can to make her happy."

I'm hopeful this means that Meredith is giving us her blessing.

Because I'm that man.

I know how amazing she is.

"I think she deserves more than that," I say.

Meredith grins. "I agree. Jake and I are going to head out." She turns to me. "Maybe we can do dinner one day next week? You know, just to get to know each other as friends, if that's okay with you?"

I smile and nod. "I'd like that."

When I first met Meredith, I told her I didn't want to take her father's place. I never could be that man after her mother took that choice from me by hiding her pregnancy. But Meredith was lucky enough to have a man who stood in, gave her the things I didn't have the chance to. My role in her life could never be any kind of parental one, but I told her we could hopefully be friends.

She wasn't sure at the time. I told her that the offer stood, and anytime she wanted, she just had to ask.

Seems we might finally have a chance at it.

"Good," Meredith says before whispering something in Tessa's ear, kissing her cheeks, and then walking off.

Tessa watches as she goes, and the two of us stand here, finally alone for the first time since I got back to the house.

I go to open my mouth to see what Meredith said, but Tessa speaks first. "Did you mean what you said in the car?"

"I meant every word I said."

"You love me?"

"With everything that I am."

And I wasn't kidding when I said her happiness means more to me than my own. I don't ever want her to be sad or hurt, and I definitely don't want to see her lose Meredith.

"Do you know that I've never been in love? Not once," she says, taking a step toward me. "I've dreamed of it, what it would feel like, how I would be consumed by it. In my head, it was this lightning bolt that would come from the sky and knock me out. I would wake up one day as this normal girl, and then suddenly, I'd be a woman in love. It wasn't exactly like that, though I do think you're a bit like a storm." Tessa grins. "I'm not sure when I fell in love with you. I'd guess it was sometime between that horseback ride out to the meadow with your incredibly sexy cowboy hat and our first date, but I know that there's not another man in this world I want to be with."

I move toward her this time. "Tessa..."

"Meredith saw me when you were gone these last few days. She witnessed, firsthand, just how devastated I was. We spoke just now, and she doesn't think I should give up on us."

My heart is pounding against my chest. "I was going to talk to her."

"You were?"

I nod. "I was going to tell her how much I love you. I hoped she'd understand this wasn't just some throwaway thing."

She laughs softly. "Which is technically what our plan was. No feelings, just a casual relationship. We really have a thing about breaking the rules."

"I think the rules don't apply to us." I reach out, take her hand, and put it on my chest, right over my beating heart. "There's no way I could keep you out of here." I tap my fingers against hers in time with my heartbeat. "You found a way into my heart, Tessa, and now it's yours."

"This isn't going to be easy," she says, her big blue eyes staring into mine.

"No, it won't."

"I don't want to give up my job."

"I wouldn't ask you to," I answer honestly.

Tessa shakes her head. "This is nuts. You know that right? It's too soon, too impulsive."

I raise my hand, cupping her cheek. "Do you love me?"

"Yes."

"Then how about we worry about the rest of the shit later and you let me kiss you?"

She grins. "I think I could live with that."

"Good."

Then I lean down, press my lips to hers, and finally kiss the woman I love.

"Are you sure there are no fish in this water?" Tessa asks as she pulls her shirt off, draping it on a rock.

I pull my pants off. "No, but I've never seen one."

She shudders. "The things I do for you."

I laugh. "Come on, you're the one who created a new company and called it Buck Wild. Let's see you put your money where your mouth is and get a little wild."

Although I'd like to do something else with her mouth.

We rode out to our spot, where I can have Tessa all to myself. Not that there's anyone at the house, but out here, it's as though no one else exists but us.

I need that tonight.

It seems she does too.

After Meredith left, the two of us spent some time cleaning up, trying to put the house back in order, and then I just couldn't stand it anymore. Looking at the destruction of my home was too fucking much, so I asked her to come for a ride and leave the past behind— even if just for a little while.

I walk into the cool water, while Tessa removes clothing, standing completely nude and then heads toward me.

With just the moonlight illuminating her body, she takes my breath away.

I hold my hand out, and she comes to me. When she's in, I pull her close and she wraps her arms around my neck.

"Hi," she breathes.

"Hi."

Tessa's fingers tangle in my hair. "I missed you so much. I know it was only a few days, but I was so worried."

I kiss her nose and then tell her the truth. "I was too, but then I saw you in the courtroom, and I don't know, I felt so much regret that you had to be there at all. I had no idea what was going to happen, but I knew I needed to see you again."

"That's behind us now."

"It is."

I wade us a little deeper as her legs tighten around my hips. I move my hand slowly up her back, pulling her chest closer. Tessa tilts her head, her eyes full of desire as I speak what's in my heart. "I want to make love to you. Right here, right now."

Her lips part and her fingers come to my face, moving along my beard. "I want that too."

"Kiss me."

She does. Her lips find mine, and I slide my tongue into her mouth. I drink her in, taking all she gives and, God, she gives me everything.

I drink in her soft moan, our tongues colliding. Her hands move to my face, holding me to her as she kisses me deeper.

I didn't know if I'd ever have this again.

I thought I lost her.

I thought I lost any chance of us.

Now I have her, and I'm never going to let her go.

"Killian, I need you," she says before her mouth is back on mine.

The two of us are frantic, desperate for each other.

I wanted to go slow, to make love to her in the water. To cleanse the past and start this anew, but I need her as much as she needs me.

I adjust her hips, lining my cock up, and she gasps as I surge up into her.

Tessa's head falls back, dipping her long brown hair into the water. I shift my hips, my right hand going to her throat, holding her there. Her eyes meet mine, and I pump into her again.

"Stay like that, Tessa, just like that," I grunt.

Her hands wrap around my wrist, holding on as I fuck her. The water splashes, rippling around us as we create a new rhythm.

I rock my hips, and she uses the motion to push down, taking me deeper.

"I'm close," she pants.

I am too. This is too much, she feels too good.

"Fuck, you're perfect."

"I love you," she says. "I love you, please, I can't hold on."

"Let go," I tell her.

Her fingers clench around my arm and she screams, her voice echoing against the rocks, I release her throat, pulling her to me. Her head is buried in my neck, and I keep pumping, so close to my own release.

I feel her lips against my ear. "I love you," she whispers.

And I fall apart.

Or maybe I finally come together.

"You know the last time we did this our entire world fell apart?" Tessa says as she's lying in my arms after I made love to her again.

This time, I did it right.

I brought her to the field after we dried off, laid out a bunch of blankets, set up the lantern, and we've been lying here since.

"All over a stupid question about our ages."

She laughs softly and tucks her head into the crook of my neck.

As exhausted as I am, and I really am freaking spent, I don't want to go to sleep. If this is a dream, I never want it to end, so I'm holding on to this version of reality, hoping it stays this time.

She pulls the blanket that's wrapped around us a little tighter. "Who knew your age would be such a hot topic?"

"I believe it was your age that really threw us the curveball," I mock, rubbing my fingers up and down her spine.

"How about we try to have a cute cuddle-after-sex talk, but without the drama after?"

I think we've had enough drama to last us a lifetime, so I'm fine with that. "All right, let's see if we can make it through this one unscathed."

She lifts up onto her elbows. "If you could live anywhere, where would you choose?"

That's an easy one. Anywhere she is. However, I don't want to spook her so I say the first place that comes to mind. "Right here."

"Ember Falls?"

I nod once. "I really feel like this place is home."

"What about Boston?"

Absolutely not. Not now. Not after all the shit I learned about the people I was around. I spoke with Anthony after I got back home, and he's already putting in the paperwork for me to get out of the real estate business. Sell it to the highest bidder. Once all of that's settled, I'll be able to move here full-time or maybe it will remain part-time if I'm in New York City with Tessa.

"Boston is my past."

"I'm sorry, baby," she says, resting her hand on my arm. "I know you and Nathaniel were close."

"I thought we were too, but…I'm trying really hard not to think about him at all tonight," I tell her.

At first, I was in denial. I *knew* him, or at least I thought I did. Nathaniel was like a brother to me, and to know that he was doing this shit behind my back seemed impossible. Then I moved to anger. To find out that someone I trusted could screw me over so badly made me see red. He fucked with my entire life all for his greed? Fuck him.

I'm pretty much still in the anger stage, and I'm completely content staying here for a while.

"All right. Where do you see your future?"

That's the easiest question she could ask. "With you."

"Killian," her voice is full of disbelief.

"I'm serious. You're who I want to build a future with. Would I love us to build a life together here? Yes. I also know that you have your job in New York, and I will never ask you to give that up, so if it means we split our time, we do that. There's only one nonnegotiable, angel."

"What's that?"

"You. I'll give up other things, but not you. Never you."

She leans down and kisses me softly. "You're my nonnegotiable too."

"Good, at least we're on the same page about this."

"We're really doing much better this time around with our cuddle talk."

I chuckle. "I agree."

I spend the next hour holding her under the stars, imagining what the rest of my life could look like with this woman who changed everything the moment she walked into it.

CHAPTER 32
TESSA

"YOU DON'T HAVE TO GO," KILLIAN SAYS AS I'M PACKING UP MY things.

"I do though."

He comes up behind me, wrapping his arms around my middle. "Hmm, I think you should stay. I bet I could find a way to convince you."

Oh, I know he can. In fact, he's done it about sixteen times since he got home eight days ago.

I laugh and place my hands on his. "I have to go back to New York. I need to figure out what the plan is with my job, and you need to do the things we've put in place for yours."

Yesterday, I laid out a detailed list of things that I think Ivy Thorn Ranch needs to do. An action plan that he can follow to get things back on track.

By some miracle, Killian's name has largely stayed out of the story that broke. He was mentioned, being Travis's boss, but it mostly laid out the arrests of the key players of a money-laundering scheme that the trainer was simply involved in.

It was a major win for Killian.

His first task is actually to find another trainer to help rebuild the program that he did start and grow into a success.

Regardless of who was buying the horses, they were still winners.

"I think you should go over the plan once again," he says as he kisses my neck.

I sigh. "You're ridiculous."

"I'm in love."

"You're ridiculous while being that," I tell him.

Although, I don't say it with all that much censure because it always makes me giddy when I hear him say it. I love this man and he loves me.

We have a lot of things to figure out, most importantly my job, but I have to believe we can do it.

My hope is that I'll be able to continue to work for Anchor Light but stay in Ember Falls where I can be close to my clients, all three of them, since Hazel signed on with me yesterday to work with her on Prose & Perk.

Which is going to be my big push.

Plus, I've already told Killian that once Brynlee returns back, I will no longer be his publicist, so our relationship won't be a conflict of interest—technically.

"What is your plan when you get back to New York?" he asks, letting me go and moving to lean against the dresser.

I sigh. "First, I'm going to meet with Brynlee and Thea and discuss working out of Ember Falls. Then, I'm going to talk to my roommate and see if she's cool with me subletting my room, if she doesn't just want to take it for herself, but that's only if I can keep my job and move down here. Otherwise, we're going to have to do long distance for a while."

"What if I have another option?"

My eyes move to his. "What?"

"What if, no matter what, you come back to Ember Falls?"

"I'm not giving up my job."

He lifts his hands. "I'm not asking you to. But I was thinking of using some of the land here for a new venture, and I think you'd be the right person to run it."

I raise one brow. In all the time I've been here, he's never mentioned wanting to do something with the land. "What's that?"

"I want to open a camp. There's a great spot in the back of the property. We could have a place where kids come, where they have time with the horses, and we can provide them with a sanctuary. We could set it up to be exactly like your old camp—and what you've dreamed of."

I drop the shirt that I was folding, staring at him. "I don't understand."

He walks up to me, taking my hands in his. "I got an offer on the real estate business today. I'm going to take it."

I blink. He mentioned that he was having meetings today, but I've been so busy with Hazel's proposal that I didn't ask and he didn't mention it.

"Okay...what was the offer?"

"A lot. They want the entire thing. I'm going to sell all of my shares and whatever Nathaniel does isn't my concern. I'm out of it and I'll be able to invest all of that money back into the ranch."

"That's great!" I say, so happy for him. "I know this is where your heart is."

He grins. "Yes, it is, but I want this to be where your heart is too."

He's so damn sweet. "You're where my heart is," I tell him.

"Then I want this ranch to be something for you too. I'm not asking you to give up your job. I want you to be able to work for Brynlee, but I just want this place to also have something for you—besides me."

I don't even know what to say. "You don't have to do that."

He brings his hand to my face, gently brushing my hair back. "In my entire life, I've never felt this way. You're who I want, Tessa. I don't just want to build my life here. I want to build our life. I heard the way you spoke about that camp, how you wanted to create something like that, to give back, and I want to create that with you. I won't have the time to run a whole camp, Buck Wild, and this new freaking rodeo thing you've apparently implemented."

I laugh. "It's a lot. You're not that savvy with the marketing."

Killian ignores that jab. "I'm saying that, no matter what happens with Anchor Light, I want us to do something good with the money and provide something for kids who need it."

I lift my arms, wrapping them around his neck. "I love you, Killian Thorn."

"Not nearly as much as I love you, Tessa Rivers. Now, go to New York and get your ass back home to me."

"You really did a great job while you were away," Brynlee says as we sit in the observatory of the most insane apartment I've ever seen.

Her husband is a billionaire and owns a luxury penthouse on billionaire row, overlooking Central Park, and I am in awe.

She's holding her son, Jameson, who is completely passed out.

"I appreciate that."

She smiles. "And you signed two new accounts. I'm...so impressed. Truly."

"I really wanted both of them. I know Aarabelle brought Penelope to the table, but thankfully she signed. With Hazel, it's a totally different project and I can see so much potential with Prose & Perk. Hazel wants to expand, and I think we're really going to be able to help her with that."

Jameson shifts and we both go silent, afraid to wake him up, until he settles.

"I had a call with Killian this morning."

That takes me by surprise. "Oh?"

Brynlee is quiet for a second. "He told me that you were vital in saving the ranch and he didn't think he could've survived the arrest and subsequent release if it weren't for you."

The tone in her voice makes me wonder if she knows there's more. I came here with the intention of being completely honest with her. I don't want to hide what happened, who we are to each other, and why I want to return to Ember Falls.

The opening sort of wrote itself. "Brynlee, I'd like to be honest."

"Okay."

"Killian and I...well, we became very close. The night before you told me anything about him, I met him at the bar. I had no idea who he was and he didn't know who I was. He was expecting Aarabelle. Anyway, we...spent the night together before we both learned who the other was."

Her eyes widen. "Oh. Well, that's definitely not what I was expecting."

"I know the company's policy on sleeping with clients, and I want to assure you that I didn't know at the time."

"Did it happen again?"

I could lie. I probably should lie for the sake of my job, but I respect my boss and I owe her the truth. "It did, and I'm sorry. I never meant to betray you or the company. I also want to say that I did everything within my power to keep things separate and help restore the image of his business in the most professional way, but my heart and my head didn't align."

Brynlee lets out a long sigh and pats Jameson's back softly. "I'll be honest, I don't really know what exactly the right thing to do is here. We do have rules for a reason. The first time isn't really the issue—it's the subsequent times you admit you were together. That said, you did your job, and you did it very well. You kept Killian's company from going under and his arrest from becoming a major news story, so all of that shows your ability to be a publicist. Plus, you signed two more companies in the time you were in Ember Falls."

"That said," I say, clasping my hands in front of me. "I know I was wrong."

"I do appreciate your honesty."

Before I can respond, Brynlee's husband knocks softly and then opens the door. "Sorry, I didn't know you had company," he says.

"Crew, come meet Tessa. She's the publicist I was telling you about."

He enters fully and walks toward me, hand extended. "Tessa, hello. I'm Carson Knight, however everyone calls me Crew."

"It's great to meet you."

Crew turns to his wife. "Everything okay? I thought you were going to take months off for the baby?"

She grins up at him. "Yes, well, Tessa just got back and we were catching up. Think of it as girl talk instead of work."

He chuckles. "Sure, love, I'll just call it that. I need to make a few calls to my employees in other locations, we'll call it the same."

Brynlee rolls her eyes. "You own how many businesses? Of course they're in other locations."

"That's the thing, I believe that good people are worth more than a location, no matter what company they work for me under." He looks back at me. "I apologize for interrupting. Anyway, it's great to meet you."

"You too."

He turns to his wife. "I'll take him so you can work."

Brynlee grins. "Uh-huh. I'll bet that's why you're taking him."

Crew shrugs and lifts Jameson into his arms. "Daddy's got you, buddy," he says as he walks out.

Brynlee watches him with a wide smile. "There's something about a man and a baby." I laugh softly, and then she turns back to me. "You know, something Crew just said really hit me. He's right, it's about good people. While I don't like that you broke the company policy regarding relationships with clients, I also know what it's like to have feelings for someone you shouldn't. Are you hoping to still have a relationship with Killian?"

My heartbeat picks up, and I nod. "Yes. I know I don't have any right to ask this, but…I'd like to ask to work remotely, from Ember Falls. It's not just because of Killian—I want to make that clear now. All of my clients are in Ember Falls and there is going to be a lot of travel back and forth. It would be best for the clients and for the company."

"I was afraid you'd say that," she says with a laugh. "I'd like to talk to Thea about this first and see how she feels. I don't want to lose a competent employee, and I understand your reasoning in being closer to your clients. It's just something we need to discuss."

That's really all I can ask for.

CHAPTER 33
TESSA

"I can't believe you're going to give all this up," Brianna says as I'm packing up the remainder of my things.

I smile at my roommate who truly made my transition into living in New York seamless. Brianna made sure I never felt alone and always made me smile. I'm going to miss her a lot.

"In a way, I really can't believe it either."

"The food, Tessa. Think of the *food*."

I laugh. "Hence why I ordered a bunch of things I know I won't get in Virginia," I tell her.

"At least I'll have leftovers," Bri says with a grin.

Yes, she will. When I got home from work, the two of us placed orders from four places. She demanded I spend the rest of my night eating all the things I won't have again. Of course, Brianna won't be here to eat with me since she has a fashion show she's working, but I'm going to have a bite of all my favorite dishes.

"You know I'm going to miss you, right?"

She moves the packed box on the floor so she can plop on my bed. "How could you not? I'm the best roommate who ever lived in the big city. Tell me again why you're moving? You hated small-town life."

"I thought I did," I admit. "Well, I know I did, but it's different in Ember Falls. It's not like Indiana. I don't hate it there. The people are kind and...there's him."

Brianna grins. "He must be something special for you to be giving up your dream here."

He is. He's very special.

"I'm not giving anything up," I tell her. "I'm keeping my job. I'm just moving where I want to be."

A week ago, Thea and Brynlee called me into the office to let me know that they made a decision. I've been given three months in Ember Falls and then we can reassess. If it's working out, with both my relationship and with Hazel and Penny, then we can extend the trial period or make it permanent.

The other part of the agreement is that I need to bring on at least four more clients in the south to make it make sense for me to be in Virginia.

I'm excited and eager to prove myself.

"If you say so, babe."

"Killian is really great. He's beyond excited that my bosses signed on to this. Even if it's just a temporary agreement for now."

Giving up my apartment was the hardest part. At first Brianna tried to convince me to keep my room since it's just a three-month trial run, but I don't see myself coming back regardless. If Killian really wants to open up the camp, that's what I would rather invest my time in.

Not to mention, I can save the money I was spending on rent and help my mother or put it toward other things I want or need. Killian wouldn't even let me finish when I said I wanted to pay rent to live with him.

"You know you can always come back," she offers.

"Yes, I'm sure your new roommate will just love that."

"She's already annoying me, and she hasn't even moved in yet."

I laugh. "Everyone annoys you, Bri."

"Yes, I know, but that's because everyone is dumb."

I'm not even remotely surprised she thinks that. "I annoy you, and I'm not dumb."

She lies back and sighs. "I know, but you do it in an...I'm so cute but annoying' kind of way. Your annoying doesn't make me want to throw things."

"I guess that's a good thing."

Brianna nods. "It is, but now you're annoying me because you fell in love and are leaving me."

"You could always come with me. I'm sure they need great hair stylists down south."

Her laugh is loud and almost like a cough. "Absolutely not! I will never leave the city—it's like my lover."

"I found a new lover."

"Yes, yes, your older, very sexy, very related to Meredith lover."

I snort. "Thanks for that last part."

"You're welcome."

I roll my eyes. "Are you going to help me?"

Bri gets up and kisses my cheek. "Nope. You're leaving me, you're on your own, kid. Plus, I have to get to work. Some of us don't have sugar daddies."

I definitely don't have that, but arguing with Bri is futile. The good part about my life here is that I don't have a lot of stuff. We have a tiny apartment, and I pretty much just have what's in this room, so packing didn't take me long.

I hear Brianna leave a few minutes later and grab my phone to video call Killian.

"Hi, sweetheart." His beautiful face fills the entire screen, and I can't help the stupid grin on my lips.

"Hi."

"Are you packing?"

I sit on the edge of my bed. "I am. I'm almost done. What are you up to?"

His long sigh, accompanied by his disgruntled look, tells me it's not something he wants to be doing. "Well, I'm preparing for a Moms' Night Out at Buck Wild. You know, that event you said you'd be back for?"

I give him my most apologetic smile. "I know, and I thought I would be. I didn't think I'd be gone for two weeks."

I wasn't really sure how long I'd be here, but Thea and Brynlee asked me to at least give them a bit of time to discuss things, and I felt I owed them that much.

As much as I really love the idea of the camp, I also love my job. I have a lot of great ideas that I want to implement and my hope is that I can do both until I can decide which I really want. The camp is going to take a lot of time to get up and running, and I explained to Killian that the one thing I promised myself was that I'd never be like my mother.

I wouldn't give up my job, my life, my hopes and dreams, and I'll never be dependent on a man. No matter how amazing he is.

Killian understood and said he supports me no matter what I decide to do. He even said he was willing to move to New York, if that's what I wanted.

Just knowing he was willing to do that meant the world to me, but when I thought about it, I realized that it wasn't what I wanted. I want to be in Ember Falls.

"It's fine. Just means I'm hanging up decorations. Also, Gary wanted me to let you know that under no circumstances is he taking these girls out to the falls after what happened with the last group."

I laugh, imagining Gary's face when they all decided skinny-dipping was on the agenda. "He does realize he works for you, right?"

Killian's huffs. "Tessa, I love you, but Gary is my only ranch hand and proving to be a trainer, and I'm not losing him over this."

"I know, I know. I'll be there in two days, and then I promise I'll handle everything with Buck Wild."

"Yeah, yeah."

"Do you miss me?" I ask, rolling onto my stomach and kicking my feet up.

"More than you can imagine."

"I miss you too."

There's a knock on the door. "Hold on, my food is here," I tell him and rush to the door.

However, when I open it, it's not my food.

It's something so much better.

"Killian?"

He grins. "Hi, baby."

I launch myself into his arms, holding on to him with everything I have. "What are you doing here?"

"I missed you."

"You said you were doing stuff at the farm."

He laughs and then kisses me. "I lied."

It's a lie that I'm not even the slightest bit upset over. "Best lie ever."

I pull him into my apartment. "Come in. Brianna just left so you won't get to meet her. I...can't believe you're here."

He wraps his arms around my waist, kissing my neck. "I didn't want to spend another day apart. Besides, I haven't been to New York for a while, so I figured maybe my girlfriend would show me around for a few days."

"A few days?" I ask. "I was heading back to Ember Falls soon."

"I think we could do with a mini-vacation, don't you?"

I don't even know what to say. I'm in shock at it all, but I'm also over the moon happy.

"If you say so."

"I do. Now, can you pack a bag for a few days? I booked us a room. We have dinner tonight and a show."

I blink. "We do?"

"Yes, angel, we have a weekend-long date."

I smile, moving closer, my hands resting on his chest. "Is this another lesson, like your date was?"

He shakes his head. "No more lessons. My hope"—he pulls me to him—"is that we're done with lessons. All you're going to have from now on is me, treating you like the beautiful, intelligent, and worthy woman that you are. You're mine, Tessa Rivers, and I'm going to keep you."

My stomach dips, but my lips tilt up. "I've waited my whole life to find a man I wanted to belong to. Someone who made me happy. Saw me, quirks and all, and was willing to love me. I never thought I'd find him, but then you sat down beside me and told me not to get fish at the bar. Little did I know that night I'd find something I wanted far more than food."

I found a man I love. A man I would fight the world for. A man who has shown me just how much I mean to him. He's here, in New York, even though I was going to be with him in just a few days. He planned an entire weekend just to be with me and give me a little more time in the city I love.

Killian and I may have had every single thing stacked against us, but somehow, we found a way to the other side, and I have never been happier.

CHAPTER 34
KILLIAN

"Are you sure you want to do this?" Tessa asks as we stand outside of the prison.

I take her hand in mine, letting her warmth envelope me and squeeze. "I think it's the only way I'm going to get any kind of honest answers."

In three months, Nathaniel's trial will begin and there's not a single doubt he's going to lie or manipulate the truth in order to get a lesser sentence for himself. I'm not naive enough to think I'll get the truth today, but maybe if it's just him and I, I'll get some answers.

She lifts up on her toes and kisses my cheek. "Then, I'll be right here when you're done."

When we first spoke about this a few weeks ago, I was completely against it. There's really no point to it other than to say what I need to say.

I'm hoping I'll figure out exactly what to say when I get in there because the scenarios that have played out in my head have gone a hundred ways.

No matter how many times I convinced myself that I didn't need or want to confront Nathaniel, Tessa could see the truth.

It's been bothering me.

It's the one dark cloud hanging in our nearly perfect skies.

Tessa keeps it away. She brings me the sun and the cloud-free days, but it's always there, just lurking and ready to dump buckets of rain once it opens.

Instead of giving it the power, I'm going to cut it open myself and let the flood come down now that I'm prepared.

"I love you," I tell her.

"I love you. No matter what information you do or don't get today, just know it changes nothing in your life."

I nod and kiss her temple, inhaling her sweet scent. "I know. I have you, the ranch, and I'm happy, I think this will just close that chapter of my life."

"I agree."

It's time to put the past behind me. I was able to fold my stake in the company without any issues thanks to the legal team I hired. Now Nathaniel is the sole owner of a pile of shit. There was no managing the PR nightmare he created for the real estate company, but Tessa decided we needed to be proactive and had Ainsley's paper cover the story. They held to the facts and kept my arrest completely out of it.

We enter the prison where he's being held, sign in, and I kiss Tessa once more before following the guard back into the visiting area.

I sit at the metal table, the room is cold and has a faint scent of rust and paint. It's the least inviting place possible. Gray, monotone, and you can feel the despair through the doors. After about three minutes, there is a loud buzzer then a clanking noise, before the door swings open and Nathaniel enters.

He has a beard that is longer than he's ever worn and the shackles cling as he enters. His hair is messy, not the normal slick back he always wore and his orange jumpsuit almost makes him look paler than usual.

We don't say a word as he is brought to the table. He keeps his hands extended as they uncuff him and then move to his ankles.

"You have fifteen minutes," the guard says.

Nathaniel nods once to him and then he sits across from me.

Looking at him, all I can think is how this isn't the man I knew.

I remind myself that I may have never really known him because the guy I was friends with for most of my life would've never done the fucked up shit he did.

He wouldn't have sacrificed his best friend for whatever goals he had.

Yet, that *is* the man in front of me.

After another few minutes of silence, he clears his throat. "I'm going to assume you weren't just in the area and wanted to visit."

I raise one brow and almost laugh. "No."

"You've never been one to beat around the bush, go ahead and ask whatever it is that brought you here."

There are so many things I want to ask from the part of me who cared about this man like a brother, hoping he's not being abused in here to the other part that partially does hope someone is teaching him a lesson.

It might be wrong. It might make me a really terrible person, but a part of me just doesn't care.

He tried to ruin my life and I'm not sure I feel all that bad about his going up in flames.

I think of Tessa, what she would say, how she encouraged me to be honest, but also be the man I am at my core.

"Are you doing all right?" I ask first, remembering that there was a time when Nathaniel was a brother to me and if I start off there, at least there's room to go.

He laughs once. "Yeah, I'm doing great."

"Good. I'm glad you're enjoying your forced vacation."

Nathaniel sighs slowly. "Is that what you drove out here to find out? If I'm enjoying prison?"

"Not really."

"I didn't think so. I'm fine, Killian. I fucked up, I'm in jail and I'll probably spend a good portion of my life paying for it. But, I'm not getting my ass kicked or anything. I stay to myself. I know how to manage."

He was also a linebacker in college and can hold his own.

"Okay then."

His eyes move to the clock and then back to me. "Time is running out for you to get to it."

Always to the point.

I guess small talk is over and I might as well jump in. "Why did you do it?"

Nathaniel's thumb bounces against the metal table and I would bet his knee is going in time with it. He does that when his mind is working quickly.

I watch him, waiting for any sign that he's lying.

"I wish I had some grand reason like a dying family member, but I don't. I knew James from high school. He was friends with the Gibrelli family's youngest son. I sold one of James's properties and he connected us because of how fast I got it done. I didn't know much about the Gibrellis other than, they were feared throughout the area. They were said to be involved in gambling and drugs. Business, though, was business. I took a few of their properties on, everything was on the up and up, like it always starts. I wasn't involved in either, so it didn't really matter what they were doing outside of me listing properties for them."

"So you were selling properties for a crime ring? Knowingly?"

He exhales heavily. "Rumors aren't facts, Killian. I heard things, but I never saw anything illegal. When one of their underground gambling rings was raided, that's when things changed."

"Changed how?" I ask through gritted teeth, already seeing where this is going.

"We had property."

"And you let them use it."

Nathaniel nods. "By this point, almost 50 percent of our sales were coming from their associates. They were using us to buy and sell like crazy. The money we were making…"

I remember. It was like one day were doing fine and the next we couldn't keep a house on the market for more than a day. People were coming to us, signing, listing, selling. I always assumed it was just that Nathaniel and I had built a solid reputation.

"Then what?"

"Well," he laughs without humor. "Then I was fucked. They threatened to pull all the listings, everything we had with them, which would've sent us into bankruptcy because I had convinced you to invest in commercial properties, but they weren't moving as fast. It felt impossible, but I also convinced myself it was fine. Prices started becoming weird and the same buyer would come in at a ridiculously low price, they'd accept, and then that seller would list the property for three times as much a month later, but always through us so the commissions were great. They needed a way to clean the dirty money, and all I was doing was selling property."

Only he wasn't just selling properties. He was using our company to help clean dirty money.

"And how did it become the horses?" I ask.

His eyes widen before he schools his features. "It was a last resort."

"How?" I ask again.

He leans back, clasping his hands in front of him. "There were rumors that the Feds were onto the game with real estate. All of this is easy to track with tax records and names. They wanted to find a way that wasn't as heavily monitored, where sales aren't documented at the state and federal levels. That's when someone mentioned racehorses."

"So you just volunteered my ranch?" Anger seeps through each word as I stare at him.

"I didn't have to. They knew who you were. The Gibrelli family doesn't not do their research. You were doing well, had a winner or two, and they took the same idea of what we were doing with the housing market and approached Travis. I know you don't care or it doesn't matter, but I refused to help if they involved you at all," he says quickly.

"You're right. It doesn't matter because it did involve me, Nate. I was cuffed, searched, held down on the ground in my fucking house while Tessa was beside me. I was put in the back of a car, taken to jail, went before a judge, and you know what? You didn't get me out of it. You didn't confess so that you spared me, the one fucking person who never betrayed you. No, you kept quiet," I say each word softly, using the tactic our college coach used—quiet rage. "You would've let me take the fall, wouldn't you?"

His jaw tenses and that was the answer I knew was coming, but it still feels like a sucker punch to the stomach. He opens his mouth, but I shut him down.

"Don't fucking lie. You would've let me go down for this. You and Travis set me up so that if this fell apart, you, at the very least, would go free." I get to my feet, done with this. The whys and whos and hows don't matter anymore. He could explain it all and at the end, it changes nothing. "I would've done anything for you, Nathaniel. We've been friends since we were eighteen. Decades of trust, loyalty, and a brotherhood you broke and for what? Money? I hope it was all worth it."

Then I walk to the door, bang a few times and wait for the guard.

"Killian?" Nathaniel calls out. "It wasn't worth it. None of it. I'm sorry."

I stare at him, wishing the door was open and I didn't hear that last part, but I dip my head and exhale. "I'm sorry too, but I don't think it's for the same reasons."

The door buzzes and then slides open, but I walk out, putting him and everything behind me so I can have the life with the woman who is waiting outside for me.

~NINE MONTHS LATER~

"This is so exciting!" Tessa says as she grabs my hand.

"It will be if we win."

This is one of the last races that will award the points Midnight Valor needs to qualify for the Kentucky Derby. When I entered him into the first prep race, I really didn't think much of it. He's a great horse, and when I decided to breed his father with Midnight, I had no idea that this would be what came. Midnight Valor has speed, agility, and I thought if I could get him to win a few races, when we went to breed him, it would yield higher returns and make it so my sister's horse could live on forever.

We won the first race. Came in fourth for the second, and we've had really consistent results each race.

This is the last one, and we need a high finish in order to qualify, which…is beyond my expectations.

"Either way, this is great for the ranch."

She's not wrong about that. When Midnight Valor started to gain traction, we sold every horse we had available.

Now our breeding program is back on track, and we are already being asked about when he'll be entered into the rotation.

"I wish my sister was alive to see this," I say, squeezing Tessa's hand. "She would've loved that Midnight helped create a winner."

Tessa smiles. "I think Alicia is with us. I think her heart, her spirit, and her tenacity live inside that horse. It's why he's a winner."

I lean in and kiss her softly. "He didn't start winning until you came into my life."

She rolls her eyes. "You're ridiculous, but I love you."

"I love you more."

I love her so much it fucking makes my chest ache.

"Killian! Tessa!" Meredith calls our names as she heads over.

That's another thing Tessa brought into my life: my daughter. We have dinner with Jake and Meredith once a month, either at their place or ours. While we ours is definitely not a father/daughter relationship, it's more than I could've hoped for.

Jake is a great guy, and he's even helping me manage the contractors who are currently building the new barn, which will become the main meeting space for the camp Tessa dreamed of.

"Hey, guys," Tessa says, giving them each a hug and kiss on the cheek.

Meredith comes to me, and we hug then I shake hands with Jake. "I'm glad you guys could make it."

"We wouldn't miss this for the world. This is freaking cool," Meredith says, looking around.

I've never seen a crowd this large for this race, but it makes sense since so many are hoping to see their favorite pull through and qualify to run in the Kentucky Derby.

"My nerves are stretched so thin," Tessa says. "I just want Midnight Valor to make it."

"He'll make it," I say, willing it into the world. "You told him to."

She laughs. "I tell him a lot of things, but he doesn't always listen."

Tessa and Midnight Valor bonded when she moved back. He was always a bit of a loose cannon and I didn't think he'd ever be able to race. Yeah, he had all the right markers, but he wasn't disciplined, and the jockey and Travis always had issues.

Then, one day, I came out to see her in his stall, petting his neck and telling him how great he was.

"You say it was me, but I think it's Gary," Tessa says with a shrug. "He's the one who got him to do what we knew he could."

Gary has become my right hand in all things, and he's an incredible trainer. Apparently, Travis taught him a lot and he soaked it all in.

The parade begins and we stand at the entrance where the spectators come to watch the horses leave their stalls and strut. A few minutes later Midnight Valor's name is called and he walks tall and proud. Tessa grips my arm, squealing a little when she sees him. "He's ready."

"He looks it."

"He is," she says with conviction.

I hope so.

"We should get to our seats," I tell the group.

The four of us head to the owners' section where we have seats reserved. A few of the other men I've met over the last few races and I exchange handshakes and waves. It's tense up here, but Tessa seems completely at ease.

She turns to me. "Take a second and soak this in."

"What?"

"Look at where we are, Killian. You have a horse in the running for the Kentucky Derby. Ivy Thorn is thriving. Buck Wild has become a sensation, and even though it's not what you wanted, it saved the ranch. We're here at this race, together, with Meredith and Jake. You did all this."

I lean in, resting my forehead to hers for the briefest moment. "*We* did, Tessa. We did. You made me a better man. You gave me the hope to save the ranch. You gave me the strength to fight when it felt like everything was caving in. I'm only here because you're beside me, baby. No matter what happens, I've already won."

She kisses me softly and then we watch Midnight Valor leave the gates and cross the finish line in second place, which means we're going to the derby.

CHAPTER 35
KILLIAN

"You think this is a good idea?" Lachlan asks.

"Of course he does, he's not going to get any better than Tessa," Miles tacks on.

Everett snorts. "He couldn't get a woman to even look at him before Tessa. Lord knows how he was able to win her over."

I often wonder about some of my choices and letting these assholes tag along with me while I went ring shopping is one of those.

"Shut up, all of you. Each one of you married out of your league."

"Won't argue with that," Miles says.

"I'm not married yet," Everett notes.

"You're engaged, and Violet is way better than you deserve," I remind him.

Today is really the only day I could sneak off, since I plan to propose before the derby this weekend. We had our Ultimate Frisbee tournament out of state this weekend and Tessa is swamped with work, so she thankfully couldn't come.

I would have asked for the girls' opinions, but Ainsley said she'd rather chew nails than come, Violet is definitely not traveling with a newborn, and Penelope was all too happy to stay back since none of the other girls were going.

So I'm stuck with these morons since we carpooled.

"I'm very aware, which is why I love her to the point of madness and treat her like a damn queen," Everett acknowledges.

Lachlan snorts. "We all got lucky."

"We did," I agree.

No one more than me. I never thought at my age I'd find someone I wanted to settle down with. I was resigned to living alone, being the eternal bachelor because it just made sense. I had loved, lost, and then just got so set in my ways that it wasn't even something I gave a shit about.

Until Tessa.

The sales attendant returns to the case where I've been eyeing this one ring. It's a pear-shaped, two-and-a-half-carat diamond solitaire with peridots lining the band. It's different, beautiful, and it just so happens that peridots are her birthstone.

More than that, it seems perfectly Tessa.

"Is there one you like?"

"Yes, that one." I point to the ring that I keep going back to.

"This is a special piece," she says. "It was designed by our in-house jeweler whose favorite color is green. It's one of a kind."

"Just like the girl I hope will accept it."

She smiles, and the guys make a variety of noises from laughs to gagging sounds.

"I apologize for them—they're all infants."

"He'd know since he could be our dad," Lachlan, I think, says from behind me.

"Fuck off," I mutter and return to the saleswoman. "This one will be perfect."

I pay for it and then the four of us head out. Miles drives the three hours it takes to get back to Ember Falls, and we drop off Everett and Lachlan. When it's just the two of us, Miles clears this throat.

"Did you know, I always thought the two of us were the most likely to be bachelors out of the group?"

I turn my head to look at him. "You thought Everett would find someone?"

He chuckles. "He was a wild card, but he at least seemed to want a family at some point. Lachlan was a goner from the beginning, but you and I, we were different. Well, that was until I met Penny. Everything changed after that."

The fact that the man who hates coffee went to Prose & Perk every single day just to see her said it all. Penelope and Miles are truly perfect for each other, and I'm so glad they battled their demons and found a way together.

"I get that. It's like the two of us found our person and knew pretty quick."

Tessa rocked my world the moment she came into my life. I didn't have any idea she'd completely become it though.

My life is infinitely better with her in it and I hope to make her my wife.

"I think the right person shows up at the right time. We just have to pray we're smart enough to know it's her. Anyway, all of this is to say, I'm really happy for you."

"Thank you."

"Good luck. Do you have anything special planned for asking her?"

I grin. "I sure do."

"Did you know that the Kentucky Derby has never been canceled?" Tessa asks as we're walking back to one of the owners' suites at the race.

"I did."

"Did you know the Garland of Roses blanket weighs around forty pounds?"

I laugh softly. "I didn't."

She sighs and walks over to the seats that are reserved for us. "This book has a ton of facts. It's really interesting."

I walk over and pluck the race book out of her hand. "Tessa, you're rambling."

"I'm nervous."

"About?"

"What if we lose?"

I shrug. "We probably will."

Honestly, our chances aren't that great, but just being here is a dream come true. The accolades and the fact that we'll be able to use this for marketing and building a strong program are going to help the ranch for years to come.

She slaps my chest. "Killian!"

"Tessa."

"You can't say that."

"I can because it's true, but also because it doesn't matter. I'm proud of our team, the horse, the program, the fact that I'm here with you, and we're going to enjoy the race. That's what I care about. Not if he wins, which would be great, but also unlikely."

Her hands move to my chest where she rests them. "I guess, but I just want this day to be perfect. I want him to win. I want to scream and cry and be so happy I can't stop smiling."

"You do, huh?" I ask.

"Yes. Don't you?" she sounds perplexed.

Of course I want the same, but I really want to see her that way—and not because of the horse, but because of us.

Because...

Fuck it.

I step back and then drop to one knee in front of her.

She moves her hand to her mouth as I reach into my pocket.

"I had this entire thing planned and how it would go, but we've never been ones to follow any kind of rules or plans. You've been the one person in my life who has managed to knock it off its axis, but at the same time, right it. In my dreams, I couldn't have envisioned a better partner. I couldn't make you any more perfect than you are because you are my other half. You're the key to my heart and the woman I want beside me every moment for the rest of my life. So, I ask you Tessa Rivers, will you let me make you the happiest woman in the world?"

She nods, tears running down her beautiful face. "Yes! Yes, of course!"

I get to my feet and take the ring out of the box, slip it onto her left ring finger, and then kiss it as cheers and applause erupts all around us.

"I'm going to make you smile every day for the rest of my life."

She lifts up on her toes, taking my face in her hands. "I love you."

"I love you."

Then the gunshot goes off, and we watch Midnight Valor take second place—and neither of us cares that we lost because we've won something so much better.

EPILOGUE
TESSA

~SEVENTEEN MONTHS LATER~

"Tessa! Goddamn it! You are supposed to be sitting down!" Meredith yells as I'm standing on the step stool, trying to hang the new curtains that came in.

We are finally opening Hope + Mane Foundation tomorrow and we have an interview with Ainsley's newspaper and a big magazine that I was able to call in a favor for. Killian paid extra to get things done quickly so I could hopefully enjoy the opening of our new foundation. What we didn't anticipate was my pregnancy. I'm on maternity leave from Anchor Light and Brynlee offered that I could work part-time once I return.

I sigh heavily and step down, knowing if Killian hears her, it'll be a million times worse.

"I'm fine, Mer."

"You're about to freaking pop!" She says through gritted teeth.

Yes, I'm thirty-seven weeks pregnant, but I can't just sit around all freaking day. It's a big, big day for us.

"I'm fine," I tell Meredith, but then, Penelope enters and gasps.

"Tessa! We have staff to do that!"

I put the curtains on the table and lift both hands. "Fine. I was just trying to help."

"Help by sitting over on the couch and putting your feet up," Penelope says, pointing to said couch.

"I just want the photos to be perfect," I explain as I flop my ever-expanding ass on the couch.

"It will be," Meredith assures me as she pats the tiny butt belonging to the baby strapped to her chest.

Two months ago, my niece, who is technically my step-granddaughter—but we're not even going to entertain that shit—was born.

"Give me Callie." I extend my hands, waiting for her to let me hold my niece.

Meredith rolls her eyes, but unstraps her and then places her in my arms. "I'm only doing it because I know you'll stay on your ass that way."

"Works for me."

Penelope and Meredith work together as I supervise, surely annoying the shit out of them. Finally after about another hour, I'm content with the way things look and feel a little more confident about today's interview.

"Give me the baby so you can do one more walk through. I'm sure you want to," Meredith says as she lifts her daughter into her arms.

Like a beached whale, I flop my top half, hoping the momentum will help me up, which it does, and I push my distended stomach forward, stretching my back. "God, I'm going to be so happy when this baby vacates my body."

She laughs. "You say that until they're out and then you dream of the quiet again."

Callie has not been an easy baby. The first four weeks were absolute hell for Meredith and Jake. Killian and I came and stayed for two days to give them both some much needed rest. I didn't know a child could cry that much.

"She's doing much better now that you found the right formula," I say, rubbing Callie's back as she sleeps against her mother.

"Yes, thank God she sleeps through the night now."

"I miss that," I say.

Meredith laughs. "I forgot that part of pregnancy where you're just miserable."

I nod. "Yes, I do miss my second trimester. I felt good, was horny, and every new change was so cute. Now, I fart when I move and I can't see my feet."

"Well, even with all that, you look stunning."

I wish I believed that lie. "Thank you. Okay, I'm going to check out the two cabins, and I'll be back."

Just then, my extraordinarily sexy husband enters, his eyes immediately narrowing.

Oops.

I told him I was going to take a nap and then…didn't.

One would think after being married for a year, he would know that I don't really ever do as I say and be used to this. Seems not.

"Tessa…"

"Hi, baby."

His jaw tics. "Don't *Hi, baby* me. You said you were going to lie down and to come wake you up in an hour. Then, I find out that you had Gary drive you out, on the damn side-by-side, to check on things. Literally one minute after I left to go pick up the food you asked for."

I smile, hoping that'll soothe him over.

It doesn't.

"I couldn't sleep. Besides, the baby doesn't like daytime naps. He gets very restless."

"You didn't try. You're going to be on your feet all freaking day," he grumbles, but no matter how much Killian blusters, he always finds a way to get over it.

I go to him, resting my hands on his broad chest. "I'm sorry, my love. I promise I sat on the couch and let Meredith and Penelope do the work."

Meredith scoffs. "Yeah, after we had to browbeat her to not hang curtains."

He pales, and then I glare at her. "Traitor."

She shrugs.

Killian's thumb moves to my chin, and he lifts it until I'm looking at him. "Please tell me she's joking."

I would love to do that, but lying to him will only make it worse. So I lift up on my toes and kiss him. "Did you bring my food?"

His heavy sigh fills the room. "I did."

Just another reason why I love him so damn much. "Where is it?"

"It's in the kitchen."

I grin and kiss him again. "I love you."

"I love you too. Go eat. The photographer will be here in twenty minutes. I'll go check on the cabin and the barn with Penelope. Just...don't get on any ladders, please."

"I promise," I say and then head into the kitchen to eat.

I have been craving one thing every day...mozzarella sticks. I swear, I can eat them for three meals a day. It's not the healthiest option, but that cheesy goodness just makes me feel so happy. Killian goes to the bar at least once a day to pick up two orders. They have to be from there too.

It's something about the oil. I swear.

A few minutes later, Killian comes into the kitchen where I'm now licking my fingers to get every ounce of deliciousness left and he chuckles. "Feel better?"

"I'm literally that old Snickers commercial where I become an angry person until I eat. I'm ready now for our big day."

He comes behind me, wrapping his strong arms around my middle. I lie my head on his chest and sigh. "We have several big days coming."

We do. Today is part of it, and then we open the camp. Thanks to some of the press I've managed to get, we're full for the summer.

The fundraising efforts helped a lot because we were able to grant all ten girls a full scholarship to attend.

That probably means the most to me.

All of the girls are struggling with the loss of their father. The camp will provide equine therapy along with group therapy. Plus, each week we'll focus on a life skill that will help them, from changing tires to electrical work, woodworking, and other things many girls learn from a male role model.

The best part is that the guys who all stepped up without even a moment of hesitation are the Disc Jocks.

Each one offered their time, and they're all excited to help mentor these girls.

After that, hopefully, we'll be having a baby.

While the timing definitely isn't ideal, it is what it is, and my husband has made sure that everything will be handled and I'm going to have to trust that everyone around me will not let this falter.

Easier said than done, but I really have no choice. My need for control is going to have to take backseat.

"I just want everything to go well, you know? Not just the camp, but also the baby, the horse race coming up, and…"

Killian kisses my neck and then my cheek. "Everything will be fine, and if it's not, someone will handle it."

"Yes, I know. But still, not the way I would handle it."

He snorts a laugh. "You are going to have something much bigger to worry about." His hands rub circles on my stomach. "Our son is going to be here, and you've said you wanted time with him."

"I know, I know. I just didn't expect to get pregnant so easily."

Seriously, we weren't even officially trying. I just decided to stop birth control and two weeks later I got pregnant.

"Well, I needed to prove my virility."

I roll my eyes. "Yes. Good job, babe. Way to prove your manliness. I'm so impressed."

He laughs and nips my ear. "Cheeky."

"It's going to be okay," I say aloud. "Everything is going to go according to plan. We'll have the magazine today. Ainsley said we can do her article anytime this week. The kids come in two days, all the guys already have their schedules, and the staff moves in today. It's going to work out. I have a few days to get things in order and…" I'm cut off as the most intense pain shoots through my body.

It holds, like a horrible freaking cramp that causes my breath to catch.

Jesus, that hurts.

"Tessa?"

It ends and I move my hand to my belly. "Ouch."

"Ouch?" Killian echoes.

"Yeah, I got a cramp. Maybe I shouldn't eat so much dairy."

He turns me, which is sort of impressive since I'm as big as a house. "Maybe that wasn't a dairy cramp?"

I shake my head. "Stop. I'm not going into labor. I have shit to do."

One of his dark brows rises. "Yes, and you can control that?"

It's not happening. I don't have time to go into labor now. I still have a few weeks to go. This is my first baby, and all the books say I will probably be a little late.

I step back out of his grasp. "It's the dairy."

Killian chuckles once. "Okay then."

"I'm going to go out there and make sure things are perfect," I inform him.

Only, that's not really what happens.

No, I take two steps and am greeted with yet another round of cramps. Only…they don't stop. And then my water breaks.

––––––––––––

"Hello, son," Killian says as he lifts Nico out of the bassinet. "You gave us all quite a scare."

My eyes are closed, after I took another nap, I'm just starting to wake.

The birth was...a lot.

I pushed for almost four hours.

The doctors wanted to make the call for a C-section at hour three, but I pleaded for just a little more time. I don't know why it was so important to me to keep trying, but it was.

Killian was near to begging, and when the doctor informed me that Nico was starting to show signs of distress, I accepted the reality and was rushed into surgery.

I lost a lot of blood, and my body just isn't cooperating on staying awake for long periods of time.

"Your mother is so brave and she fought so hard for you," Killian tells him.

I move my head to the side and slowly open my eyes, looking at my husband holding our son. I smile softly. "I didn't know you could look any hotter, but here you are."

Killian comes over, brushing my hair back. "Are you feeling better?"

I inhale and groan a little. "Tired, but...okay."

He kisses my forehead. "You should rest, Tessa. You went through a lot and I was worried we might lose you both."

I force my arm to extend and rest my hand on his. "I'm not going anywhere."

The bed depresses as he sits beside me carefully and places Nico between us. "He needs you. I need you."

I push away the remnants of sleep. "I need you both, too." Nico fusses a little. "Can you put him on my chest?"

Killian does as I ask, placing our son on me, and instantly I feel more at ease.

He's here and he's absolutely perfect.

All the pain, fear, struggles, and worries were worth it. I have more than I could've dreamed of.

I look up into my husband's green eyes and smile.

"What is it, love?" he asks.

"I was just thinking how lucky I am."

"I think I'm the lucky one."

I smile and kiss the top of Nico's head and then crook my finger so Killian will come close. He leans down, his mouth just hovering over mine. "You have given me everything, Killian Thorn, and I love you more than you'll ever know."

His lips just graze mine. "I think I know, sweetheart, because if it's anything like how I feel about you, then I think we both are the luckiest people alive. Now rest and I'll be here to watch over you and Nico for the rest of our lives."

As though all the weight of the world was lifted, I close my eyes and drift to sleep, knowing nothing will harm me as long as he's here.

BONUS SCENE
TESSA

"THESE ARE PERFECT!" I SAY AS I PULL OUT THE BOMBER JACKET that is so ridiculous that it's amazing.

"I can't believe we're going to wear these," Penelope says as she lifts hers up.

Ainsley grins. "Believe it. We're going to be the talk of the Ultimate Frisbee world."

"This is a good thing?" Violet asks.

"It's something," Penny adds, clearly not as excited as Ainsley and I are.

The Disc Jocks have made it to the Ultimate Frisbee playoffs. Yes, it's a thing. One that they are very proud of getting to. Of course, it means that as their wives, we had to come out in support.

Violet slips hers on and turns, giving us a full showing. Each one of us has a cream-colored bomber jacket with a Frisbee embroidered on the back and their last name above it. The right sleeve has the words: Big Disc Energy going down it and the left sleeve has their number, which we just gave them for fun. The front is really where the magic is. There, we put the name of the era they wore when they played their tournament against the Swiftbees. We had to honor them in a way that is sure to embarrass them as well. Ainsley's jacket says: Lover. Violet's says: Fearless. Penelope's has: Reputation. Mine says: 1989—which is comical in so many ways.

They are truly perfect.

I can't wait to see the guy's faces when we stroll up wearing them.

"Your friend is a magician," Ainsley says as she grins broadly. "These are fantastic."

I called Brianna a few months ago when Penelope mentioned WAGs jackets that she saw on social media for hockey teams. She was telling us about how Miles always wished he would've gotten to see the woman he loved wearing one.

We couldn't let that go, so I called in a favor. Brianna has spent the last few years cultivating relationships in fashion. She said she knew of the perfect person who was up-and-coming and would love to make jackets for us if we would share them on social media.

I truly never expected them to be this on the nose.

"Seriously, Tessa, the guys are going to flip," Violet chuckles softly. "Oh, look, mine even has Brutus!" She looks at the wrist area where we had a tiny emblem that represents each guy.

Ainsley gasps and she holds hers up. "Awww, a fire truck!"

Penelope laughs and shakes her head. "A tree. Cute."

"What do you have?" Ainsley asks as she moves toward me.

"A horse."

"You guys are too cute."

I wink at her. "I think the best part of today is not only the jackets, but the new jerseys the guys will be wearing."

We decided to take their old jerseys so they have no other options but to wear what we made. Well, I wouldn't put it past them to go shirtless, but I'm sure there's a rule about clothing—I hope.

We all get our jackets on, link arms, and walk out to the field.

The guys are warming up and as soon as they see us, each one stops to look. Killian's smile is broad and he laughs before making his way toward me.

"Hi," I say with a grin.

"You had jackets made?"

"Of course, we are WAGs, are we not?"

He lets out a deep, throaty laugh. "You are."

Ainsley cuts in. "This is a very serious sport, Killian. We have to represent our men."

His brow raises as he. Nods. "I see. Well, you are all beautiful and all of the Disc Jocks are proud to have such stunning women on our sideline."

I look over at the very empty sideline. "You have no one else."

Killian snorts. "It's early."

"Oh, okay. I thought maybe you just didn't have any fans..."

Hazel makes her way off the field, grumbling and then her eyes widen. "What the hell? You had jackets made?"

I shrug. "Don't feel left out, we had something made for you and your husband."

If looks could kill, Hazel would have me ten feet under. Of course we didn't make Caspian a jacket, because that would've been a total waste, but he does have a jersey with her name and number on it. Since he pretty much deemed himself the coach anyway.

"No, no, you didn't have to do anything. I'm only on this stupid team because I lost a bet."

She says that, but it's been years now and she still shows up. Hazel would've found an out, so we all know she secretly loves it.

"Sure you are," Everett scoffs. "Nice digs girls. Looking hot. You're going to make all the other teams jealous."

"That was our intent," I say with a grin.

Miles has Penelope lifted in his arms with the biggest smile. It's clear he likes the jacket.

Killian laughs and pulls me to him. "You always look hot."

I stare up at my handsome husband and wink. "And I'm getting bothered thinking about you in your new uniform."

His smile drops and eyes narrow. "What did you do?"

"Me?" I ask with all the innocence I can muster.

"Yes you. When did we get new uniforms?" Killian asks.

That's a fair question and one that only makes this even more fun.

"Well, remember a few days ago when you asked me to wash it?"

"Yes, and you told me it was in my bag."

"I lied," I inform him.

"Tessa…"

"Killian…"

A low growl comes from his chest and I stifle a laugh. "Now, we had WAGs jackets and it was only fair that you guys got some new merch too. Part of my job as a publicist is to gather new customers, is it not?"

"I'm going to hate this, right?"

"Absolutely," I tell him.

I grab the bag that is on the ground and the girls pull the other guys over. "The wives and I wanted to do something nice for you all, to show how much your league of old—er—extraordinary talented Frisbee players means to us. So, we thought, what better way to show our support than to have new jerseys made for you."

I pull out the bright pink jersey with their names across the back and the numbers we gave them, which were their college numbers for their sport. On the front it says their team name, with a new addition.

"And Hazel?" Killian asks with a laugh.

Hazel groans. "The Disc Jocks & Hazel? That's the team name now?"

Everett laughs and pulls her to his side. "Aww, look at you, officially part of the team." He pulls his jersey on. "I'll rock the pink."

Miles and Lachlan follow suit, clearly not caring.

Killian winks at me then puts his on. "Still hot?"

Oh, this man could wear anything and I'd still think he was the sexiest thing to walk this Earth. I move to him, placing my hands on his chest. "Scorching."

"Good. Give me a good luck kiss."

I do as he asks, lifting up on my toes and pressing my lips to his. When he turns, I slap his ass. "Give 'em hell, baby."

He turns, smirks, and blows me a kiss. "Oh, I will and later, when we win, I'm going to give you something."

"Promise?"

Killian's sly grin sends tingles through me. "Absolutely."

And my man always keeps his promises.

ACKNOWLEDGMENTS

My husband and children. I love you all so much. We've been doing this a long time together and I couldn't survive without you.

My assistant, Christy Peckham, for always keeping my life together, even when I'm falling apart. I love you and am so grateful you came into my life all those years ago.

To Page and Tori, thank you for your endless support and guidance. You guys are the best managers a girl could have.

Melanie Harlow, you are truly one of my best friends in the world, and I don't know what I would do without you. Thankfully you're stuck with me until the end of time, so I'll never have to know what that would feel like.

My beta readers: Salma and Catherine. Thank you for loving me and these characters. You all made this book better and pushed me hard. Thank you.

My daily writing loves: Lauren Blakely, Laura Pavlov, and Natasha Madison. This little group of misfits is my favorite thing in the world. You have no idea how much I love you guys.

My agent, Kimberly Brower, thank you for having my back and always being on my side.

To Aimee Ashcraft for your editing and support on this story. I'm so grateful for the guidance.

The team at Sourcebooks, thank you for believing in this story and my work, I am beyond grateful.

To my author friends who are truly the best support system I could ever wish for. Thank you for showing what women uplifting women looks like. Catherine, Elsie, Lena, Chelle, Amy, Willow, Laura, Kandi, Rebecca, Samantha, Amber, Kennedy and so many more.

Every influencer who picked this book up, made a post, video, phoned a friend...whatever it was. Thank you for making the book world a better place.

ABOUT THE AUTHOR

Corinne Michaels is a *New York Times*, *USA Today*, and *Wall Street Journal* bestselling author of romance novels. Her stories are chock full of emotion, humor, and unrelenting love, and she enjoys putting her characters through intense heartbreak before finding a way to heal them through their struggles.

Corinne is a former Navy wife and happily married to the man of her dreams. She began her writing career after spending months away from her husband while he was deployed—reading and writing were her escape from the loneliness. Corinne now lives in Virginia with her husband and is the emotional, witty, sarcastic, and fun-loving mom of two beautiful children.